"INDESTRUCTIBLE," HE REMA
NIBBLING HER EARLOBE. "THA

"Irresistible, too."

"You are." Gazing deep into her eyes, he murmured, "How did I live so long without you? I look back at all those empty years . . ." He shook his head. "But now you're here and it's like I've been reborn."

Abbey looked up at him, her throat thick with unshed tears. "Was it really so awful?"

He drew her down on the grass beside him, then pulled her close to his side. "You have no idea. After Mara left me, I wandered aimlessly from place to place. I hated what I'd become and yet—I probably shouldn't be telling you this—I loved the blood. The taste of it on my tongue, the power of it! I loved the hunt, and yet, at the same time, I hated it. . . .

D0204590

Night's Surrender

AMANDA ASHLEY

ZEBRA BOOKS
KENSINGTON PUBLISHING CORP.
http://www.kensingtonbooks.com

ZEBRA BOOKS are published by

Kensington Publishing Corp.
119 West 40th Street
New York, NY 10018

All Kensington titles, imprints, and distributed lines are available at special quantity discounts for bulk purchases for sales promotion, premiums, fund-raising, educational, or institutional use.

Special book excerpts or customized printings can also be created to fit specific needs. For details, write or phone the office of the Kensington Sales Manager: Attn.: Sales Department. Kensington Publishing Corp., 119 West 40th Street, New York, NY 10018. Phone: 1-800-221-2647.

Zebra and the Z logo Reg. U.S. Pat. & TM Off.

First Printing: September 2015
ISBN-13: 978-1-4201-3735-4
ISBN-10: 1-4201-3735-2

eISBN-13: 978-1-4201-3736-1
eISBN-10: 1-4201-3736-0

10 9 8 7 6 5 4 3 2 1

Printed in the United States of America

Chapter One

Abbey Marie Cordova stood on the balcony of her small New York apartment. Gazing at the bright lights of Broadway, she admitted what she had suspected for some time—she wasn't cut out to be an actress, great or otherwise. All those acting classes had been a waste of time and money. She just didn't have the necessary drive or the ruthless ambition to claw her way to the top, nor was she willing to surrender her morals for a bit part in a movie.

She could have asked Uncle Logan to grease the way for her. He had produced a dozen hit movies, even won an Oscar. He wielded a lot of influence with several major Hollywood producers and directors. But she didn't want any favors, not from her family or from anyone else.

Standing there, she knew giving up her childhood dream was the right decision. She had heard too many horror stories of talented young actresses who had made it to the big time, then slid down the slippery slope of fame and fortune into drug addiction, or worse. She had seen their photos splashed across the nightly news, read their obituaries.

Twenty-six years old, Abbey thought with a sigh, and what did she have to show for her years of study? Nothing. No career. No job. No special someone in her life.

Truth be told, she had been feeling blue ever since attending Derek's wedding last month. The whole family had been there to see Mara's son marry the woman of his dreams—the DeLongpres, the Blackwoods, the Cordovas—all of them looking blissfully happy and deeply in love.

All of them vampires.

Until the wedding, Abbey hadn't been home for three or four years and it had been a bit of a shock, seeing her parents and the others and realizing that she now looked the same age as her father; in time, she would look older than her mother.

At the reception, her father had taken her aside and asked, without actually saying the words, if she had given any thought to becoming a vampire.

As a teenager, Abbey hadn't thought much about accepting the Dark Gift. After all, she was young and healthy. She had plenty of time to decide if she wanted to be a vampire. But she wasn't a young girl any longer. She aged with every passing day. Did she want to wait until she was in her thirties? Her forties? Her fifties? She suppressed a shudder. Who wanted to look old forever? Of course, she didn't have to get a day older. Her mother or father would gladly bestow the Dark Gift on her. The whole family took it for granted that Abbey would eventually become one of them. The only thing was, she wasn't certain it was what she wanted.

Going into the bathroom, she studied her reflection in the mirror. Her skin was still taut and smooth and clear. Her hair, the color of dark chocolate, fell past her shoulders in thick waves. She ran her hands over her breasts and down her hips. Her figure was still firm, but for how long?

Frowning, she switched off the light, her steps heavy as she went into the bedroom. After changing into her favorite sleep shirt, she crawled into bed. But sleep wouldn't come. Every time she closed her eyes, she saw her hair thinning and turning gray, her skin growing wrinkled and spotted, her energy waning, until, in the end . . .

She bolted upright, her breath coming in ragged gasps. She told herself people weren't meant to live forever, that growing old and passing on was the natural order of things. The way life was meant to be.

Unless you were a vampire . . .

Chapter Two

He had been a vampire for over two thousand years. As such, he was one of the oldest of his kind. Only Mara, the so-called Queen of the Vampires, had survived longer.

For centuries he had searched for her, but to no avail. He had to admire her skill at eluding detection, whether by hunters or those of her own kind.

She was a legend among the Nosferatu—fearless, stronger, more powerful and more cunning than any of them. It was rumored that she had regained her humanity, that she had given birth to a child, but he had dismissed both possibilities out of hand. Such things were impossible, even for the Queen of the Vampires. No doubt she had spread the rumors herself, knowing it would only add to her mystique.

But he couldn't ignore the niggling voice in the back of his mind that wondered if it could be true.

He stared at the goblet in his hand, at the thick red liquid it held. What would it be like to be able to consume something besides blood after so many centuries? To sample the various foods and drinks he saw advertised on TV and in magazines? To eat something that required chewing? He often sat in restaurants, sipping a glass of wine, watching men and women as they ate, envious of the culinary pleasure he read on their faces. Just once, he thought, just once he would like to bite into a thick, juicy steak.

Mara was the answer. If she had truly found a way to regain her humanity—no matter how briefly—he wanted to know how she had accomplished it.

And if it was impossible, what then?

He leaned back in his chair and closed his eyes. He had lived as a vampire long enough. He was ready to die, but as one of the Nosferatu, his options were not pretty. He could let a hunter stake him or take his head. Or he could walk out into the light of a new day. As old as he was, he wasn't sure it would even be fatal. He could always set himself on fire. . . . Grimacing, he quickly discarded that alternative.

Better to become human again if at all possible, and spend his final years as a mortal before he breathed his last.

He sipped his drink. It all came back to Mara. She was the answer. If she couldn't restore his humanity, then she could grant him a quick, painless death.

She owed him that much.

And a helluva lot more.

Chapter Three

Tossing the want ads onto the kitchen table, Abbey blew a stray wisp of hair from her brow. She had learned to use a computer in high school, though she had no real aptitude for anything beyond the basics. She wished now she had paid more attention, since it seemed every job required at least some degree of computer savvy, and she was woefully lacking. All her friends were into the latest social media, but she had never gotten the hang of finding her way in the digital world. As for texting . . . Abbey shook her head. She much preferred talking to people face-to-face.

With a sigh of resignation, she phoned for a cab. Her father had offered to buy her a car, but she had no real need for one. Most of the places she had to go were within walking distance of her apartment.

Even after all the years she had lived in New York, the sights and sounds of the city filled Abbey with excitement. After paying the cab driver, she stepped out of the car and quickly became part of the crowd. These days, most stores were open 24/7, so whether it was day or night, the streets were swamped with cars that drove themselves, the sidewalks packed with people who were always in a hurry—rushing to get to work or eager to go home, dashing off to see a movie, a Broadway show, a free concert in the park.

Hitching her handbag over her shoulder, Abbey stared at the gleaming glass-fronted façade of the computer store. Her knowledge of digital devices started and ended with her iPod, which was nothing like the current high-tech phones, iPads, and computers. She could find music, text when she had to, and read the latest news on her iPod; anything else was beyond her.

Taking a deep breath, she opened the door and stepped into a world that was totally unfamiliar to her.

A quick glance around showed computers in all types and sizes—small towers with enormous screens, monitors that didn't need a tower, wireless laptops, and devices that were no bigger than a cell phone.

You could buy a keyboard if you were old-school, but newer computer models responded to voice commands. She had heard that, in another year or so, those would be obsolete and man and computer would communicate with thought waves.

Shelf after shelf held nothing but computers, monitors, keyboards, software programs and gadgets, and stacks of technical manuals. It looked like geek heaven, she mused. All around her, people chatted enthusiastically about the latest software, the newest addition to this or that. They might as well have been speaking a foreign language, because Abbey didn't understand a word they were saying.

With a shake of her head, she turned and headed for the exit. Maybe she could get a job in Beverly Hills as a house sitter or a dog walker. Cash only. She wouldn't need any computer skills for that! She could stay in Hollywood with Mara and Logan until she found a place of her own.

Lost in thought, Abbey didn't see the man coming through the door until she slammed into him. It was like crashing into a mountain.

"Whoa, girl," he exclaimed. "Are you on your way to a fire?"

"I'm so sorry. I wasn't . . ." Abbey glanced up—and up. He was a *tall* mountain. Blinking up at him, she took a step back. She was used to handsome men, but this guy . . .

He looked like the *GQ* Hunk of the Month with his long black hair, broad shoulders, trim waist, and vibrant blue eyes.

He reached out a hand to steady her. "Are you all right?"

"What? Yes. No. I mean, of course."

He grinned, sending her temperature rising and her pulse racing. It was disconcerting, the effect he had on her. She had met a lot of good-looking men. None of them had made her feel like throwing herself into his arms.

"Can I buy you a drink?" he asked. "There's a club just down the street. Dante's. Do you know it?"

"Yes." She knew it all too well. Dante's catered mainly to out-of-work musicians and down-on-their-luck actors and screenwriters.

"Shall we?"

It was a tempting offer—sharing a drink with an incredibly handsome man. But gorgeous or not, he was a stranger.

He cocked his head to the side. "Is there a problem?"

"No." What could go wrong? Dante's was just two blocks down, the sidewalks were crowded with people. She had a .22 semi-automatic in her purse—a going-away gift from her father. Smiling up at him, she said, "Lead the way."

He took her hand as they threaded their way down the street to the club. The touch of his fingers twining with hers made her heart race and her toes curl with pleasure.

Inside, he guided her to a small table in the back, held her chair as she sat down. "I'm Nick." His voice, deep and whiskey-rough, moved over her like a caress.

"Abbey."

"It's a pleasure to meet you, Abbey."

"Even though I almost knocked you down?"

A laugh rumbled deep in his throat. "I don't think I was in any real danger from a little thing like you."

She would have been offended if any other man had called her a "little thing," but the way he said it, the admiration in his dark blue eyes, made it sound like high praise.

Their waitress arrived then. Abbey ordered a dry martini, Nick ordered a glass of Pinot Noir.

When the waitress left to turn in their order, Nick leaned forward, his forearms crossed on the table, his gaze intent upon Abbey's face. "Tell me about yourself."

"There's not much to tell. I wasted the last five years trying to be something I'm not cut out for."

"Oh? What's that?"

"I thought I wanted to be an actress, but I recently came to the realization that I just don't have what it takes." She shrugged, thinking how good it felt to finally admit it out loud. "I guess I just don't want it bad enough to make the tough choices."

He nodded. "So, what are you going to do now?"

"I'm not sure. Go back home, I guess."

"Where's home?"

"Northern California. My parents have a ranch there. But enough about me. What about you? What do you do?"

"Nothing much. You might say I'm footloose and fancy free. No job. No family. No prospects."

Abbey bit down on her lower lip, uncertain how to reply. Was he recovering from some horrible tragedy? An entrepreneur down on his luck? Or just some incredibly handsome drifter with no goals and no ambition?

She was still trying to think of a suitable response when the waitress arrived with their drinks. Nick smiled at the woman, tossed twenty-five dollars on the tray, and told her to keep the change.

He might be a drifter, Abbey thought, but he didn't appear to be strapped for cash.

"What were you looking for in the computer store?" he asked.

"Nothing, really. I was thinking about getting a job and thought I should try to get up-to-date on the latest technology, but . . ." She smiled self-consciously. "I have no talent in that area, either. It's all Greek to me. I have trouble remembering to charge my cell phone. The new computers . . ." She shook her head.

He laughed softly. "Maybe I can help with that. I know a bit about computers and software."

"You do?"

"I was a computer programmer in another life."

"Really?" She would never have pegged him as a computer nerd. "Well, I'd appreciate any help you could give me. Of course, I'll have to buy a new computer first. I'm afraid mine is woefully archaic and past repair."

"Well, when you're ready to make the plunge, just let me know."

Abbey sipped her drink. Who was this man, really? He appeared to be in his mid-thirties, yet there was something about him that made her think he was older.

Perhaps it was his eyes—they seemed world-weary, and wise beyond his years.

The silence between them made her uncomfortable. She was scrambling for something witty to say when the DJ selected a love song.

Nick set his glass aside. "Care to dance?"

Abbey's heartbeat kicked up a notch at the thought of being in his arms. She nodded, her throat suddenly dry as he took her by the hand and led her onto the tiny dance floor.

He drew her into his arms, holding her far closer than was proper between strangers. His arm around her waist was solid—protective, not imprisoning. His thighs brushed hers, his breath was warm when it caressed her cheek.

She looked up and his gaze met hers—intense and deep blue. For a moment, she imagined him probing her mind, uncovering her deepest secrets. For a moment, she imagined she could read his thoughts in return, imagined that he was alone and lonely, that only she could ease his pain.

Blinking rapidly, she looked away, and now she was acutely aware of his body pressed so close to hers, of how intimately he held her. Only a breath apart, she mused. And it was too far. His hand lightly stroked her back, up and down, and she sighed with the sheer pleasure of his touch, of being in his arms. She felt warm and achy in the deepest part of her being and she wished suddenly that they were alone in her apartment. In her bed . . .

Blushing furiously, she glanced up at him, grateful that he couldn't read her mind.

He smiled at her, his arm tightening around her waist as the music ended and they returned to their table. "If I asked you out, what would you say?"

"Ask me and see." She had intended for her reply to be saucy and flirtatious; instead, it emerged as a husky whisper. What was there about this man that she found so irresistible? It was more than his devastating good looks, more than the rich timbre of his voice. Something primal within him called to something wild and untouched within the deepest part of her being in ways she recognized but didn't understand. She was meant to be his, she thought, as he was meant to be hers.

"Would you go out with me tomorrow night, Abbey Marie?"

"I'd love to."

"Pick you up at eight?"

Nodding, she pulled one of her business cards from her wallet and handed it to him. His fingers brushed hers as he took the card.

"Eight," she said breathlessly.

It wasn't until Nick had put her in a cab and she was on her way home that Abbey stopped to wonder how he knew her middle name.

Nick lingered on the sidewalk long after Abbey's cab was out of sight. She was a lovely young woman with an air of innocence that was remarkably rare these days. That she was human, he had no doubt. And yet the scent of vampire clung to her, almost too faint to detect, but there nonetheless, which led him to wonder if she was in the habit of associating with vampires, or if she had simply, unknowingly, been in contact with one earlier that day.

He grinned wryly as another thought crossed his mind. Unlikely as it seemed, she might be a hunter.

His grin turned to laughter as he pictured a little bit of a thing like Abbey trying to take down an angry vampire, or lop the head off a sleeping one. Of course, anything was possible. He hadn't lived this long by underestimating his enemies, however unlikely they appeared.

He would do well to remember that, Nick mused as he strolled down the street. In recent months, the vampire community had again gone underground. Several prominent hunters had been slain, among them Louise McDonald and her sister. He had never had any contact with Lou McDonald, but she had been a legend among the Undead—ruthless in the hunt, merciless in the kill. A group of hunters had recently put out a contract on whoever had killed her and her sister. Odds were good that it had been a vampire, though no one in their community had come forward to claim the honor.

He paused at the corner, his gaze drawn to a group of young adults exiting a dance club. Their combined scents stirred his hunger. And his memories. Memories that shamed him now. There had been times, in the distant past, when he would have preyed upon them all, drained them dry and tossed the empty husks aside without a qualm.

Those days were long gone, but the ubiquitous need to feed remained. Nick fell into step behind them as they moved on, laughing and weaving down the street. Had he ever been that young, that carefree? His days in mortality had been spent trying to keep body and soul together.

He fell back a little as one of the couples broke off from the others. His hunger spiked as he trailed soundlessly behind them.

They never realized he was there, never suspected they were in danger until it was too late.

* * *

Back at home, he poured himself a glass of red wine and settled into his favorite chair. Thoughts of days gone by had tempted him to drain the couple dry. Doing so in the past had become an addiction. For his kind, taking a life was a high like no other—to drink a man's life, his memories, his strength—the rush was indescribable. And he had been sorely tempted. But he hadn't killed in centuries unless it was in self-defense. These days he took only what he needed and moved on.

He shook the ancient memories from his mind and focused instead on Abbey Marie. He had been drawn to her the moment her eyes met his, though he couldn't say why. Still, he had been shocked by the almost mystical sense that he had not met her by accident, that she was meant to be his, body and soul.

He sat there until dawn teased his senses. In his bedroom, he undressed down to his briefs, then stretched out on the bed. In days past, he had slept in caves, abandoned hovels, burned-out buildings.

Muttering an oath, he closed his eyes. Enough about the past. He dragged a hand across his jaw. An indrawn breath reminded him of the woman. Abbey. The scent of her skin lingered on his, a scent that was uniquely hers. It conjured images of sunshine and children at play, of close-knit families gathered together in love and laughter, things that had never been his. Would never be his.

He murmured her name as the thick darkness closed around him, sweeping him into oblivion.

Abbey woke early with a smile on her face. Sitting up, she hugged her pillow to her chest. It was Friday and she had a date. With Nick.

Bounding out of bed, she showered and dressed, ate

a quick breakfast, then hurried down the street to the loft where her acting class met.

She nodded to her friends, but didn't stop to chat lest they weaken her resolve.

Taking a deep breath, she knocked on the coach's door, hesitated when he bid her enter. Did she really want to do this?

Another deep breath and she stepped into his office. Peter Abbot sat behind a large walnut desk. Autographed photographs of world-famous actors and actresses covered the wall behind him. Abbey had hoped that her own photo would one day join the others, but it had been nothing but a pipe dream. She knew that now.

Abbot listened quietly to what she had to say, nodding from time to time, "I can't say I didn't see this coming," he remarked. "I believe you have the talent necessary, but you're right, you don't have the drive, the hunger, to make it to the top." Rising, he came around the desk and gave her a hug. "You may never be a great actress," he said, "but you will always be a star in my eyes."

Blinking back her tears, Abbey gave him a quick smile, then hurried out of the studio.

She spent the rest of the day scrolling through the want ads on her iPod, only to realize that not only wasn't she cut out to be an actress, she wasn't fit for much of anything else, either. Save for a few menial jobs in food services or child care, or those that required physical labor, most of the jobs these days were strictly high-tech, requiring complicated computer and software skills.

Tossing her iPod on the sofa, Abbey glanced at her watch, then grabbed her handbag, and headed out the door, all thoughts of finding a job erased in the excitement of her upcoming date with Nick. She couldn't wait to see him again. She wanted to wow him tonight, make him really sit up and take notice, and with that in mind, she hailed a cab and went shopping at her favorite boutique.

The doorbell rang at eight sharp. A million butterflies took flight in the pit of Abbey's stomach as she quickly applied her lipstick, took a last glance in the mirror, then ran to answer the door.

Nick whistled softly when he saw her.

"You didn't say where we were going," Abbey said, blushing as his gaze moved over her. "I hope this is appropriate."

"You're beautiful." And indeed, she was. The black dress emphasized her curves and displayed a generous amount of shapely leg. Her hair fell over her shoulders in silky soft waves. "Are you ready to go?" he asked.

Abbey nodded. Outside, he handed her into a blood-red, late-model sports car, making her think that, for a man without a job or prospects, he seemed to be doing pretty darn well.

He drove to a high-class nightclub in a posh section of the city. One look and Abbey knew it was a place made for lovers. The lighting was discreet, the high-backed booths arranged for privacy.

A small band occupied a raised dais at one end of the room. Lights twinkled around the floor of the dais. A long bar, also outlined by tiny twinkling lights, took up one wall at the opposite end. The same tiny, twinkling lights ringed a large dance floor.

A hostess attired in a long black gown guided them to a booth. A waitress came quickly to take their order—a Manhattan for Abbey, a glass of Cabernet Sauvignon for Nick.

"I've never been here before," Abbey said, glancing around. "It's lovely."

"As are you." Nick gestured at the dance floor. "Shall we?"

She nodded, eager to be in his arms. Taking her hand in his, he led her onto the floor. It was like a dream come true, Abbey thought, being in his arms again. The music was soft and low yet carried a sensual undertone that made her think of lovers entangled in silken sheets. He held her close, his body brushing intimately against hers. The air between them was charged with tension, making it hard to breathe. She looked up at him, wondering if he was as aware of it as she, felt his desire wash over her in a wave of longing.

Lost in the heat of his eyes, she pressed herself against him, wanting to be closer, hating the clothing that separated them. When he lowered his head to hers, she closed her eyes in anticipation of his kiss. His lips were cool, yet warmth suffused her from head to heel. She was only scarcely aware that they had stopped moving. There were only his arms tight around her, his mouth boldly claiming hers.

She stared up at him, dazed, when he pulled away.

"The music's stopped," he murmured.

"Has it?"

Nick brushed her cheek with his knuckles, then took her hand and led her back to their table. She might be young, he mused. She might be small in stature, but she was all woman.

Smiling, he lifted his glass in a toast. "To us."

"To us," Abbey repeated. They were, she thought, the two most beautiful words she had ever heard.

They danced and talked for hours, until Abbey's eyelids grew heavy.

"I should take you home," Nick said when she yawned yet again.

"No."

"You're falling asleep, sweetheart."

"I know, but I don't want this night to end."

"There's always tomorrow night."

"Same time?" she asked.

He nodded. "Come on, I'll take you home."

Abbey felt a tingle of awareness as they waited, hand-in-hand, for the valet to bring Nick's car around. It had rained while they were inside; dark gray clouds scudded across the sky, the sidewalk and streets glistened wetly in the moonlight.

She couldn't stop looking at Nick as he drove to her apartment, one hand on the wheel, his other hand holding hers. Would he kiss her good night?

Lost in daydreams that went beyond a mere good-night kiss, she didn't see the car careening toward them, wasn't aware of any danger until a black SUV swerved to miss the car and clipped their fender.

Nick hit the brake to avoid going onto the sidewalk, but the tires had no traction and went skidding over the wet street, then came to a jarring stop when it smashed into the side of a building.

Abbey cried out as her head slammed against the side window, and then everything went black.

Nick hissed a vile oath. He was sorely tempted to go after the idiot who had side-swiped him, but a quick look at Abbey changed his mind. Blood oozed from a shallow gash in her right temple and trickled down her cheek.

Getting out of the car, he hurried around to her side, opened the door, and lifted her into his arms.

Utilizing his vampire senses, he assured himself that she had no serious injuries and no concussion before he called upon his preternatural powers and transported the two of them to his favorite lair on Park Avenue.

Abbey woke with a groan, one hand pressed against her throbbing head.

She opened her eyes, squinting against the light. Where was she? A glance at the window showed it was still dark outside.

She started to sit up, only to fall back on the mattress as the room spun out of focus.

"Easy, now."

She recognized that whiskey-rough voice. "Nick?"

"I'm here. How are you feeling?"

"Awful. What happened?"

"Don't you remember?"

She frowned. The movement made her wince. "We were in an accident . . . somebody hit us . . . but how did I get here?" Wherever "here" was.

"I brought you home. My home," he clarified. "You're not badly hurt. Bit of a cut on your forehead is all. You were lucky."

She didn't feel lucky. Her head hurt like sin. And she was in a man's bed. A man she scarcely knew. "I should go home." It was one thing to imagine being in Nick's bed; quite another to wake up and find herself there. He was, after all, little more than a stranger.

"Tomorrow." He eased her back down when she tried to sit up again. "You need someone to keep an eye on you tonight."

She wasn't up to arguing with him. She had never been in an accident before; it left her feeling vulnerable.

Nick placed a cool cloth on her forehead. "Get some sleep. I'll be here if you need anything."

She wanted to tell him that she was fine, that she didn't need a nursemaid, but trying to form the words was suddenly too much trouble. The best she could manage was a murmured "Thank you" before her eyelids fluttered closed.

Nick stood beside the bed, his hands shoved into the pockets of his jeans, his brow furrowed as he watched her sleep. Although she wasn't badly hurt, he intended to stay by her side until dawn.

Bemused by his urge to protect her, he watched her sleep. He should have taken her back to her apartment, or to the hospital. With her in the house, he would have to take his rest elsewhere.

Why had he brought her here?

Why, indeed?

Closing his eyes, he inhaled the flowery fragrance of her silky hair and skin, the enticing scent of her life's blood.

The slow, steady beat of her heart was like music to his ears as he lowered his head to her neck. He would only take a little, he promised himself, just enough so that he would be able to sense it should she need him when she woke in the morning.

Just enough to discover if she tasted as good as she looked.

Chapter Four

"Hey!" Logan Blackwood made a hasty grab for his wife, but his hand closed on empty air as she deftly slid out of bed. "Where are you going?"

Mara moved to the window. Drawing back the curtain, she stared out into the darkness. "Abbey's hurt."

"Are you sure?"

She glanced at him over her shoulder, one brow arched. "Are you doubting me?"

"Of course not, but . . ." Logan shook his head. He had known Mara for over nine centuries, yet her preternatural abilities continued to amaze him. They were in California; Abbey was in New York City. In spite of the vast distance between them, Mara was able to sense her godchild's distress because of the blood link they shared. Still, he thought it remarkable. She shared a similar blood link with her godsons, Rane and Rafe, as well. It allowed her to find them no matter where they were. "Is Abbey okay?"

Mara nodded as she slid back under the covers and into his arms. "It's nothing serious."

"Good." He kissed her cheeks, the tip of her nose, trailed his tongue down the length of her neck. She was a woman like no other. He never tired of looking at her, or making love to her. Even after all the years they had shared, she still had the power to excite him. To surprise him. "So," he murmured, tucking her slim body beneath him, "where were we?"

She gazed up at him, her deep green eyes sparkling with mischief as she raked her nails down his bare back. "You don't remember?" She pouted, hips undulating in a way meant to drive him wild.

"Honey," he growled, "how could I ever forget?"

Chapter Five

Abbey woke abruptly. One minute, she was dreaming about making love to a tall, dark handsome man who looked remarkably like Nick and the next she was wide awake, with the sun brightly shining in her face, and her cell phone ringing.

After sitting up, she looked around for her phone. Spying it on the bedside table, she checked the display before answering. "Dad? What's wrong?"

"Where are you?"

"I'm at . . . at a friend's house."

"Are you all right?"

She lifted a hand to her head, winced when her fingers brushed the bandage on her temple. "Yes, why?"

"Mara called me late last night. She said you'd been hurt, that it wasn't serious. I've been calling you all morning."

"I . . . I guess my phone was off." Had Nick turned it off last night? Nick. She glanced around the room. Where was he?

"Do you need me to come there?"

"No. Listen, Dad, I'm going home. I'll call you when I get there, okay?"

"You're sure you're all right?"

"Yes. Love to Mom."

After disconnecting the call, Abbey got to her feet, very carefully. She stood there a moment. When she didn't feel dizzy, she smoothed her hair and her clothes, then searched for her sandals. She found them, and her handbag, on the floor at the foot of the bed.

After stepping into her shoes, she went looking for Nick. The condo was large, sparsely furnished with what she thought might be genuine antiques. Although there was little furniture, the walls were covered with paintings. She didn't know much about art, but the paintings—mostly seascapes and scenes of ancient cities—looked incredibly expensive.

There was no sign of Nick, leaving her to wonder where he was at such an early hour. Not at work, since he'd told her he didn't have a job. Jogging, perhaps?

Feeling suddenly uneasy, she went outside to hail a cab.

Her father was pacing the floor in the living room of her apartment when she got home.

"Dad! What are you doing here?"

He opened his arms. "Do I need a reason to come and see my girl?"

"Of course not! I'm glad you're here." After dropping her handbag on a chair, she hurried toward him, sighing as his arms enveloped her in a bear hug. He was, Abbey thought, the best, most handsome father in the whole world.

He released her after a moment, his nostrils flaring as he cupped her chin and turned her head to the side. He sniffed the shallow cut on her forehead. "Are you sure you're all right?" he asked dubiously. "Maybe you should sit down."

"I'm fine." With a shake of her head, Abbey sat in her favorite chair, her legs tucked beneath her.

Rane sat across from her, his hands resting on his knees. "Tell me about this man you met."

"There isn't much to tell. I mean, I hardly know him."

"Where did you meet him?"

"In a computer store," she said, grinning at the memory.

"Does he know who you are?"

Abbey frowned. "What do you mean?"

"I smell vampire on you."

"What?" Abbey blinked at him. "Are you sure?"

"New York City's a big place. There's no way for me to detect his or her identity. It could be your friend, it could have been some vampire who brushed against you by accident."

Abbey stared at her father. Could Nick be a vampire? Even as she told herself it was ridiculous, she knew it was true. "That's how he knew my middle name," she muttered.

Rane's head jerked up. "What?"

"The night I met him. He called me Abbey Marie. I never told him my middle name."

Rane nodded, his expression troubled. "I don't want you to see him again."

"Come on, Dad, you're a vampire and you don't want me to date one?"

"Abbey . . ."

"You're not suggesting he knew who I was and met me for some nefarious reason, are you?"

"Stranger things have happened."

Stalling for time because she couldn't think of a valid counterargument, she kicked off her sandals, made a fuss about lining them up side by side next to her chair. It wasn't always easy, being the adopted daughter of a vampire and the only mortal in the family. They knew things she didn't know, possessed supernatural powers she sometimes envied.

"So, what's the big deal if he knew who I was?" she asked at length. "What could he hope to gain by meeting me?"

"It depends. He could be one of those rare vampires that hunt their own kind. He could be looking for Mara. He could be looking for that will-o'-the-wisp cure of Pearl's." Rane leaned forward and pinched her cheek. "Maybe he just wanted to seduce a pretty girl."

"Right."

"Listen, why don't you come home for a while? We haven't seen much of you lately. Your mom misses you."

"I know. I miss her, too. Why didn't she come with you?"

"I decided to come on the spur of the moment. She was still resting when I left."

Abbey nodded. Her mother, Savanah, hadn't accepted the Dark Gift until the year after Abbey graduated from high school, making Savanah the youngest vampire in the family. Because Rane had sired her, and because he had consumed Mara's blood, Savanah was able to be up during the day. However, she usually rested when the sun was at its zenith. Abbey had often wondered if her mother regretted giving up her humanity, though she had never found the nerve to ask.

"So, what do you say, honey? Will you come home for a while?"

Abbey nodded, thinking how foolish she had been to leave in the first place. After selling their home in Porterville, her parents had bought a beautiful place near Auburn. The two-story ranch-style house sat on ten acres. Besides the house, there was a big, old barn, a chicken coop, and several corrals. A stream ran through the back of the property; pines and oaks covered the gently rolling hills. It was the perfect place for her mother to fulfill her secret dream of raising horses.

"Your mom bought a new mare," Rane remarked, hoping to tip the scales in his favor.

"Really?" One of the things Abbey missed in New York was riding across open country. Until now, she hadn't realized how much she had missed it. True, you could ride in Central Park, but riding some plodding stable hack just wasn't the same as riding a horse with some spunk.

"All right, Dad," Abbey said, grinning. "You convinced me."

She would miss seeing Nick again, but what if her father was right? What if Nick was up to no good?

Besides, there were enough vampires in her life. She didn't need another one.

It didn't take her long to pack. She had been staying in a furnished, rented apartment; all that belonged to her—her clothing and personal effects, her books and a few knickknacks—fit easily into two large suitcases.

Since she had already paid the last month's rent, all she had to do was let her landlord know she was leaving. When that was done, she took one last look around to make sure she hadn't forgotten anything and she was ready to go.

Rane held one of her suitcases, Abbey held the other, along with her purse.

A rush of anticipation swept through her when her father wrapped his arm around her waist.

"Ready?" he asked.

Abbey nodded.

"All right, then. Here we go."

Abbey felt a rush of nervous excitement as her father called upon his preternatural power and transported the two of them from her apartment in New York to their living room in Northern California. It was an awesome experience, hurtling through time and space. It always left her feeling slightly disoriented and a little queasy.

She dropped her suitcase and her handbag on the floor, then sank onto the nearest chair while she waited for the world to right itself and her head to stop spinning.

"You okay, honey?" Rane asked.

"Fine." What was it like, she wondered, to be able to think yourself anywhere you wished to go?

They had left New York City at four, but in California, it was only one in the afternoon, Pacific time. Her mother was still resting.

Abbey glanced around. The room was just as she remembered it. The walls were still white, the carpet a light blue plush, the curtains—heavily lined to block the sun—were a darker shade of blue. A pair of high-backed sofas covered in a flowered print flanked the fireplace; a pair of easy chairs covered in the same shade of blue as the drapes faced the hearth.

Rane dropped her second suitcase beside the first. "I'll take these up to your room later."

"Thanks, Dad, but I can do it."

"You always were an independent kid."

"Well, I guess I learned that from you."

"Is that right? I always thought you got it from your mother's side of the family. Oh, you might want to go pick up some groceries," Rane suggested, handing her the keys to his car.

Abbey glanced at the keys, then grinned at him. "Really, Dad? Another new car?"

"She's fast. Take it easy on the curves. Maybe we'll try out that new mare when you get back," he said with a wink. "She's fast, too."

"Sounds great. I won't be gone long."

Thinking how good it was to be home again, Abbey tucked the keys into her purse and went out to the garage. She whistled softly when she saw her dad's new car. Like his father and his brother, Rane Cordova loved fast cars. This one was as black as sin, with black leather upholstery and every extra imaginable.

When she slid behind the wheel, the dashboard lit up as the onboard computer sparked to life, and asked for her destination.

"Howard's Market, no faster than the speed limit."

"Yes, miss."

Abbey buckled her seat belt, then sat back, and let the car do the driving.

She had a lot to think about. She knew she was welcome to stay with her parents for as long as she wished. A visit was one thing, but she was too old to live at home and sponge off Mom and Dad. Not that they would mind, but she needed to do something with her life, make her mark on the world before she was too old. . . .

Abbey shook her head. Why was she so obsessed with aging all of a sudden? She was still young; she had a good long life ahead of her. Places she wanted to go. Things she wanted to do.

The car pulled up in front of the grocery store a short time later. Inside, she selected a shopping cart and strolled through the market. She loved shopping, whether it was for clothes, shoes, gifts. Or food. As she filled her cart, she couldn't help wondering, as she had so many times before, if her parents ever missed the pleasure of sitting down to a good meal.

Savanah had made sure they celebrated all the holidays while Abbey was growing up. Turkey and all the fixings at Thanksgiving and Christmas, ham at Easter. Her father had joined them at the table, sipping wine while Abbey and her mother ate until they couldn't hold another bite.

Savanah never mentioned those bygone holiday feasts, but sometimes, when Abbey was eating something her mother had once loved, Abbey glimpsed a hint of longing in her mother's eyes.

An hour later, Abbey was back home and putting her groceries away. She found a note from her father on the fridge. It read: *I'm at the barn, waiting for you.*

After quickly stowing the last of the canned goods in the cupboard, Abbey hurried up to her room and changed into a pair of jeans and a T-shirt, pulled on her favorite riding boots, and ran out the back door, heading for the stable.

As she passed the corrals, she noted there were three yearlings in one, and a couple of black-and-white heifers in the other. A large yellow cat dozed in the shade beside the barn.

Abbey found her father outside the barn, currying a lovely Appaloosa mare. His favorite mount, a long-legged bay gelding, whinnied softly as Abbey approached.

"What do you think of her?" Rane asked, resting one arm on the mare's back.

"She's beautiful!" The mare was predominantly black, with one white stocking. A spotted white blanket covered her hindquarters.

"She's yours."

"Mine? But I thought you said Mom bought her."

"She did. She bought the mare for you."

Abbey stroked the Appy's neck, ran her fingers through the short, silky mane. "Hi, girl," she murmured. "Have you got a name?"

"Her previous owner called her Freckles, but I suppose you can call her anything you like."

"Freckles suits her."

"Well, saddle her up and let's go," Rane said.

The mare had a smooth, rocking chair gait. She responded quickly to the touch of Abbey's heels and seemed to be bomb-proof, unruffled by a jack rabbit that darted across her path, unperturbed when a flock of birds burst from cover and took to the air.

Abbey glanced at her father as they rode across the pasture, side by side. He was a handsome man, with chiseled features, a strong jaw, and long black hair. Years ago, he had been a magician, performing as The Remarkable Renaldo, The Marvelous Marvello, The Amazing Antoine, and Santoro the Magnificent. Of course, the magic he had performed wasn't magic in the usual sense of the word, merely a display of his preternatural powers.

Sometimes she forgot that he was a vampire, that he had to drink blood to survive. He rarely spoke of his past, but Mara had once told her that he regretted every life he had taken as a young vampire, that for most of his life he had refused to walk in the sun's light because he thought of himself as evil.

He wasn't evil, she thought, but the kindest, sweetest man in the whole world.

And then there was her mother, Savanah, a direct descendent of that infamous vampire hunter, Abraham Van Helsing.

As always, thinking of her parents brought a smile to

her face. It just didn't seem possible that a vampire and the descendent of a vampire hunter could ever find happiness together.

"What's so funny?" Rane asked.

"I was just thinking about you and Mom. Yours has to be the strangest love story I've ever heard."

"I can't argue with that," her father agreed.

"I guess opposites really do attract."

"So they say. Are you ready to let her out?"

At Abbey's nod, Rane touched his heels to his mount's flanks. With a toss of his head, the big bay gelding broke into a lope.

With a whoop, Abbey urged her own mount into a gallop. It was wonderful, exhilarating, racing across the ground with the wind in her face, the sound of the mare's hooves pounding over the ground, the sense of freedom that engulfed her.

They rode until the horses broke a sweat, then turned back toward home.

"So, what do you think you'll do now?" her father asked after a time.

"I don't know." Abbey shrugged. "Got any ideas?"

"Your mom can always use help with the horses. Right now, we're paying a college kid to come by and feed the stock in the morning, but he's starting a new job tomorrow, so today was his last day."

Abbey chewed on her lower lip. It did sound tempting.

"If you don't want to feel like you're mooching off of us, we can make it a business deal. I can even put it in writing. I'll pay you a fair salary. And if you want a place of your own, you can live in the cottage out back. If it'll make you feel better, I'll even charge you rent. What do you say? Do you need to think it over?"

What was there to think about? It was the best offer she'd had since she'd left home.

It was only later, alone in her room, that Abbey had second thoughts. If she stayed in California, she would probably never see Nick again.

Chapter Six

At sundown, Nick left his secondary lair located in New Jersey. A thought took him to his condo. Even before he opened the door, he knew Abbey was gone.

He grunted softly. He wasn't surprised that she wasn't there. After all, he hadn't really expected her to spend the day waiting for him. What surprised him was the depth of his disappointment. He hardly knew the girl, and yet he was drawn to her in ways he couldn't explain.

After leaving the condo, he strolled the crowded streets to her apartment. He loved hunting in New York. A vampire could find prey on every corner, he thought with a wry grin, and there was no end of variety. Male and female—and some who hadn't yet made up their minds—people of every ethnic origin imaginable. A veritable smorgasbord of humanity to choose from.

But it wasn't prey on his mind just now.

He took the stairs to Abbey's apartment two at a time. An indrawn breath told him she wasn't here, either. A second breath told him another vampire had been there not long ago.

Frowning, Nick returned to the street. He had smelled vampire on her before, but not this particular vampire. Was she in the habit of keeping company with the Undead? The thought that she might be a hunter skittered, unwanted, across his mind again.

Was it possible that the lovely Abbey Marie was not the innocent she seemed?

Determined to see her again, hunter or not, he opened his vampire senses, homing in on the blood link that bound them together.

Chapter Seven

Abbey woke early on her first day back at home. For a moment, she lay in bed, listening to the familiar sounds of the house. Outside, a rooster crowed. Smiling, she threw back the covers, bounded out of bed, and headed for the shower. It had been a long time since she'd gotten up with the chickens, she thought with a grin.

After showering, she pulled on a pair of jeans, donned a red sweatshirt over a white T-shirt, and tugged on a pair of well-worn boots. A cup of coffee and a doughnut served as breakfast.

Although her parents could both be up and about during the day, they preferred to sleep late, often not rising until midafternoon.

With that thought in mind, Abbey grabbed three apples and hurried down to the barn, eager to ride while the air was still cool. She could move into the cottage later. Right now, she wanted to see her horse.

Freckles whinnied softly when Abbey entered the barn. Her father's gelding and her mother's chestnut added their greetings to the Appy's.

"Hey, girl." Abbey offered the apples to the horses,

idly scratched the mare's neck while Freckles quickly devoured hers, then sniffed Abbey's hand, looking for more.

After dropping a halter over the Appy's head, Abbey led her out of the stall. She picked the mare's feet and gave her coat a quick going-over with a dandy brush before lifting the heavy Western saddle into place.

Abbey tightened the cinch, gave Freckles an affectionate pat on the rump, and swung onto her back. Nudging the mare with her heels, she rode out of the barn and into the cool, misty morning.

Holding Freckles to a walk, Abbey wondered why she had ever left home. She loved it here, loved the horses, the cattle, the sense of freedom that riding gave her. How had she ever thought to find happiness in a small apartment in a crowded city?

When Freckles tugged on the reins, Abbey loosened her hold and the mare took off running. As they flew across the dew-damp grass, laughter bubbled up inside Abbey. Oh, how she had missed this! The sting of the wind in her face, the power of the animal beneath her, the rhythmic pounding of hooves. It was exhilarating.

Abbey let Freckles run flat out until, sides heaving, the mare slowed of her own accord.

Abbey reined Freckles to a halt in the shade of a tall oak. After dismounting, she stood there a moment, idly scratching the mare's ears while taking in the beauty of the land that stretched away into the distance, the vast blue vault of the sky. The air was crisp, redolent with the scents of earth and grass, trees and sage.

After a time, she started walking back toward the barn, leading the Appy to give her time to cool out.

Abbey hadn't gone far when she had the uneasy feeling that she was being watched. She glanced behind her and from side to side, but saw no one, yet the feeling remained. Someone was watching her. She was sure of it.

As nonchalantly as she could, she stepped into the saddle, took up the reins, and kicked the mare into a gallop. Heart pounding, Abbey leaned over Freckles's neck, afraid to look behind her. She told herself she was being foolish. There was no one there, but she didn't stop until they reached the barn.

Once safely there, she felt like an idiot.

After unsaddling the mare, Abbey walked Freckles around the corral until the mare had cooled off, then led her into the barn. She forked hay to the horses, topped off the water barrels.

Humming softly, Abbey fed the rest of the stock, then sat in the shade, her thoughts turning to Nick.

Was he really a vampire?

Had they met by chance?

Would she ever see him again?

Nick, Nick, Nick. He had probably forgotten all about her. With a huff of annoyance, she went up to the main house. In the kitchen, she sorted through the groceries she had bought the day before. She packed half to take to the cottage and left the rest behind so she'd have something to snack on when she was here.

It was a short walk to the cottage, tucked within a small copse of trees. She loved her parents, but she'd grown accustomed to her independence in New York and liked the idea of having a place of her own.

The cottage was just as she remembered it. Three steps led up to a railed porch. There was a two-person swing in one corner. The house, white with yellow trim, had a red tile roof, a red brick chimney, and a bright green front door. The interior rooms were all painted white, something Abbey intended to change as soon as possible.

She wasn't surprised to find the front door unlocked. The living room furniture was a hodgepodge of colors and styles that somehow managed to blend together. A satellite screen was mounted on the wall across from a small fireplace.

In the kitchen, she opened the window over the sink, then quickly put the groceries away. There were dishes and pots and pans in the cupboards, silverware and dishtowels in the drawers. A toaster, a coffeemaker, and a blender occupied a corner on the marble countertop.

She found her suitcases in the larger of the two bedrooms. The furniture—chest of drawers, nightstand, and small desk—was cherrywood. Pink curtains draped the windows, a matching quilt covered the double bed.

A flush climbed up her neck when she imagined Nick sharing that bed with her. Abbey pressed her hands to her burning cheeks. Where had *that* thought come from? In spite of the few kisses they had shared, she really didn't know the man.

But she had to admit that, since the night they'd met, he had never been far from her thoughts.

Hurrying out of the bedroom, she went into the kitchen and poured herself a glass of cold water, then stood at the sink, staring out the window, her wayward thoughts returning to Nick. Always Nick.

She had to stop thinking about him. Until she decided when—or if—she wanted to become a vampire, she didn't want anything to do with the Undead community, save for those who were already a part of her family.

She wanted a normal life—a husband, children,

grandchildren someday. Of course, first she had to find a man.

Nick was a man. . . .

She slammed her hand against the edge of the sink. "But he can't give you children! Or a normal life."

So what? asked a rebellious little voice in the back of her mind. *What's so great about a normal life? As for children, Mara has a son,* the voice reminded her. *Your mother had you. Cara had twins. Anything is possible.*

With a sigh of exasperation, Abbey left the cottage. A path lined with white rocks led to a small pond surrounded by wildflowers and shaded by the overhanging branches of a massive oak. It had always been her favorite place, a miniature Eden without the serpent.

Sitting on one of the wrought-iron benches, she closed her eyes and listened to the hum of insects. It was quiet here. Peaceful. As a young girl, she had often come here to read or to daydream; as a teenager, it had been her favorite place to be alone with her thoughts.

Back then, she had worried about grades and homework and how to persuade her father to let her stay out after ten. It was here that she had first been kissed, here that she had come to shed copious tears when the boy she had a crush on asked her best friend to the sixth grade dance.

Abbey smiled at the memory, remembering how brokenhearted she had been. And now she couldn't even remember the boy's name.

She was about to go up to the house to see if her parents were awake when she was overcome with the same sense of unease she had felt earlier.

Someone was out there, just beyond the trees, watching her.

She was sure of it.

* * *

Rane leaned forward in his chair, his gaze intent on his daughter's face. "You didn't see anyone?"

Abbey shook her head. "But I know someone was there."

"All right. You stay here with your mother. I'm going out to have a look around."

Savanah laid a hand on her husband's arm. "Be careful."

"That's my middle name," Rane said, patting her hand. "I won't be long."

Rane took his time getting to his destination, all his senses on high alert. It had been a while since any hunters had been spotted in the area, but you could never be too careful. He didn't see or sense anything out of place until he reached the pond.

The vampire's scent was strong, impossible to miss. Jaw clenched, hands balled into fists, Rane followed it to the tree line.

Oh, yeah, he recognized that scent. It was the same one he had detected on Abbey back in New York City.

Chapter Eight

Mara's gaze swept the area. Rane had called her earlier, requesting her help. She and Logan had arrived at the ranch shortly after dusk. Now, the three of them were gathered outside.

It wasn't possible, she thought as she paced from the pond to the tree line and back again. *He couldn't be here.* "What did you say this vampire's name was?"

Rane shrugged. "Abbey said he introduced himself as Nick."

"Nick?" Mara shook her head. *Could it be?*

Logan looked at her sharply, his eyes narrowing when her voice spoke to his mind. *Not now.*

"Does the name mean anything to you?" Rane asked.

"I knew a Niccola Desanto a long time ago," Mara replied, her voice carefully neutral.

"Who's Desanto?" Rane glanced from Mara to Logan and back again. "How come I've never heard of him?"

"He's old," Mara said. "Ancient."

"How old?"

"Older than Logan," she said, careful not to look at her husband. "Not quite as old as I am."

Rane swore under his breath. "He must have followed Abbey from New York. Dammit, I don't like this at all."

"She's a lovely young woman," Mara said. "You can hardly blame him for being interested."

"I can understand that. What I don't understand is why he's skulking around out here in the woods."

"It's not the *why* that bothers me," Mara said. "It's the *how.*"

Rane's head snapped up, his brow furrowing as he met Mara's gaze.

She nodded. "Unless Abbey told him about this place, there's only one way Desanto could have tracked her here over such a long distance."

"He took her blood." Rane clenched his hands until his knuckles went white. What else had Desanto taken from his daughter?

"Maybe she offered."

Rane glared at Logan. "She wouldn't do that! She just met the man." But what if he was wrong? How well did he really know his daughter? She had been living away from home for the last five years. Times changed. People changed.

"We need to talk to Abbey," Mara said. "Find out what happened between her and Nick before we make any rash decisions."

Logan looked at Mara, his expression carefully blank. "Maybe it's another man with the same name."

"Who just happens to be a vampire?" Rane asked.

A faint breeze stirred the leaves on the trees. Mara sighed as Nick's familiar, never-forgotten scent filled her nostrils and opened the floodgates of her memory. He had been here not long ago. Nicky, with his beautifully expressive dark eyes, and that whiskey-rough voice that no woman over the age of puberty could resist.

"It's Desanto," she confirmed, meeting her husband's eyes.

And that ended the discussion.

Abbey looked up when the front door opened, her eyes widening when she saw the Blackwoods. What were Mara and Logan doing here?

Savanah sent a questioning look at her husband before welcoming Logan and Mara.

Abbey put her iPod aside, a shiver of alarm skittering down her spine as she glanced from Mara to Logan to her father. All three wore the same serious expression.

"What's going on?" Savanah asked.

Rane dropped onto the sofa beside his wife. "Abbey met a man in New York."

Savanah lifted one brow. "I'm sure she met a lot of them."

"This one is a vampire," Rane said. "A very old vampire. Mara thinks he followed Abbey here."

"Followed me?" Abbey exclaimed, unable to contain a rush of excitement at the thought of seeing Nick again.

Rane nodded. "You thought you were being watched. You were right. It's Nick."

"How could he have followed me here?" Even if he had checked her driver's license while she was asleep, it listed her home address in New York City. She didn't carry anything with her parents' address on it.

"There's no point in dancing around the issue." Mara's gaze settled on Abbey. "The only way he could have followed you is if he's tasted your blood. Has he?"

"No! I mean, I don't think so. . . ." But it was possible. He could have drunk from her while she slept. She shuddered at the thought. Such a thing shouldn't have bothered her so much. She had grown up in a family of vampires, after all. She knew what they did to survive, though they had always been careful not to talk about it in detail in her presence. Of course, knowing wasn't the same as seeing. Or doing.

"So, it is possible," Mara said.

Abbey nodded, her stomach churning. "I guess so. We were in a car accident. I hit my head and he insisted I stay the night at his place so he could make sure I was okay."

Nick had taken her blood while she slept. How could he have done such a despicable thing? He had seemed so nice, so charming . . . and now he was here! Why had he followed her?

A dozen reasons sprang to mind, none of them good.

Choosing his words carefully, Rane asked, "Did anything else happen that night?"

Abbey stared at her father. "What do you mean?" Her cheeks flamed when she realized what he was asking. "I didn't sleep with him! I told you, I just met him." She glared at her father. "And even if I slept with him, which I didn't, it's none of your business!"

"All right, all right, I'm sorry." Clearing his throat, Rane turned to Mara. "So, since this guy is ancient, I'm guessing he's a day-walker."

Mara nodded.

"That means we'll have to be on guard day and night," Savanah remarked.

Abbey fidgeted with a lock of her hair, uncomfortable and embarrassed at being the center of attention. All she'd done was have a drink with a handsome man. How could she have known that something so innocent, so ordinary, would cause such a tempest in a teapot?

She was only vaguely aware of Logan and Mara taking

their leave. A short time later, Rane said he needed some air.

Looking up, Abbey met her mother's gaze. Of all the people in the family, surely Savanah would understand her attraction to a vampire. "Mom? Do you ever miss being human?"

"Sometimes," her mother admitted quietly, and then she sighed. "Most of the time."

She should have been surprised by this revelation, Abbey thought. Why wasn't she? Had she known, on some unconscious level, that her mother had regrets about her decision? "Does Dad know how you feel?"

"I'm not sure. We've never discussed it, and I try not to have any negative thoughts when we're together. It would hurt him to know how I feel."

"Would you do it over again?"

Savanah smoothed a nonexistent wrinkle from her skirt. "I . . . I honestly don't know."

"If you weren't sure it was what you wanted, why did you ask Dad to bring you across?"

"Because I love him, of course." Savanah shook her head. "We were married for eighteen years before he turned me. I knew what he was. I knew his family." She shook her head again. "I thought I knew everything there was to know about being a vampire, but of course, I didn't. It's like jumping out of an airplane. No matter what people tell you about it, you can't really know what it's like until you've experienced it for yourself."

"What do you miss the most?"

"Little things. Seemingly unimportant things I once took for granted. Like being able to enjoy a latte. Or eating a bowl of popcorn while watching a movie. Or seeing my reflection when I pass a mirror. It was frightening the first time I looked in a mirror and saw the room behind me and nothing else. I felt like . . . like

I didn't exist anymore." She smiled wistfully. "Not being able to see how you look in a new dress takes all the fun out of shopping."

Abbey rose from her chair and went to sit beside her mother. Wondering how she could have been so blind all these years, she took her mother's hand in hers. "I'm sorry you're unhappy, Mom."

"I'm not unhappy," Savanah said, patting Abbey's hand. "I have a good life, a loving husband, a wonderful daughter."

"But?"

"I don't want you to see Nick again."

"Why not?"

"This isn't a life I would choose for you. I know how exciting dating a vampire can be. They have an innate glamour, an allure, that's hard for mortals to resist. And then there's his age. Your father said he's ancient, which means he must be over five hundred years old. That's quite an age difference, don't you think?"

Abbey licked her lips. Was it possible he was that old? She thought of Mara, who looked like she was twenty but was, in reality, over two thousand years old. What if Nick was that old? Did he even remember what it was like to be human?

"It's better to end it now," Savanah said. "Before you get in so deep you can't get out."

Abbey nodded, but she was afraid it was already too late.

Logan confronted Mara in the Cordovas' guestroom later that night. "It's him, isn't it?"

"Yes." There was no point in lying. Mara had kept secrets from Logan in the past, but her acquaintance with Nick wasn't one of them. However, she had never discussed her relationship with the other vampire with Logan. He knew only that she had turned Nick and left him, as she had left so many others.

"Dammit. I thought he was dead."

"Aren't you overreacting just a little? I haven't been with Nick since I met you."

"Do you think it's just coincidence that he met Abbey? How do you know he isn't stalking her to find you?"

"Don't be ridiculous."

"It's not beyond the realm of possibility," Logan insisted. "Most of the vampire community knows about your close relationship with the Cordova family. If he couldn't find you, all he had to do was find one of them."

"To what purpose?"

"How the hell should I know?"

Suddenly thoughtful, Mara stroked a finger across her lips. What if Logan was right? What if Nick was looking for her?

She had a sudden flashback to the nights she and Desanto had spent together. When they'd parted centuries ago, she had banished him from her mind, refusing to think of him. She had driven him so completely from her thoughts that it hadn't occurred to her to mention him in the story she had written about her life. Save for Logan, she had never told anyone about Nick. Only Logan knew that she and Desanto had once been lovers, but that was all he knew.

What quirk of Fate had brought Nick into her life again?

And what was she going to do about it?

* * *

It was a question that lingered in Mara's mind long after Logan had fallen asleep beside her. She had never loved anyone the way she loved Logan Blackwood. He was the other half of her soul. The better half. He was an honorable man, and far too good for her. It never failed to amaze her that, in spite of all he knew about her, in spite of the callous way she had treated him in the past, he still wanted her. Still loved her.

And she loved him. So why did the thought of seeing Nick again fill her with such excitement? Such trepidation?

Niccola. He was the first man she had seduced after being turned by Dendar. She had taken Nick while she was still a young vampire, still confused over what had been done to her. Filled with anger and a burning need for vengeance, she had taken Nick for her lover, kept him against his will, venting her anger on him one moment and seducing him the next. And when she started to care for him, she had left him without a word or a backward glance, just as she had left so many others after him.

And now he was here. Was it truly coincidence that her old lover had met her goddaughter? Or was Logan right? Had Nick somehow discovered her ties to the Cordovas and followed Abbey here, hoping Abbey would lead him back to her?

Which led to the nagging question—why?

And why now, after all these years?

Chapter Nine

Abbey woke late after a mostly sleepless night. She had met a man she liked, but both her father and Mara were convinced that Nick had some ulterior motive for asking her out. What if they were right? More importantly, what if they were wrong? What if Nick was exactly as he seemed—a nice, sweet, sexy guy.

Who just happened to be a stalker? A vampire who had stolen her blood while she slept?

Try as she might, she couldn't ignore the little voice in the back of her mind that said if he was on the up-and-up, he would have knocked on the front door instead of lurking in the bushes, spying on her.

After showering, she ate a peanut butter and jelly sandwich for breakfast, washed it down with a cup of coffee heavily laced with cream and sugar, and went out the back door, heading for the barn.

She quickly fed the stock, then spent a few minutes scratching her mare's ears before going to the cottage. It was time she settled in. She needed to unpack her clothes, do a little dusting, vacuum the rugs, change the linens on the bed.

The same bed she had imagined sharing with Nick.

She rounded the corner of the cottage, let out a shriek when she saw him standing on the front porch.

She stared at him a moment, then whirled around and sprinted back up the gravel path, shrieked again when his hand closed on her shoulder, bringing her to an abrupt halt.

"Easy, now." Taking a firm hold on her wrist, he drew her back toward the cottage, pulled her gently up the porch stairs, only to stop at the threshold. "Are you going to invite me in?"

"No!"

"We need to talk."

"What are you doing here?"

"Looking for you, of course. Why else would I be here?"

"You drank my blood, didn't you? That's how you found me."

"I only took a little." And he had been wanting more—much more—ever since.

She glared at him. "How could you do such a despicable thing?"

"Despicable?" He lifted one brow. "Coming from a family of vampires as you do, I wouldn't think you'd give it a second thought."

"Well, you thought wrong!" She tried in vain to wrench her arm from his grasp, but he had a grip like iron. "How do you know about my family?"

"I can smell them on you." It was the truth, but it wasn't how he'd known that she was related to the Cordovas. Her mind was an open book. Someone really should teach her how to block her thoughts.

"Let me go!"

"Calm down, Abbey. I'm not here to hurt you."

"What do you want from me?"

"How about that second date you promised me?"

Abbey stared at him. A date? He had caused all this trouble and confusion for another date? "My father thinks you want something else from me."

"Oh?"

"Do you? Want something?"

A smile twitched his lips. "Maybe a kiss good night when I bring you home?"

"Stop joking! This is serious."

"I'm not *after* anything, Abbey. I just want to get to know you better."

"Mara thinks . . ."

His hand tightened around her wrist, his gaze spearing hers. "Mara's here?"

"You're hurting me!" Abbey exclaimed.

"I'm sorry." He released her immediately. "What is she doing here?"

Abbey shook her hand, which had gone numb. "She's a friend of the family."

Nick stared at her as if he had seen a ghost. "Mara. Here. After all this time." His nostrils flared. "How did I miss her scent?" he wondered aloud.

Abbey took a step backward. When he didn't seem to notice, she took another. And then another. Reaching behind her, she opened the door and darted across the threshold. Inside, she breathed a sigh of relief, knowing he couldn't enter without an invitation.

Nick shook his head as if to clear it; then, regarding her across the threshold, he said, "So, how about that date?"

"I don't think so."

He leaned one shoulder against the jamb, ankles crossed negligently, as if he was prepared to stay there all day. "What can I say to change your mind?"

"How do you know Mara?"

"It's a long story. Maybe I'll tell you about it one of these days."

Intrigued, Abbey cocked her head to the side. "Why not now?"

"I don't think so. Not until I know you better."

"My father said you're an old vampire. Is that true?"

A shadow passed behind Nick's eyes, and then he shrugged. "I guess it depends on what you call old."

"Just tell me!"

"Does it matter?"

Abbey nodded, her hands clenching. The man was impossible. "I'm afraid so."

"I've been a vampire almost as long as Mara."

Feeling suddenly light-headed, Abbey swayed on her feet. Mara had been alive during the reign of Cleopatra. She wasn't sure why she was so shocked to learn that Nick was ancient, except that Mara had always been a law unto herself. One of a kind. And Nick was almost as old. What had he seen in that vast amount of time? How many lives had he taken? How many women had he loved and lost?

Nick pushed away from the jamb, his eyes narrowing. "Abbey, I think you'd better sit down."

"I think you're right," she murmured, and after quietly closing the door in his face, she sank down on the floor, knees bent, her face buried in her hands.

"Abbey? Abbey! Dammit, answer me!?"

"Go away, Nick. Please, just go away."

"All right," he replied. "But I'm not going far. You still owe me another date."

Nick paced away from the cottage, melting into the cool shadows beneath the trees. He could be active during the day, but only when the moon was high in the sky did he feel fully alive.

Mind spinning, he stared at the distant mountains.

Mara was here. His thoughts traveled back in time to that fateful night when he had met a beguiling young woman with hair like black silk and eyes as green as the grassy banks of the Nile. As if it had happened yesterday, he remembered being seduced by her. Remembered the sting of her fangs at his throat, the horror of learning what she was. What he had become. The fear that engulfed him when he woke one night to find her gone.

Abandoned by his maker after only a few months, he had been lost, uncertain of what he truly was, ignorant of most of the powers that were now his. Driven by an insatiable lust for blood, he had savaged those he fed upon, killed indiscriminately before he discovered that he didn't have to take a life to sustain his own, that he could make feeding pleasurable for those he preyed upon. How many lives had he needlessly taken before he learned to control his hunger? Even now, centuries later, the guilt rode him with whip and spurs. Yes, she owed him, he thought, owed him for the lives he had taken. For the life she had stolen from him.

He glanced back at the cottage. Only a few short days ago, he had yearned for death, had intended to spend the rest of his existence seeking Mara's whereabouts and an end to his damnably long life. Now the means to that end was here, but death no longer held any appeal because Abbey was also here.

Abbey. Her smile was brighter than the sun, her life's blood sweeter than honey.

He would not court death now. Not while she drew breath.

Abbey sat on the floor for a long while, her mind blessedly blank. Eventually, the hard floor drove her to her feet. She stood there a moment, then shook her head. Needing something to take her mind off Nick, she went into the bedroom and unpacked her suitcases, hanging her clothes in the closet, carefully folding her underwear before putting it in the dresser.

She stripped the linen from the bed and tossed it into the washing machine located in a small alcove off the kitchen, dusted the furniture, vacuumed the carpets. And when that was done, she took a quick shower, slipped into a pair of jeans and a T-shirt, pulled on her boots. A nice long ride was exactly what she needed to clear her head.

After peering out the front window to make sure Nick was gone, she went to the barn and saddled Freckles.

The Appy was eager to run. Giving the mare her head, Abbey surrendered to the sheer joy of racing over the gently rolling hills, reveling in the kiss of the afternoon sun on her cheeks and the warm wind blowing in her hair. It was exhilarating, liberating.

Gradually, Freckles slowed to a canter, then a trot, then a walk.

Murmuring, "Whoa, girl," Abbey drew rein in the shade of a tree. Dismounting, she ground-tied the mare, loosened the saddle cinch, then flopped down on the grass. She sat there a moment, then fell back, arms outstretched, and closed her eyes.

When she opened them again, Nick sat beside her.

Startled, she jackknifed into a sitting position, her heart pounding. "Go away."

"Abbey, please . . ."

"Please what?"

"Don't be afraid of me. You've nothing to fear from me, I swear it on the memory of my mother."

"You had a mother?" she asked flippantly.

He shrugged. "I barely remember her."

Overcome with guilt for her sarcastic remark, Abbey laid her hand on his arm. "I'm sorry."

"Like I said, I barely remember her."

His fingers stroked the back of her hand. Warmth flowed in the wake of his touch.

"I'm sorry I scared you earlier," he said quietly. "As for taking your blood . . . it was a temptation I couldn't resist. I should have asked you first."

"Apology accepted."

His smile went straight to her heart. When he reached for her, it seemed the most natural thing in the world to settle into his embrace. For a time he simply held her, one hand lightly stroking her hair. And that quickly, all her doubts faded away. His gentle touch, the tender expression in his eyes, assured her that he would never hurt her. It no longer mattered what anyone else thought. If her Uncle Roshan could fall in love with a photograph of a witch, then she could fall in love with Nick.

"What are you smiling at?" he asked.

"Nothing. I'm just happy you're here."

He stroked her cheek with his knuckles, ran his fingertips over her lower lip. "Women," he muttered with a shake of his head. "I'll never understand them. Aren't you the same girl who told me to get lost just a short time ago?"

"It's my prerogative to change my mind. Didn't you know?"

He laughed softly, then swooped down to claim her lips in a long, slow kiss. She wrapped her arms around his neck, holding him tightly as he ravaged her mouth. He nipped her lower lip, his tongue slipping inside to duel with hers, sending frissons of heat spearing through every fiber of her being.

"What the hell is going on here!"

At the sound of her father's voice, Abbey pushed Nick away and scrambled to her feet, her cheeks burning. "Dad!"

Nick rose slowly to stand beside her.

Rane glared at him. "Get off my land. Now!"

A muscle throbbed in Nick's jaw. He was taller than Rane Cordova. Older. Stronger. But Rane was Abbey's father. There was nothing to be gained—and much to be lost—by fighting with the man.

Nick gave Abbey's hand a squeeze and then, in a move too quick for her to follow, he was gone.

"Do you want to tell me what you're doing rolling around out here in the grass with a perfect stranger?" Rane demanded, his voice tight.

Abbey lifted her head, hands clenched at her sides. "He's not a stranger. And I have every right to 'roll around in the grass' with him if I want to. I'm not a little girl anymore. I'm twenty-six. Old enough to do whatever I please."

"Abbey . . ." He took a deep breath, knowing that he had to be careful. Saying the wrong thing now could damage their relationship, send her back to the city where she was liable to do something stupid just to spite him.

"I never believed in love at first sight," she whispered, "but I do now."

Her declaration left him speechless. Not knowing what else to do, he drew her into his arms.

The situation was even worse than he had feared.

* * *

Mara, Logan, and Savanah were waiting for Rane and Abbey at the main house.

"What's happened?" Abbey asked, glancing anxiously from one sober expression to the next. "Did someone die?"

"Not yet." Mara shook her head. "Why is it bad things always happen in threes? First Nick shows up, and now this."

At the mention of Nick's name, Rane and Abbey exchanged glances.

Savanah looked at Mara. "What's happened?"

"I just got a message from an informant of mine," Mara said, closing her phone. "Were any of you aware that a coalition of hunters has posted a reward for the capture and/or heads of the persons or vampires who killed Lou McDonald and her sister?"

Logan grunted. "No shit. I guess Edna and Pearl better lay low for a while."

"I don't think they're in any danger," Rane remarked. "We're the only ones who know they killed the McDonalds."

"Unless they let something slip," Mara pointed out. "Edna never could keep a secret."

"What's the third thing?" Savanah asked.

"Pearl and Edna are missing."

"And that's a bad thing?" Logan muttered.

Rane looked at Mara. "There's more, isn't there?"

"It seems those meddling old fools are very popular this week. The coalition wants them dead, but there's a rumor that an unknown hunter is offering a thousand credits for information on their whereabouts."

"I'd be happy to turn them in."

"Forget it, Blackwood," Rane said brusquely. "Edna and Pearl are like family."

Logan shook his head. "Not to me." He held up his

hands in a gesture of surrender when Rane glared at him. "Okay, okay. You win."

"Enough, you two," Mara said. "We need to find out if Pearl and Edna are in hiding, or if they've been captured, and if so, who has them."

"If the coalition found them, they're no longer a problem," Logan stated. "They're already dead."

"And if the other hunter has them?" Savanah asked. "What then?"

"I don't know, but I'd love to know why a hunter would want to take a vampire alive."

"I can think of several reasons," Mara said. "Maybe he wants to change sides. . . ."

Logan snorted. "Yeah, right."

"Maybe he's looking for the cure," Rane suggested. It wasn't well known, but Edna and Pearl had concocted some mysterious brew rumored to restore a vampire's mortality.

"The cure?" Savanah murmured. "Why?"

Mara lifted one shoulder in an elegant shrug. "Who knows why mortals do what they do."

Logan slapped his hands on his knees. "So, do we look for them, or let 'em sink or swim on their own?"

"We ask around," Rane said, "and see what we can find out. Right, Mara?"

She nodded, none too enthusiastically.

Sighing, Savanah murmured, "It never rains but it pours."

Near dawn, when Logan and the rest of the family were occupied elsewhere, Mara went in search of Nick. His scent—so familiar, so easy to follow—led her to a deserted shack at the edge of Rane's property.

She should have known he would be outside, waiting for her.

"You look the same," he remarked. "Just as beautiful as I remember."

She smiled, pleased by the admiration in his eyes. "What are you up to, Nicky? Why are you here?"

"I came to see Abbey."

"Is that the only reason?"

"Do you think I've got some ulterior motive?" His eyes narrowed. "Revenge, perhaps?"

"Why are you really here, Nicky?"

"I told you. I came to see Abbey. I met her in New York a few days ago, and I wanted to see her again."

"You had no idea she's my goddaughter?"

"How would I know that?"

"You tell me."

"If I hadn't met Abbey, I'd think it was a nice twist of fate that I found you."

"Oh?"

"I'd heard you regained your humanity. I was weary of my life, and I wanted to know how you did it. And if you couldn't tell me, I was going to ask you to destroy me."

She hadn't expected that. The very thought of destroying him made her gasp with surprise. "That's why you're here? You want me to end your life?"

"Not anymore."

Mara regarded him for several moments. "I see. Abbey's given you a reason to go on."

He nodded. "How did you do it? How did you regain your humanity?"

"I don't know. It just . . . just happened, but the more I think about it, the more certain I am that it had to do with conceiving a werewolf's child. I gradually lost my powers and one day I woke up and I was human again."

She frowned thoughtfully. "You were hoping I could tell you how it happened so you could be mortal again, weren't you? Because of Abbey."

"I want her and I intend to have her, one way or the other."

"Just like that?"

"Just like that."

In the blink of an eye, Mara's hand curled around his throat. "I don't think so."

He didn't flinch, merely stared at her. "She was meant to be mine, and I will have her."

"What if she doesn't want you?"

"She wants me, all right. Besides, you owe me," he said, his voice little more than a growl. "You owe me more than you can ever repay."

"Shut up!"

"You seduced me. You turned me against my will. And then you abandoned me. Do you know how many lives I took? How many people I killed because I didn't know I could control the lust for blood?"

"I will not use my goddaughter to repay my so-called sins against you."

"I'm not going to hurt her. I care for her."

Her hand tightened around his throat, her gaze probing his, her fingers digging deeper into his flesh before she released him. "If you hurt her . . ."

"I know," he said with a wry grin. "You'll rip out my heart."

"And feed it to you," she added sweetly.

"I've missed you, Mara. We had some good times." His hand cupped her cheek, his thumb caressing her lower lip. "Even after everything that happened, I missed you."

"I'm sorry, Nick. I was young. Angry. I never meant to hurt you."

"We've both come a long way," he said. "It's all in the past."

Mara nodded. Rising on her tiptoes, she kissed him lightly. "Remember what I said."

"I will."

She was gone before the words left his mouth.

Logan was lying in bed, hands clasped behind his head, a sheet pooled around his hips, when Mara entered their room. "Is there anything I need to worry about?" he asked quietly.

"Of course not. I needed his forgiveness, that's all." She frowned. "You don't believe me?"

"Should I?"

"You've never doubted me before."

"Nick was never here before."

Mara cupped Logan's face in her palms, then opened her mind and her heart to his gaze. "There's no one for me but you, Hektor," she whispered. A pair of tears, tinged with blood, slid down her cheeks. "There never has been. There never will be."

He smiled faintly at her use of his ancient name.

And then he took her in his arms and kissed away her tears.

Chapter Ten

In the morning, after putting on her work clothes, Abbey poured herself a cup of coffee. Carrying it into the living room, she stared out the window. How had things gotten so complicated? She wasn't even sure what was going on. She was the youngest member of the family, the only mortal, and yet she had always known that everyone loved her, that they would always be there for her, and yet last night made it crystal clear that she didn't really know anything about them.

She had lived with vampires her whole life and she knew most of the basics. They were practically immortal. They healed rapidly when they were wounded. They drank blood to survive. They could move faster than the human eye could follow. They could turn into mist, change shape, scale tall buildings with a single bound. Holy water burned them. The old ones could only be killed if you drove a wooden stake into their heart, took their head, or burned them to ash. Younger ones could be destroyed by dragging them into sunlight.

Abbey had never asked her parents any but the most fundamental questions, had never wanted to know the intimate details. Not knowing made it easier to pretend the Cordovas were just like everyone else. She had clung to the belief that ignorance was bliss, at least where vampires were concerned.

Until she discovered Nick was a vampire.

Now she wanted—needed—to know everything because, as impossible as it seemed, what she had told her father was true.

She was falling in love.

The thought made her smile. After rinsing out her cup, she put it in the dishwasher, then went out the back door. She strolled toward the barn, pausing now and again to appreciate the beauty around her—the vast blue sky, the wildflowers, the rolling hills. She laughed as a squirrel darted across her path and scampered out of sight. Overhead, birds chirped merrily in the trees.

Using both hands, she opened the barn door. It was time to earn her keep, she thought. Time to get to work. Although getting paid to do something you loved really didn't seem like work.

She mucked the stalls. She fed the stock. She filled the water barrels. She exercised the horses. And all the while, her thoughts were on Nick. Everyone seemed opposed to her relationship with him, but she didn't care.

She wanted him.

It wasn't quite noon when her stomach growled, reminding her she hadn't had any breakfast. After cooling out the horse she had been exercising, she made her way to the cottage.

In the kitchen, she washed her hands and packed a lunch. Hurrying back to the barn, she saddled Freckles, stowed her lunch in one of the saddlebags, and rode to a secluded glen where she could relax and sort out her thoughts. It was her second favorite place on the ranch.

Dismounting, Abbey tethered the mare to a low-hanging branch, then loosened the cinch. The Appy immediately lowered her head to nibble on the thick grass.

Giving the mare a pat on the neck, Abbey moved a few feet away. After finding a shady spot, she sat on the grass to eat her lunch, her mind filling with the events of the previous night.

A coalition of hunters was offering a reward for whoever had killed Lou McDonald and her sister. It didn't mean anything to Abbey; she had never met the McDonalds. She didn't know who had killed them or why. But the thought of hunters in the area gave her cause for concern. If there was one thing she did know, it was that hunters were often more ruthless than the vampires they hunted.

Edna and Pearl were missing. Again, Abbey had no idea how or if that should worry her, since she had never met either one of them.

And then there was Nick. Always Nick. Was he somehow involved in all this? Was that why the family was so upset? She frowned as she pulled two apples from her bag. She tossed one to Freckles, then bit into the other. What possible reason would Nick have to kill the McDonalds, or offer a reward for their killer? By the same token, what would he want with Edna and Pearl? Surely he had no designs on them. Abbey knew little about them other than that they had both been in their seventies when her Uncle Rafe had turned them. They had recently concocted a potion they hoped would cure Derek of being a werewolf, but Sheree had refused to let him take it.

Abbey shook her head. Her father had mentioned a cure for vampires. Was Nick looking for it?

Too many questions without answers. Taking a last bite of her apple, she tossed the core to Freckles, who quickly gobbled it up.

With a sigh, Abbey gained her feet. She stowed the trash in her saddlebag, then tightened the cinch and swung onto the Appy's back.

She turned the mare toward home, only to abruptly change her mind. It would be hours until her parents were up. Might as well do a little exploring. If she remembered correctly, there used to be an old line shack not far from here. Was it still there, or had her father finally torn it down?

Nick stirred as a wayward breeze penetrated the chinks in the shack's walls, carrying Abbey's scent with it. He started to rise, thought better of it, and rolled onto his side, his gaze on the door. Abbey's scent grew stronger as the sound of hoofbeats drew closer. Nick propped himself on one elbow, listening. A horse whinnied softly. Tentative footsteps approached the door.

She was here. Why?

The rusty hinges creaked as Abbey nudged the door open and peered inside. The room was in shadow, the ragged curtains drawn across the cracked window. She glanced around, then opened the door wider, allowing more light inside.

A faint movement caught her eye. Startled, she took a step backward, her eyes widening when she saw Nick watching her from the cot. She pressed one hand to her breast. "What are you doing here?" she exclaimed.

"I could ask you the same thing." He sat up, the sheet pooling in his lap.

Abbey stared at him, her mouth going dry. He had the upper body of a Greek god. Toned and well muscled. With six-pack abs any bodybuilder would envy.

He lifted one brow in wry amusement. "Wanna see the rest?"

"Of . . ." She swallowed hard. "Of course not."

He slid one long, muscular leg out from under the sheet. "Are you sure?"

Abbey bit down on her lower lip as a flush spread up her neck and into her cheeks. She clenched her hands at her sides to keep from ripping the sheet from the bed and satisfying her curiosity. She had to get out of here, she thought desperately.

Before she did something totally out of character. Before her father found her . . .

That thought sent her backing out of the shack. Taking a deep breath, she closed the door.

She was trying to convince herself to jump on her horse and get the heck out of there when Nick stepped outside clad in nothing but a pair of jeans that rode dangerously low on his hips.

Oh, Lord, he was just as sexy and desirable partially clothed as naked.

Caught in the web of his gaze, she stared up at him, helpless to resist as two short strides closed the distance between them.

Murmuring, "Mornin', darlin'," he wrapped her in his arms.

With a sigh, she rested her head against his chest, no longer caring if her father or anyone else saw them. She was in Nick's arms, and that was all that mattered.

He held her close, his hand lightly caressing her back, his breath warm against her skin.

"How did you know I was here?" he asked after a while.

"I didn't. I was just out riding and I stopped by to see if this old place was still standing. I used to play here when I was younger."

He grunted softly. "Another hope crushed."

She smiled up at him. "What are *you* doing here?"

"I needed a place to spend the day." He stroked her cheek. "Someplace close to you. Come on," he said, shielding his eyes against the sun, "let's go inside."

Ignoring the little voice warning her that being alone with Nick in a room with a bed was a bad idea, she followed him into the shack, her teeth worrying her lower lip as he closed the door, shutting out the rest of the world.

He lifted one brow. "I can hear your heart beating a mile a minute. What are you afraid of?"

"I'm not afraid."

"No?"

When she shook her head, he crossed the short distance between them.

"Maybe you should be." His gaze moved to the pulse beating rapidly in the hollow of her throat.

Abbey swallowed hard. What was she doing here, alone with a vampire she scarcely knew? His gaze was compelling and she glanced away, only to come face to face with the bed he had so recently occupied.

Nick laughed softly as her cheeks turned pink. The scent of her desire, mingled with her uncertainty, teased his nostrils. She wanted him, but she was afraid—afraid of him. Afraid of her own desire.

"Ah, Abbey," he murmured, "you tempt me almost beyond reason."

"Do I?"

"You are so incredibly lovely. And you smell so damn

sweet." Lifting a lock of her hair, he let it sift through his fingers. "Your hair is like silk." His knuckles brushed her cheek. "Your skin is soft and smooth." His gaze moved over her, lingering on her breasts, her narrow waist, the flare of her hips. "Do you have any idea how much I want you?"

Incapable of speech when he was looking at her like that, as if he were a starving man and she his next meal, she could only stand there, mute. Waiting.

"Tell me what you want, Abbey."

She curled her hands into fists to keep from reaching for him. "I want you, but . . ."

"Go on."

"How do I know what I'm feeling for you is real? My Mom told me vampires have an innate allure that's hard for mortals to resist. How do I know you're not manipulating me in some way? Making me feel something that doesn't really exist?"

Nick blew out a breath. Damn, how was he supposed to answer that?

"Nick?"

"It's true," he admitted. "I have the power to compel you to do whatever I want. I also have the power to attract you. It's part of being a predator. But I've never compelled you or used any preternatural power to attract you. Whatever you feel for me is real."

"I want to believe that, but we hardly know each other. It doesn't seem possible that I could care for you so quickly."

"Haven't you ever heard of love at first sight?"

"Of course." Hadn't she admitted as much to her father? "But I don't want to end up like my mother."

Taking her by the hand, Nick led her to the small wooden table in the corner. He held out a chair for her and when she was seated, he took the other one. "Tell me about her."

"Her father was fascinated with magic when she was growing up, and with one magician in particular. That magician happened to be my dad. She saw him several times through the years as she was growing up. And even though he used a lot of different names, she always recognized him. Eventually, she became a reporter, and being the curious type, she was determined to find out why he never aged. She started waiting for him outside his dressing room. One night, she finally met him and the rest, as they say, is history. When I turned eighteen, my dad turned my mom."

Abbey paused. "I always thought my mom liked being a vampire, but we had a talk the other day and it seems she's not as happy about it as I thought."

"Being a vampire isn't for everyone," Nick remarked. "I take it you've given it a lot of thought."

"What do you think? I grew up surrounded by them. My mom was always warning me that I couldn't tell anyone the truth, plus she was very protective of me. I had to come straight home from school. I wasn't allowed to spend the night at my friends' houses. I know she worried about me, always afraid that I'd say something I shouldn't, or that some hunter would find out who I was and use me to get at my dad."

Abbey sat back in the chair, hands tightly folded on the table. "Sometimes I think I should ask my dad to turn me, but then I think of all I'd be giving up, and . . ." She blew out a sigh. "Once it's done, it's done."

"I don't imagine it's an easy decision for anyone who's given the choice."

"What made you decide to become a vampire?"

"I didn't." A muscle ticked in his jaw. "Someone decided for me."

"Would you undo it, if you could?"

He nodded. "In a heartbeat."

"I always wished I could have all the preternatural perks—without actually becoming a vampire. I mean, it would be great, being able to read minds, move faster than the eye can follow, turn into mist, never grow old."

"Yeah, that is nice," he agreed.

"What do you miss most about being human?"

"A lot of things. The change in seasons. Summer or winter, hot or cold, it's all the same to me. I miss sleeping and dreaming. I miss the innocence that mortals have, the sense of wonder that I no longer possess." He paused. "I would have liked the chance to be a father."

"It's not impossible. Look at Mara. She has a son. And my uncle Vince and his wife had twins."

"I guess miracles happen now and then," Nick mused. He was silent a moment, and then asked, "So, where does that leave us?"

Where, indeed? Did she really want to pursue a relationship with a vampire? Even one as gorgeous as Nick Desanto? What if they got married . . . Married! Where had *that* thought come from? She had just met the man. She hardly knew him, and since she didn't believe in casual sex, there didn't seem to be any point in seeing him again if it wasn't going to lead to something permanent . . . And if it did, was she prepared to make the hard decisions sure to follow?

If she was going to call it quits, now was the time, before she started to care more than she already did.

But she couldn't form the words.

Leaning across the table, he covered her hands with one of his. "Will you go out with me tonight?"

Her heart made the decision before her brain had time to think it over. "Yes."

"Pick you up at seven?"

"I'll be ready."

Rising, Nick drew Abbey to her feet, then wrapped her in his arms again. He held her for a long moment before he claimed her lips with his.

And in that gentle, lingering kiss of possession, Nick knew his fate was sealed.

As was hers.

Chapter Eleven

When Abbey returned to the cottage, she found her father sitting on the swing on the front porch.

"Hi, honey," he said, rising. "Where have you been?"

"I was out riding. Have you been waiting long?"

"Not really." He gave her a hug, then drew back, nostrils flaring. "You've been with him, haven't you?"

Abbey's gaze slid away from his. Having a vampire for a father made lying useless. Not that she would have lied to him. But without his preternatural senses, he never would have known she'd been with Nick.

Rane glanced around the yard. "Where is he?"

"Dad . . ."

"Where is he?"

"Out at the old shack." She grabbed his arm when he started to turn away. "What are you going to do?"

"I'm going to ask him what his intentions are toward my daughter."

"Dad! I just met the man!"

"He's got no business on my property," Rane said. "Or any business stalking my daughter."

"He's not stalking me."

"No? What do you call it when he follows you here and then sneaks around like a thief in the night?"

Abbey bit down on the corner of her lip. Not long ago, she had used the word *stalker* herself. She took a deep breath. "He asked me to go out with him tonight."

"I suppose you said yes."

She nodded. "I don't know where this is headed, but there's something between us, a connection. I can't explain it, but it feels right."

Rane drew a ragged breath, let it out in a long sigh of resignation. "Like you've said so often, you're old enough to make your own decisions."

"Did Mom know what she was getting into when she fell in love with you?"

Rane looked at her sharply. "What does that mean?"

"Nothing. But Mom was human when the two of you met. If you're so set against humans and vampires dating, why did you go out with Mom?"

Rane grunted softly. *Why, indeed?*

Walking toward the old shack, Rane found himself thinking about what Abbey had said. He had never intended to get involved with a mortal female. But Savanah had been hard to ignore.

He had first seen her when he was performing as The Remarkable Renaldo. He had invited several volunteers to come onstage to witness one of his most popular tricks, in which he stepped through a doorway and disappeared. Savanah's father, William Gentry, had volunteered, at his daughter's urging. Gentry had asked if his daughter could accompany him and after a moment's hesitation, Rane had agreed.

In the years that followed, he had seen Savanah and her father in the audience in a number of cities. He had watched her blossom from a gangly nine-year-old into a lovely young woman with hair the color of moonlight, eyes as blue as a robin's egg, and a figure that went in and out in all the right places. The first time he had seen her, all grown up, he'd wanted to know her better.

After graduating college, she became a reporter. As such, she became more interested in discovering the secrets behind his so-called tricks than in being entertained.

He recalled the night that had changed his life forever. Savanah had been in the audience, front row center. Wanting to show off a little for her benefit, Rane had left the stage and strolled up the center aisle. He had stopped here and there, asking men and women chosen at random to think of something no one else could possibly know about them and then, using his preternatural power to read their minds, he had revealed their secrets. From time to time he had glanced at Savanah. Annoyed by the skepticism in her eyes, he had made his way to the front row.

She had stared at him in surprise when he greeted her by name. She had blushed furiously when he asked if he should tell the audience what she was thinking. She had responded with a vigorous "No!" He had laughed, because she had been thinking he was the handsomest man she had ever seen, and that she wanted to run her fingers over his bare chest. Rane grinned at the memory.

She had waylaid him in the alley after the show, requesting an interview for her newspaper, and he had invited her to have a drink. He had been smitten by her beauty, her sense of humor, and, later, when she learned the truth about what he was, her courage.

Pausing, he stared into the distance. It might have

been a mistake to court Savanah, to make her his wife. Though they had never discussed it, he knew that, in some ways, she regretted her decision to become a vampire, just as he knew that she loved him, body and soul, as he would always love her.

He only hoped that whatever decision Abbey made in the future, she would never regret it.

Rane paused when he reached the shack. Was he doing the right thing? Abbey had been living on her own for the last five years. What right did he have, really, to tell her how to live her life? He had raised her the best way he knew how. It was time to trust her. Time to let go.

He was turning away when he felt the other vampire's presence.

"Something I can do for you, Cordova?" Nick asked.

Rane drew a calming breath. "I want to know what your intentions are toward my daughter."

Nick didn't know what he'd been expecting Abbey's father to say, but this definitely wasn't it. "My intentions?"

"She's my only child. I don't want to see her get hurt."

"Neither do I."

"Are you in love with her?"

Nick raked his fingers through his hair, reluctant to put his feelings for Abbey into words. "I've only known her for a few days."

"That's not what I asked you."

"All right, dammit, I'm in love with her."

"I was afraid of that." Rane shoved his hands into his pants' pockets. "Listen, Abbey might have grown up in a family of vampires, but there's a lot about our kind that she doesn't know. I want your word that you won't take advantage of her ignorance, or use your preternatural powers to seduce her. If you haven't already."

Nick shook his head. "Stop worrying, Cordova. We haven't gone there," he said, but couldn't help adding, "Yet."

"Abbey told me you're taking her out tonight."

"You got a problem with that?"

"Plenty of them, but that's neither here nor there. I'd like you to pick her up at our place."

"Sure," Nick said with a wry grin.

Nothing like spending a little time with Mom and Dad.

Chapter Twelve

Pearl stared at the middle-aged hunter, but he refused to meet her gaze. Smart man. She had tried to read his mind earlier, but he had managed to block her. She wondered how he had done that. More importantly, she wondered if she would live to see another night.

She glanced at Edna, who sat on the floor on the other side of the room. Like Pearl, Edna's hands and feet were bound with silver.

Pearl glared at the hunter. "Who are you? What do you want from us?" She was stalling for time. She knew all too well who he was—a hunter, and a seasoned one, at that.

"I'll ask the questions here," he said curtly. "I've heard about the two of you."

"Is that right?" Edna asked.

Pearl scowled at her friend. She loved Edna Mae Turner like a sister but the woman was easily swayed. A smile, a compliment, and she behaved like a silly teenager.

Pearl shifted uncomfortably on the hard floor. "Just what have you heard?"

"They say you've developed a cure, a vampire cure. Is it true?"

"Maybe. Why do you want to know?"

"Someone turned my daughter night before last. When she came home, she tried to attack her brother. I have her locked in her room, chained up so she can't hurt anybody. So, I'm asking you again. Does it work?"

Pearl jerked her chin toward the gun in his hand. She could smell the silver bullets. "Why would I help you?"

"Because you're dead if you don't."

"And dead if we do," she retorted, anger swamping her fear.

"I'll let you go. Both of you."

Pearl snorted. "Why should we believe you?"

"You've got the rest of tonight to think it over," he said. "After that . . ." Shrugging, he left the room.

Pearl's shoulders slumped when he closed the door.

"We have to give it to him," Edna said. "We don't have any other choice."

"Really? And what if it doesn't work?"

"What if it does?"

"This is all your fault, dear."

"*My* fault?"

"You're the one who flirted with him. You always were crazy for tall blond men with blue eyes." Pearl shook her head. "You certainly fluttered your eyelashes at the wrong man this time."

"He didn't smell like a hunter," Edna said. "How was I to know?" Some hunters were born, some chose the occupation on their own. Vampires were able to detect those born to the trade. Hunters and vampires alike had discovered scents to disguise their true natures.

"I wonder what he used to mask his scent. I didn't recognize the smell."

"So they found something new. What difference

does it make now?" A single, blood-red tear ran down Edna's cheek. "Damn silver shackles are burning my skin."

"I know, dear. Mine, too." Pearl frowned thoughtfully. "Does he look familiar to you?"

Edna shook her head. "I don't think so. I'm sure I would have remembered him."

"I guess so, but I can't shake the feeling I've seen him somewhere before."

Edna glanced at the narrow, barred window set high in the wall. It was covered by a thin curtain.

Pearl's glance followed Edna's. If the sun found them in the morning, the hunter would never get his cure. "Maybe you should try calling Derek."

Edna glared at her. "Don't you think I've been doing that?" She had taken Derek's blood when he was a child; it had formed a link between them. "I don't think the bond is working anymore."

"Keep trying," Pearl said quietly. "He's our only hope."

Chapter Thirteen

Abbey was a nervous wreck when she left the cottage and made her way up to the main house. Her father had informed her that Nick was picking her up there instead of at her place. Needless to say, she was not thrilled with the prospect of sitting down with her parents while they gave Nick the third degree—something she was sure was bound to happen.

She hesitated at the front door, took a deep breath, and stepped into the foyer. Her parents were already there, of course, sitting side by side on one of the sofas. Mara and Logan were holding hands on the other couch. At first glance, the vampires looked like anyone else. A closer look revealed that their skin was unblemished and unlined, their hair unusually lustrous and thick, and that they didn't breathe as deeply or as often as ordinary mortals.

A quick glance around the room showed that Nick had not yet arrived.

Smiling, Savanah rose to embrace her daughter. "How pretty you look!"

"Thanks, Mom."

"Come, sit with us," Savanah said, taking her by the hand.

Abbey sat on the sofa between her parents. The tension in the room was palpable.

Looking at her father, she said, "Please don't turn this into an inquisition. It's just a date." She shook her head. "I don't believe you're doing this. It's not like I'm a teenager going out with a boy for the first time. And it's not like I need your permission."

Savanah patted Abbey's hand. "I just want to meet him, honey, nothing more."

Abbey nodded, but her mother's assurance did nothing to calm her nerves. If her mother just wanted to meet Nick, what were Mara and Logan doing here?

"Has there been any news about Pearl and Edna?" Abbey asked, hoping to get everyone's mind off Nick and onto something else.

Mara shook her head. "It's like the earth just swallowed them up. No one I've talked to knows anything, which is hard to believe."

"Maybe they found out they're being hunted and they're masking their scent," Rane suggested. "They did it when they kidnapped Derek years ago. And it was a common practice years before that, during the War."

The old war between the vampires and the werewolves, Abbey thought. Something else she knew little about. Her Uncle Rafe and his wife had been heavily involved, but they never spoke of it, at least not in Abbey's hearing.

The conversation came to an end when the doorbell rang. Abbey fidgeted with the hem of her sweater as her father went to open the door.

The sound of Nick's whiskey-rough voice greeting her dad banished her anxiety. She smiled up at him as her father introduced her mother to Nick, then invited him to sit down.

Appearing completely at ease, Nick winked at her as he dropped into the chair catty-corner to the sofa.

"Nick, please tell us a little about yourself," Savanah said. "Mara tells us you're old friends."

Abbey couldn't help grimacing at her mother's emphasis on the word *old*.

"I'm not sure we're friends," Nick said pleasantly, "but we have known each other a long time."

Abbey glanced at Mara, who avoided her gaze. Frowning, Abbey noticed that Logan seemed to be studying the pattern in the carpet. What was going on? Was there some sort of vampire feud between Nick and her godmother?

"Where are you from, originally?" Savanah asked.

"My father was born in a small town in Italy that no longer exists. He was a soldier, captured in Egypt. I was born a slave."

"Abbey said the two of you met in New York."

He nodded. "I've made my home there for the last few years."

"What do you do with your time?" Rane asked.

Nick shrugged. "It depends. When I'm bored, I find a job. Sometimes I travel. Sometimes I hole up somewhere and rest awhile."

"We should be going," Abbey said. Jumping to her feet, she grabbed Nick's hand. "Don't wait up."

"Abbey . . ."

Ignoring her father's voice, she pulled Nick toward the door. "See you later, everybody," she called over her shoulder. To Nick, she whispered, "Now would be a good time to use some of your vampire power and get us out of here."

Muttering, "Hang on," he wrapped his arm around her waist.

Abbey's stomach roiled as the world spun out of focus. Sight and sound were lost as they careened through time and space.

"Are you all right?" Nick asked when the world stopped spinning.

"Yes. I don't think I'll ever get used to that," Abbey said, blowing a wisp of hair off her brow. "I remember when I was a little girl, I thought it was some kind of magic trick. I was always asking my dad to zap me from one place to another." She glanced around. "Where are we?"

"Santa Barbara. Would you like to go to dinner?"

"Maybe later."

"Come on." Taking her by the hand, Nick strolled down the street.

Abbey had never been to Santa Barbara before. It was a lovely old town located on the Pacific Coast. Aside from several hotels, most of the businesses were surf shops, restaurants, or antique stores.

When she spied a place that made fudge, she pulled Nick inside. After sampling several varieties, she bought half a pound of dark chocolate fudge with marsh-mallows.

Nick watched indulgently as she took one bite and then another. He shook his head as an expression of pure pleasure crossed her face. He had often wondered what it was about chocolate that modern women found so irresistible.

"Too bad you can't have a bite," she remarked as they strolled along the beach. "You don't know what you're missing."

"I have to admit to a certain curiosity. I'll bet you

didn't know that cocoa originated in the Amazon over four thousand years ago."

"Really?"

He nodded. "According to legend, the Aztecs believed that their god, Quetzalcoatl, gave them a cocoa tree stolen from paradise."

"Good for him!"

"Chocolate in those days wasn't what it is today," Nick said with a grin. "The Mayans and the Aztecs used cocoa to make a cold, unsweetened drink called xocoatl."

"Unsweetened?" Abbey shuddered. "I've tasted candy bars that were eighty percent cocoa. They were way too bitter for my taste."

"As I recall, it was the Europeans who first sweetened it by adding sugar and milk."

"For a man who can't eat chocolate, you certainly know a lot about it."

He shrugged. "I've done a lot of reading over the years."

Of course, she thought. Sometimes she forgot how old he was.

"Do you want to sit down for a while?" Nick asked, gesturing at a flat rock big enough for two.

"All right."

Nick spread his jacket over the rock and they sat side by side. Abbey licked fudge from her fingertips, then dropped the sack into her handbag. "Do you know Edna and Pearl?" she asked.

"I know about them, but we've never met. Why?"

"They seem to be missing and my family is concerned."

"Really? Why?"

"My uncle Rafe turned them during the War and now he considers them family."

"Family," Nick mused. "It's an odd concept for most

vampires, you know. We tend to be solitary creatures most of the time, although there are covens here and there."

"Really?" It was hard to imagine living like that, Abbey thought. The Cordova-DeLongpre clan were a close-knit bunch, even by human standards. "Why haven't you ever married? You've lived such a long time. Why did you choose to remain alone?"

He lifted one brow, his dark eyes glinting with amusement. "Who said I was alone?"

"Silly of me," she muttered. And realized how true that was. Nick was a gorgeous hunk of male—chiseled features, sensuous lips, dark blue eyes that a woman could get lost in . . . as she was lost.

He slid his arm around her waist and drew her closer. "I won't lie to you. There have been a lot of women, Abbey, so many I've lost count. But none of them were important to me."

"None of them?" she asked skeptically. "Not even one? In hundreds of years?"

He shook his head. "I cared for some of them. I made love to many of them. But I was never in love with any of them. Not even Mara."

"Mara!" Abbey stared at him.

"I thought you knew. She turned me."

Stunned, Abbey stared into the darkness. Mara had turned Nick. Had they been lovers before she turned him?

"It was centuries ago," Nick said quietly. "Long before you were born." He stroked her cheek. "It has nothing to do with us, or my feelings for you."

"Did you . . . ? Were you . . . ?" Abbey shook her head. "Never mind. I don't want to know."

But he knew what she was thinking. "Believe me

when I say there's no love lost between us. She turned me against my will and abandoned me soon after."

"So, she's your sire. Isn't that an unbreakable bond?"

He nodded. "A vampire's sire has power over him or her so long as one of them lives."

"So, if she ordered you to do something, you would be compelled to do it?"

"Yes. In theory."

"And in practice?"

"Mara's very strong, but since she made me, and I've survived such a long time, so am I."

"So you could resist her?"

"Possibly. She also has the ability to find me wherever I might be."

"Does my father have that power over my mother?"

"Yes. Which is why it's always nice if you're turned by someone you care for. Someone who cares for you."

She nodded absently, her thoughts chasing round and round like a hamster on a wheel. Nick knew Mara, had known her for centuries. No doubt they had been lovers. She didn't know whether to laugh or cry at the thought of the man she loved being turned by her godmother. If it didn't hurt so bad, she might have laughed. But there was nothing funny about it. Nick said it had nothing to do with the two of them. Was she wrong to let something that had happened centuries ago bother her?

"You look a little pale," Nick remarked. "Come on," he said, taking her by the hand. "I think you need a good stiff drink. And maybe something to eat."

Lost in thought, Abbey paid little attention to where they were going, but her breath caught in her throat when they arrived. One wall was entirely made of glass, providing a spectacular view of the ocean. Moonlight shimmered on the cresting waves.

The hostess showed them to a booth. Abbey scooted in and Nick slid in beside her, so close his thigh brushed intimately against hers.

When the waitress came, Nick ordered a mojito for Abbey and a glass of red wine for himself.

"Are you hungry?" he asked.

"No." She couldn't think of food now. She was still reeling from what he had told her earlier. "Can I ask you something?"

"Fire away."

"Have you ever turned anyone?"

"Are you afraid I'll turn you? If you are, stop worrying. I've never made another vampire, willing or not."

Abbey nodded, still stunned by his revelation about Mara.

"I can see all this talk about Mara has upset you." Taking her hand in his, he gave it a squeeze. "I'm sorry, Abbey. Would you like me to take you home?"

"Yes. No." She shook her head. "I don't know what I want."

"Yes, you do." He brushed a kiss across her lips. "You just have to decide if you've got the courage to take the next step."

He was right. She wanted him. But was she brave enough to tie her life to his? Could she live with the knowledge that he had a past with Mara, however long or short or passionate it might have been? How was she ever going to face Mara and Logan again, knowing what she knew now?

Mara and Logan. They had been unusually quiet up at the house earlier. Abbey remembered the tension in the room before Nick arrived and she suddenly understood the reason for it. Logan was jealous of Nick, and understandably so. She hadn't missed the veiled look that passed between Mara and Nick.

"Abbey?"

Filled with uncertainty, she looked at him, all her doubts fading when her gaze met his. She wanted him. He wanted her, and nothing else mattered.

Closing her eyes, she murmured, "Just kiss me."

"Don't ask me twice, darlin'." Grateful for the booth's high back, which shielded them from the other diners, Nick cupped her face in his hands and kissed her gently; then, wrapping his arms around her, he kissed her more deeply. Kissed her until she was breathless, trembling with desire.

"Nick . . ."

He heard the yearning in her voice, knew he could have whisked her to his place and made love to her all night long. It was tempting, oh, so tempting. But she wasn't a woman to be pleasured for a night, but a lifetime. He had told Mara he meant to have Abbey, and have her he would.

But, like it or not, he was afraid that meant winning her parents' approval.

Chapter Fourteen

"He seemed nice," Savanah remarked. "Polite."

Rane sat back on the sofa, his legs stretched out in front of him, one arm draped around his wife's shoulders. "You think so?"

"Don't you?"

"I don't know. There's something about him . . ." Rane shook his head. "I can't help thinking he's up to no good. And then there's his history with Mara."

"It was a long time ago," Savanah said.

"Maybe so, but did you see Logan's face when Nick showed up? He's not so sure it's over."

"That's ridiculous. Mara's crazy about Logan. She always has been. Everybody knows that."

"Maybe. Maybe not."

"I didn't notice any sparks between Mara and Nick. Quite the opposite."

"I guess. But we were talking about Nick and Abbey. He's too old for her. Too worldly wise. It's like pairing a pit bull with a kitten."

Savanah smiled faintly. "I can't argue with that. It bothers me that he has centuries more experience than she does, but . . ." She took a deep breath and let it out in a long sigh. "The more we object, the more determined Abbey's going to be to prove us wrong. You know how she is. And maybe, just maybe, he'll be good for her."

"The way you're good for me?" Rane asked, nuzzling her neck.

"Could be."

"*Could* be? What do you mean by that?"

"I'm just teasing you. Honestly, Rane, I think you've lost your sense of humor."

"Maybe I have. I've got a lot on my mind just now, what with Nick and . . ."

She drew back, her gaze searching his face. "And what?"

"I overheard your conversation with Abbey."

Savanah went very still. "What conversation?"

"You know what I'm talking about. Why didn't you tell me you're unhappy?"

"I'm not unhappy!"

He lifted one brow. "No?"

"Rane . . ."

"You didn't have to become one of us," he said, his voice tight.

"Of course I did! How else were we going to have a life together? What would I have done, how would I have felt, when I grew old and you didn't?"

"I wouldn't have stopped loving you."

"I know that. But I couldn't have stood it, getting older, having people think I was your mother, your grandmother, and all the while you'd still be young and virile while I just shriveled away!"

"Savanah, honey . . ." He shook his head, at a loss for words. "I had no idea you felt this way all these years."

Rising, he paced away from the sofa to stare out the window. "I don't know what to say except I'm sorry."

"There's nothing for you to be sorry about. It was my choice, not yours. I knew what I was doing."

"Did you?"

"Well, not entirely, of course. How could I?" She moved up behind him and wrapped her arms around his waist. "I admit, there are still days when I miss being human, but I wouldn't give up what we have, or all the years ahead for anything in the world. I love you, Rane Cordova. I loved you when I was human. I love you now."

He turned to face her, his gaze searching hers. "You mean it? You're not just saying all that to make me feel better?"

"Of course not."

Relieved, he drew her into his arms and held her close. "Why don't you go on up to bed?"

"Aren't you coming?"

"I'll be along in a minute. I just want to make sure Abbey's home safe."

"Do you think that's wise?"

"I don't know, but I'm going over to the cottage just the same."

"It wasn't much of a date," Nick remarked as they strolled along the path to the cottage. "I'll try and do better tomorrow night."

"That's not necessary. I mean, I'd love to go out with you again. But I'm glad everything's out in the open."

"Are you?"

She nodded. "I was thinking about it on the way home and you're right. You and Mara, it was a long time ago. If you say it doesn't matter, then I believe you."

When they reached the front door, Nick wrapped her in his arms and drew her close, one hand tenderly stroking her cheek. "That's my girl," he murmured.

"Actually," said a familiar voice from the shadows. "She's *my* girl."

"Dad! You're spying on us? Really?" Stepping out of Nick's embrace, Abbey peered into the darkness.

"I wasn't spying," Rane said, materializing at the bottom of the porch stairs. "Just making sure you got safely home."

"Okay, now you're sure. Good night."

"Good night, Abbey. Nick."

"Good night, sir."

"Is he gone?" Abbey asked, grateful for the darkness that hid her flushed cheeks.

Nick pulled her into his embrace. "We're quite alone."

"I can't believe he was waiting for me. I'm not a child anymore. I wish he'd let me grow up!"

Nick laughed softly. "He's your father. He loves you."

"Are you defending him?"

"It's natural for him to worry about you. Would you rather he didn't care?"

"Of course not." Shaking off her annoyance, she smiled at him. "Aren't you going to kiss me good . . . ?"

Nick's mouth covered hers in a searing kiss that made Abbey forget everything else. She gasped when his hands cupped her buttocks, drawing her body tight against his while he ravaged her mouth.

Moaning softly, she locked her hands around his neck, holding on for dear life as the world she knew disappeared and there was only Nick's mouth on hers, his hands caressing her.

When he let her come up for air, she leaned into him, her knees weak, her breathing erratic.

"Are you okay?" he asked, amusement evident in his tone.

"Who, me?" She blinked up at him. "I don't think I'll ever be all right again."

Nick laughed softly. Abbey was delightful, he thought. Innocent and wanton at the same time, like Eve in the Garden before the fall.

And she was his.

Chapter Fifteen

Abbey sat in the kitchen, sipping a cup of hot chocolate, and thinking about her date with Nick the night before. They hadn't done much, but she had learned a lot. More than she had ever wanted to know, she mused glumly. Mara had turned Nick against his will. Someday, she wanted to hear the whole story of Mara, Nick, and Logan. No doubt their history would play out like a vampire soap opera.

She had to laugh when she recalled her father popping out of the shadows. *Who's the stalker now, Dad?* She had to hand it to Nick, though. He had been polite and respectful, even calling her father—who was centuries younger—sir. She admired that.

After drinking the last of her cocoa, she rinsed the cup, then headed out the back door. It was time to look after the stock.

Abbey stretched her arms out to the side and then over her head. She had been working steadily for the last three hours and she was developing a whopper of a backache. It was time to take a break before she began exercising the horses.

She glanced at the sky as she took off her gloves and tucked them in the waistband of her jeans. Gray clouds were building in the east; there was a promise of rain in the air.

Deciding to skip lunch in favor of a short ride before she worked the other horses, she led Freckles out of the barn.

She was lifting the heavy saddle onto the mare's back when Nick appeared beside her. Taking the saddle from her hands, he set it in place and fastened the cinch.

"What are you doing here?" Abbey asked. "Shouldn't you be resting?"

"I rest during the day by choice. It's not a necessity."

"Oh. Do you ride?"

"Of course. Cars are a relatively recent invention, you know. In my day, it was ride or walk." He glanced at the barn. "You got a horse for me?"

"One of my Mom's horses is a remarkably stubborn, high-strung mare mistakenly named Serenity. I haven't exercised her today. Do you think you can handle her?"

"Are you kidding? I can handle you, can't I?"

Abbey punched him in the shoulder before returning to the barn for the troublesome mare.

Nick watched the horse with interest as Abbey led her out. Serenity was a true black, with one white stocking, and stood a good seventeen hands. The mare eyed him warily as he saddled her, pinned her ears when he took up the reins, tried to bite him when he stepped into the leather.

He gave a sharp tug on the reins to bring her head around, then jabbed his heels into her flanks. With a toss of her head, the mare took the bit between her teeth and lined out in a dead run.

Muttering, "Holy cow!" Abbey leapt onto the Appy's back and gave chase, all the while admiring Nick. He rode with the grace of a born horseman, his body moving in perfect rhythm with that of his mount. Once, he threw back his head and loosed a wild cry filled with the joy of the moment. And she loved him all the more because of it.

He let the mare run flat out until she broke a light sweat, then he eased her down to a slow lope, then into a trot before reining her to a halt on a grassy knoll.

Dismounting, he patted the horse's neck, then looped the reins over a low-hanging branch.

He was grinning when Abbey drew rein beside him.

Dismounting, she exclaimed, "I guess you *can* ride!"

"I'd forgotten how much I loved it."

"If it had been anybody else on her back, I'd have been worried sick," Abbey remarked as she ground-tied Freckles. "But I knew if Serenity stepped in a hole and broke her fool neck, or yours, you'd walk away from the fall."

Laughing, Nick pulled Abbey into his arms. "Indestructible," he remarked, nibbling her earlobe. "That's me."

"Irresistible, too."

"You are." Gazing deep into her eyes, he murmured, "How did I live so long without you? I look back at all those empty years . . ." He shook his head. "But now you're here and it's like I've been reborn."

Abbey looked up at him, her throat thick with unshed tears. "Was it really so awful?"

He drew her down on the grass beside him, then pulled her close to his side. "You have no idea. After Mara left me, I wandered aimlessly from place to place.

I hated what I'd become and yet—I probably shouldn't be telling you this—I loved the blood. The taste of it on my tongue, the power of it! I loved the hunt, and yet, at the same time, I hated it. For years, I was wracked with guilt for what I was, what I did to survive. After a while, I vowed never to kill again and that's when I learned I could take what I needed from a few instead of taking it all from one.

"I met other vampires as I traveled the earth. A few knew Mara personally. It seemed I wasn't the only one she'd seduced and abandoned. Like me, they all hated her for it. Others, those who didn't know her, were awed by the fact that she was my sire. She had a reputation, even then." He paused, his thoughts obviously turned inward. And then he said, "Not long ago, I was determined to end my existence . . ."

"No!" Abbey couldn't imagine why anyone, even a vampire as ancient as Nick, would seek death. Life in any form was sacred.

"Ironically, I was hoping to find Mara and ask her to destroy me. And then I met you."

Tilting her face up, he kissed her, a gentle kiss that was little more than the whisper of his lips against hers, and yet she felt it burn deep into her soul.

"I love you," he whispered. "I would never have believed I could fall in love with anyone so quickly, but I love you, Abbey. I'll love you until the end of time."

With a sigh, she rested her head on his chest and closed her eyes. It humbled her to think that he loved her so deeply. He had seen everything, been everywhere. He was a gorgeous, sexy, supernatural being who could have any woman he desired.

And he wanted her.

The thought that she also wanted him frightened her in ways she didn't understand. She told herself he would never hurt her, and yet . . . what if she decided she didn't want to spend her life with a vampire?

What if he refused to let her go?

What if he turned her against her will? She would hate him if that happened.

He had said he loved her. That he had intended to end his life before he met her. That was a heavy burden to bear.

"You're awfully quiet," Nick remarked as they rode back toward home. "Is something wrong?"

"No."

"You're troubled by what I said earlier."

"No. Well, yes, a little. I mean, we've only known each other a short time and yet, all of a sudden, things are kind of intense, what with you declaring your undying . . ." She grimaced, thinking *undying* was a poor choice of words. "Declaring that you'll love me forever."

"I'm sorry I upset you. Vampires tend to be over zealous when they see something—or someone—they want."

"Oh." It wasn't the most intelligent reply she'd ever made, but she was at a loss for words. Had all the men in her family compelled the women they loved to marry them? She had heard their courtship stories. No long engagements for any of them.

Thunder rumbled in the distance as they drew closer to the cottage. Not wanting to be caught in the rain, Abbey urged Freckles into a trot. They reached the barn a short time later.

Dismounting, Abbey led the mare into the barn.

Nick followed her.

Side by side, they unsaddled the horses. Abbey passed Nick a brush and they spent several minutes grooming the mares. Abbey was acutely aware of Nick beside her. She loved watching the play of muscles in his back and shoulders as he ran the dandy brush over the mare's sleek coat, the way a lock of hair fell over his brow as he stroked the brush down the mare's legs, the way his jeans stretched over his taut buttocks. Oh, yeah, she had it bad.

Her cheeks felt like they were on fire when he caught her staring. His lips curved in a knowing smile.

He tossed the brush into the box at his feet, then reached for her. Eyes wide, Abbey looked up at him, her heart pounding like a wild thing as his arms enfolded her. She released a deep, shuddering breath as his gaze searched hers.

"Abbey?"

With a sigh, she leaned into him, closed her eyes as he lowered his head to press kisses to her cheeks, her brow, the curve of her throat.

"It's been a long time since I made love in a hayloft," he murmured, nibbling her earlobe.

"I guess you'll have to wait a while longer," she retorted, although the thought of climbing into the loft and making love to Nick was tempting indeed.

"I guess you want to be courted first."

"Courted?" Taking a deep breath, she smiled up at him. "That's an old-fashioned concept."

"Well, I'm an old-fashioned guy."

"Very old."

He laughed softly as he put her away from him. "I can wait until you're ready." Untying the mare, he led her into a stall and closed the door.

"Nick . . ."

"It's all right, love." He kissed her lightly on the cheek. "I'll see you tonight."

Abbey stared after him as he left the barn, wondering how much longer she would be able to resist the blatant desire in his eyes, the yearning of her own body. She reminded herself that they were still strangers in many ways, but it didn't help. Right or wrong, whether she had known him for a week or a year, she would always want him.

A thought took Nick home. Though he would miss being close to Abbey while at rest, staying in the shack no longer seemed wise now that her father knew he'd been there. He couldn't hide from Mara, of course, but she had no reason to come looking for him. And even if she did, the threshold would, hopefully, prevent her from entering uninvited. Of course, she might be able to compel him to go to her. But it seemed unlikely.

After taking a shower, he changed into a pair of black jeans and a black T-shirt, pulled on a pair of boots, and went into the city. Dark clouds covered the sun, turning the day to night. The rain fell in a steady drizzle.

He hadn't hunted in several days. The hunger grew inside him, an aching need that burned like fire in his veins. He hadn't lost control in centuries, but with Abbey in his life, it wasn't a risk he was willing to take.

Oblivious to the weather, he strolled the downtown streets in search of prey, bypassing the elderly, the sick, the very young. His prey of choice had always been women in their late twenties or early thirties.

The sidewalks emptied as the rain fell harder, Thunder rumbled across the skies. Lightning split the heavens, filling the air with the smell of ozone.

Ducking into an upscale bar, he found an empty booth in the back and ordered a glass of wine.

The room was rapidly filling with shoppers seeking shelter from the downpour. He scanned the room and selected his prey—a dark-haired woman sitting alone near the end of the bar. He spoke to her mind, summoning her. A moment later, she slid into the booth beside him.

Slipping his arm around her shoulders, he drew her close and bent his head to her neck. Anyone seeing them would think they were lovers.

He drank quickly, savoring the rich taste of her blood on his tongue, the way it warmed him. He took only what he needed, sealed the tiny wounds, wiped his memory from her mind, and sent her on her way.

He sat there a moment, his thoughts turning to Abbey. Her blood was sweeter and more satisfying, making it dangerous for him to drink from her too often lest he get lost in the moment and take too much.

Knowing he would soon see her again, kiss her again, he ordered another glass of wine. It wouldn't do to go to her with the smell of blood on his breath.

Chapter Sixteen

Pearl woke to find the hunter standing over her, gun in hand.

She looked across the room at Edna, then up at the hunter.

"Well?" he asked curtly. "What's your decision?"

"We'll do it," Pearl said. "We'll give you the cure."

He glanced from her to Edna and back again. "How do I know I can trust you?" He paced the floor for several moments. "Where is this cure?"

"At our home."

"Where's that?"

"Outside Houston."

He stared at her for several moments, then, muttering, "Dammit!" he took a key from his pocket and released Pearl. "You go get the cure." He pressed the muzzle of his weapon against Edna's left temple. "You've got fifteen minutes. If you're not back by then, she's dead."

Pearl smiled at Edna. "Don't worry, dear. I'll be back in plenty of time."

"I'll be here," Edna said dryly. She watched Pearl

leave the room, then closed her eyes and sent out a desperate cry for help, praying, as she did so, that Derek would hear her this time, since he hadn't responded to any of her urgent calls last night.

True to her word, Pearl returned less than fifteen minutes later.

The hunter gestured at the small brown bottle in her hand. "Is that it?"

She nodded.

"How does it work?"

"You give it to your daughter tonight."

"And then what?"

"When she wakes tomorrow night, she should be human again."

"Should be?"

Pearl held out the bottle. "There are no guarantees."

The hunter took the container and slipped it into his pants' pocket. "Sit down and put those shackles back on."

"What? I gave you what you wanted. Now let us go."

The snick of the gun being cocked sounded like thunder in the small room. "Do it."

Eyes blazing indignantly, Pearl sat down. She hissed as she locked the shackles in place. "Now what?"

"If it works, I'll let you go."

"And if it doesn't?"

"I think you know the answer to that."

Pearl stared at him. Why had she ever believed him, she thought, and then her eyes widened as Mara's son materialized behind the hunter. Before the man knew he was there, Derek plucked the weapon from his hand.

Exclaiming, "What the hell!" the hunter whirled around, his face going pale when he saw the vampire.

Derek nodded at Pearl and Edna. "Evening, ladies."

"I knew you'd come!" Edna said, beaming at him.

Derek glanced from the hunter to Edna. "What's going on here?"

"He wants our cure for his daughter," Edna explained. "And we agreed to give it to him, and then he said if it didn't work, he was going to kill us."

"And what do you want me to do?" Derek asked.

Edna looked at him as if he wasn't too bright. "Get us out of here, of course."

"I meant, what do you want me to do with him?"

"Nothing, dear," Pearl said. "He's just a father worried about his daughter. Let him take the cure and leave."

"Must be your lucky day, hunter," Derek remarked. "What's your name?"

"Thad Rivers."

"Turn the ladies loose, Rivers, and get the hell out of here."

The hunter released Pearl and Edna and then, looking like a man who expected to be shot in the back with his own gun, he hurried out the door.

Edna threw her arms around Derek. "Thank you for coming."

"No problem," he said. "But you're not out of the woods yet. Word on the street says a coalition of hunters is offering a hefty reward for whoever killed the McDonald sisters."

"Cindy was very tasty," Edna murmured.

Pearl sent her a withering glance. "This is serious, dear!"

"It is that," Derek agreed. "If I were you two, I'd make myself scarce."

Pearl nodded. "Sounds like remarkably sound advice.

It was good to see you again, Derek. Say hello to your lovely wife for us."

"Will do. If you need a place to stay, call me."

"Thank you again," Edna said.

With a wave of his hand, Derek took his leave.

Pearl stared after him a moment, then looked at Edna. "I didn't think he was coming."

"Me, either. I was so afraid. Maybe that kept him from hearing me right away. At least now I know the link between us still works," she said with a grin. "Eventually."

"Well, I guess all's well that ends well, dear. Let's get out of here."

"Where are we going to go?" Edna asked. "If what Derek said is true, there's a whole pack of hunters looking for us."

"We need a safe place to hide," Pearl mused, tapping one finger against her cheek. "Somewhere no one will ever think to look for us. But where?"

Chapter Seventeen

With one eye on the clock, Abbey showered and shaved her legs, then spent thirty minutes trying on one outfit after another. In New York, she hadn't had much call for a lot of fancy clothes. She had spent her days at acting classes and auditions and most of her evenings at home, memorizing lines—or sitting in all-night coffee shops exchanging hopes and dreams and condolences with other wannabe actors.

She finally settled on a long black skirt with a modest slit in the side, and a silky white blouse with a V-neck. A pair of black heels and a hot pink bracelet completed her outfit.

At seven o'clock, the doorbell rang.

A thousand butterflies took wing in the pit of Abbey's stomach. Buoyed up with anticipation, she hurried to answer the door and came face to face with an enormous bouquet. "Nick? Are you in there?"

He peered around the flowers to hand her a two-pound box of chocolates tied with a big white bow.

"Flowers *and* candy?" Abbey asked, smiling. "Wow, what's the occasion?"

"You said you wanted to be courted," he reminded her.

"So I did."

"Just doing my best to please my lady." He cocked his head to the side. "May I come in?"

"What? Oh, of course." She took a few steps back, frowned at the odd vibration in the air when he stepped across the threshold.

In the living room, she put the box of candy on the coffee table, then reached for the bouquet. "Thank you for the chocolates. And the flowers." She brushed her thumb over a velvety red petal. "They're beautiful. Why don't you sit down while I put these in water?"

Hurrying into the kitchen, Abbey searched for a vase. The flowers—three dozen long-stemmed red roses—must have cost him a fortune. Men had brought her flowers before, but never so many at one time—or as lovely as these.

She carried the vase into the living room and placed it on the table beside the sofa.

"I hope you like roses," Nick said, patting the cushion beside him.

"They're my favorite, especially red ones."

"I'm glad they please you." He jerked his chin toward the box of candy. "I wasn't sure if you liked milk chocolates or dark, so I bought both."

"Either one is good, but dark is definitely better."

"I'll file that away for future reference. So, where would you like to go this evening?" he asked. "Dining? Dancing? Perhaps a walk in the moonlight?"

"A walk?" She glanced out the window. "I don't know if you've noticed, but it's raining."

"True, but the moon is still there," he said with a wry grin.

"Very funny. You won't mind if I get a jacket?"

He winked at her. "Not if you think you'll need one."

Shaking her head, Abbey ran to get her jacket from the closet, then grabbed her keys.

She put the hood up as she followed Nick outside. "Do you do this often?" she asked, locking the door behind her.

"I like storms, the more violent, the better," he said, taking her hand in his. "This little drizzle hardly qualifies as rain."

"Why do you like storms so much?"

"The sound and the fury, I guess." He sent her a wicked grin. "It appeals to me on some dark, sinister level."

She punched him on the arm. "Stop that."

"It's true. There's something primal about wind and rain, thunder and lightning. What about you? Do you like storms?"

"Yes, when I'm curled up in front of a cozy fire." She jumped as lightning crackled across the sky, followed by a deafening crash of thunder that shook the ground.

Laughing, Nick pulled her into his arms. "Don't be afraid, I'll protect you."

She looked at him curiously. "Would getting hit by lightning kill you?"

"I don't know. I never thought about it." He kissed the tip of her nose, then reclaimed her hand and they started walking again.

"Vampires don't get cold, do they? I remember my dad used to put on a coat when it was cold outside even though he didn't need it. And he always wore wool shirts in the winter and T-shirts in the summer so he'd blend in with everyone else. He doesn't do it so much anymore."

"It gets old, trying to pretend you're something you're not. So does relocating every twenty or thirty years, changing your name, trying to remember the last time you were in a particular city . . ." He shook his head.

"My parents have never done that. Well, we moved from Oregon to California, but they've never changed names." She looked up at Nick thoughtfully. "What's your real name?"

"Niccola Desanto. I use it every hundred years or so to remind me who I really am."

Brow furrowed, Abbey squeezed his hand. "I guess my folks will have to move, at least temporarily, in a few years."

"Yeah, that's one of the drawbacks to living a long time. But you get used to it."

"My dad said Mara's never changed her name," Abbey remarked, then wished she could call back the words. If there was one thing she didn't want to discuss with Nick, it was her godmother. She was suddenly glad that Mara and Logan had gone back home.

"Mara's always been a law unto herself."

"Were you in love with her?"

"I was never in love with her. But I was fascinated by her. She's a beautiful, bewitching woman, who's also arrogant, outspoken, and ruthless. I hated her for a lot of years."

"And now?"

Nick pulled Abbey under the shelter of an overhanging rock. Tilting her face up, he gazed deep into her eyes. "There's nothing between Mara and me. Not love. Not hate. Just, I don't know, acceptance, I guess. She's my sire, and she'll always be a part of my past. I can't undo that. But like I told you before, she has nothing to do with the two of us. Okay?"

"Okay."

"I have a lot of years behind me," Nick said quietly.

"I've done a good many things I'm ashamed of, things I'd like to forget. But when I'm with you, none of that matters. It's like starting over." His knuckles caressed her cheek. "Does that make any sense?"

"I'm not sure, but . . ."

"But?"

"I like knowing that being with me makes you feel better."

A flame seemed to burn in the depths of his dark eyes as he drew her close, his arms like steel as they tightened around her. "Honey, you have no idea what you do to me."

Abbey stared up at him, suddenly breathless as his body pressed intimately against hers, leaving no doubt of his desire for her. "I think I have a pretty good idea."

He grinned wryly. And then he cupped her face in his hands and kissed her.

Abbey's knees turned to jelly as his lips claimed hers. He had kissed her before, but never like this. The rain, the thunder, the lightning—all faded into the distance as his mouth ravished hers again and again. She felt his hunger for her, his need, and then, amazingly, images flashed through her mind—battlefields littered with bodies of the dead and dying, mounted knights jousting on the lists, banners flying, a stone castle high atop a windswept crag.

Nick drew back abruptly. "What the hell! How'd you get inside my head?"

She stared at him. "What are you talking about? That's impossible."

"It should be," he muttered. "What did you see?"

"I don't know. Just disjointed images. There was a castle on a hill and a battlefield . . . and knights jousting . . ." She frowned, then exclaimed, "One of them looked like you! It was you, wasn't it?" Her gaze searched his. "I was seeing your past, wasn't I?"

Nick scrubbed his hand over his jaw. "So it would seem."

"You put those images in my mind, didn't you?"

"No." How the devil had it happened? He could read her mind because he was a vampire. There was a link between them because he had tasted her blood, but it only went one way because she had never tasted his. So how the hell was it possible for her to slip inside his mind and glimpse scenes from his distant past? He took her in his arms again. "What do you see now?"

"Nothing."

"Try harder." They had been kissing before, he thought, and pressed his lips to hers.

He felt her presence in his mind like the flicker of a candle in a dark room, lighting dark, distant corners, illuminating bits and pieces of his life that he had tucked away and forgotten.

He broke the kiss, cursing softly. "Why didn't you tell me you were a mind reader?"

"I didn't know. It's never happened before. Anyway, I'm the one who should be upset," she muttered. Whatever this power was, she wasn't sure she wanted it.

"I'm not upset." It was only a small lie.

"Then what's wrong?" She tapped her finger against his temple. "Got something in there you don't want me to see?"

"Damn right." He'd done things—horrible things that would likely make her despise him if she ever found out. He didn't like keeping secrets from her, but some of his escapades and exploits were best left buried.

Taking her hand in his, he started walking back toward the cottage.

Abbey slid a glance in Nick's direction. What was he hiding? He had admitted he had done things he was ashamed of. Being female, she couldn't help being curious about what those things might be, but she didn't really want to know.

She knew about Mara. What else was there?

When they reached the cottage, Abbey hurried inside. She felt chilled clear through and it wasn't because of the rain, she thought as she shrugged out of her wet jacket and hung it on the hall tree. She couldn't help being a little unsettled by the thought that Nick might be hiding some horrible secret, even though she was certain she was better off not knowing what, if anything, it might be. What was even more troubling was the knowledge that she had somehow slipped inside his mind. She wasn't psychic. She didn't have any paranormal talent. So how had such a thing happened?

She jumped when flames sprang to life in the hearth, though why it startled her, she had no idea. She knew Nick had the ability to ignite fire at his will. Everyone in her family had the same power.

"You should go change into some dry clothes," Nick suggested.

"Yes, I think I will."

"Do you want me to be here when you get back?"

"Of course. I won't be long."

In her room, Abbey undressed quickly. After tossing her wet clothes in the sink, she pulled on a pair of sweatpants and a sweater, stepped into a pair of fuzzy pink slippers, shook out her hair. And all the while she wondered what was happening to her that she had been able to glimpse flashes of Nick's past.

When she returned to the living room, Nick and her father were standing on opposite sides of the room, not quite glaring at each other. They were both handsome men, both tall and dark, though Nick was a little taller, a little broader through the shoulders.

"Dad! What are you doing here?"

"I need to talk to you."

"Oh? Well, sit down."

Nick moved toward the door. "I'll be going."

"I'd rather you stayed," Rane said.

Nick hesitated a moment, then sat on the sofa, his legs stretched out before him, one arm draped across the back of the couch. Abbey sat beside him, her hands folded in her lap. Her father took the chair.

"What's this about?" Abbey asked. "Is something wrong?"

Rane leaned forward. "I'm not sure. I went into Auburn to pick up some horse liniment earlier today. While I was there, Cal told me some woman's been going around town asking questions about your mom and me."

"A former lover?" Nick asked, just to rile the other man.

Rane glowered at him.

"Sorry," Nick said, serious now. "Probably a hunter."

"Maybe, maybe not." Rane shook his head. "Cal said she had some old newspaper clippings from my days as a magician."

"Maybe she's a reporter," Abbey suggested, though she had no idea why a reporter would be interested in her father after all this time . . . unless, as Nick suggested, the stranger was also a hunter.

"Did you get the woman's name?" Nick asked.

"No. But whoever she is, I don't like it." Rane stroked his jaw thoughtfully. "What really disturbs me is that the articles she showed Cal were written by Savanah."

Nick whistled softly. "What do you plan to do about it?"

"I haven't decided. I'm not sure whether I should try to find out what she's up to, or just let it go."

"If she's still in town, it should be easy enough to track her down and find out what she's after."

"Yeah. I just came down here to tell the two of you to be careful. You, especially, Abbey. I know I used to tell you this when you were a little girl, but it's still good advice—don't talk to strangers."

"I won't."

"Well, then, I'll say good night, you two."

Abbey followed her father to the door and gave him a hug. "I love you, Dad."

"I love you, too." He glanced toward the living room where Nick waited. Then, looking back at her, he asked quietly, "Are you all right?"

"Of course." Abbey smiled. "He's courting me. He brought me all those roses. And candy, too."

Rane nodded. "Be careful, Abbey. I couldn't bear it if anything happened to you."

"Stop worrying. I know what I'm doing."

"I hope so. Good night, honey."

Returning to the living room, Abbey resumed her place on the sofa. "Good thing I don't always listen to my dad," she mused, poking Nick in the ribs, "or we never would have met."

"I would have found you, one way or another."

She snuggled against him. "Like lovers fated to be together?" she teased.

He nodded. He had told Mara that Abbey was meant to be his. He believed it now more than ever.

"Do you really think whoever's asking questions about my parents is a hunter?"

"That would be my guess. It's the only thing that makes any sense, but I wouldn't worry about it. I'm sure your dad can take care of you and your mother." Nick gave her a reassuring squeeze. "And if he can't, I sure as hell can."

Chapter Eighteen

Savanah climbed the stairs to the attic. Turning on the overhead light, she glanced at the remnants of her past. Her mortal past. A small gray velvet box lined in satin held the silver rings, chains, and bracelets she could no longer wear but couldn't bear to part with, like the beautiful silver chain and crucifix her mother had bequeathed her. Funny, she hadn't thought about these things until now. *I should have given the chain to Abbey years ago,* she mused. But soon after becoming a vampire, Savanah had boxed up her past and put it out of her mind—a neat amputation of memories.

Moving deeper into the attic, she knelt before a dusty old, iron-bound trunk, took a deep breath, and lifted the lid. Memories, like butterflies, took wing from inside.

There was an old theater playbill advertising Santoro the Magnificent, and another touting the wonders of The Remarkable Renaldo. She smiled faintly, remembering how incredibly handsome he had looked on stage. Clad in a pair of tight black trousers, a white muscle shirt that clung to his upper body like a second skin, and a pair of knee-high black leather boots, he

had been—and still was—the most handsome man
Savanah had ever seen.

The white lace dress Abbey had been blessed in was
wrapped in tissue paper, along with her first pair of
shoes, a pink Easter bonnet, her favorite stuffed teddy
bear.

Beneath that, neatly folded in a garment bag, was
Savanah's wedding dress and veil.

A small wooden box held a few of her father's personal belongings—his favorite books, an antique letter
opener, several awards he had won as a reporter, his
wedding ring, and that of her mother. And there,
sealed in a plastic bag, was the letter that had turned
Savanah's life upside down.

She removed it from the bag and carefully unfolded it.

*My darling Savanah ~ I had hoped never to have
to tell you these things but after what happened last
month, I feel the need to write them down, that you
may know the truth.*

*There are many things about your mother that I
never told you—things she could have explained so
much better than I.*

*Your mother's maiden name was not Johnston,
but Van Helsing. Yes, she is a direct descendent of the
well-known vampire hunter, Abraham Van Helsing.
And like her predecessors, she, too, was a vampire
hunter.*

*Her passing was not from some mysterious disease,
as I told you. It was a vampire who was responsible
for her death.*

*You may remember that I left you with your Aunt
Ramona shortly after your mother passed away. I spent
the time hunting for information, trying to track down
the monster responsible for your mother's demise, but to*

*no avail. I'm sorry to say that I'm not the hunter your
mother was. As my grief ebbed, I realized that my
daughter needed a father more than I needed to
avenge your mother's death, and so I came home.*

*Your mother told me that vampire hunting is in
your blood, that the day may come when you will feel
the need to take up where she left off. Whether you
choose to accept the call will, of course, be up to you.
I hope you do not follow in your mother's footsteps.
It is a nasty business, but the decision, ultimately,
must be yours.*

*Under the tree to the right of where we buried your
bunny, you will find a box. Inside is a silver crucifix
on a silver chain. It belonged to your mother. Wear it
always. You will also find several wooden stakes and
a number of other implements used for destroying the
Undead, together with two books. One contains a list
of known vampires; the other is a book of instructions
written by your mother.*

*The house and everything in it is yours. All the
legalities have already been taken care of. Always
remember that I love you and, according to my faith in
the Almighty, I know that I will see you again, just as
I know that I am now in paradise with your mother.*

*God bless you, my darling daughter. Always your
loving father, Will.*

After carefully refolding the letter and replacing it in
the bag, Savanah removed a large, square metal box
from the bottom of the trunk. She stared at the lid for
several moments, her fingertips tracing the initials
inscribed on the top: *BG*. Barbara Gentry.

Taking a deep breath, Savanah lifted the lid. Inside
were several sharp wooden stakes, a mallet, a long,
heavy-bladed knife in a leather sheath, several bottles

filled with holy water. A wooden box, its lid carved with ancient runes and symbols, held two leather-bound books, one black, one brown.

She picked up the brown book and thumbed through the pages, remembering how stunned she had been the first time she read it. It was a primer of vampire facts written in her mother's precise hand. The pages contained a wealth of information on how to identify a vampire, what supernatural powers they possessed, and listed the various ways—none of them pretty—to destroy the Undead.

She had learned that vampires were remarkable creatures. They could change shape or cross great distances in the blink of an eye. Turn into mist. Scale the side of a building like a spider. Hypnotize a person with a look. They had the ability to confuse or control a person's thoughts. Control the weather. If not fatal, their wounds healed overnight. The touch of the sun's light turned all but the very oldest to dust.

Toward the back of the book was a list of vampire hunters. Savanah skimmed over the names, though she knew them well—Abraham Van Helsing, Pearl Jackson, Travis Jackson, Rick McGee, Edna Mae Turner, Edward Ramsey, Tommy Li, Barbara Van Helsing Gentry. On the next page, written years ago in Savanah's own hand, were the names Louise and Cynthia McDonald.

A small section in the back of the book dealt with werewolves.

Putting the brown book aside, she picked up the black one. It was far older than the other book. The ink was faded, the pages yellow with age. The flyleaf read: *I take pen in hand that my heirs might finish the work I have begun.* It was signed *Abraham Van Helsing.*

The pages of this book contained a record of all known vampires up to the time Savanah had given up hunting. Columns listed the date each vampire had been turned and, if applicable, the date it had been destroyed. There was also a place to note who had sired the vampire, if known, as well as a place to include the name of the hunter who had destroyed it. The first name on the list of vampires was Mara.

Savanah frowned. How had Niccola Desanto managed to stay under the radar all these years?

She sat back on her heels, remembering the first time she had perused these pages, and how what she had learned had changed her life. It had been while searching these pages of known vampires that she had found Rane's name.

Savanah could still remember her shock, her disbelief, at learning what he was.

With a sigh, she returned the brown book to the box; then, deciding she should update the black one, she carried it downstairs.

Throughout the ages, vampires and hunters alike had sought the whereabouts of these books.

She was suddenly certain that the stranger asking questions in town was one or the other. But was she a vampire, Savanah wondered, or a hunter?

Rane swore under his breath as he paced the living room floor. He had buried Savanah's books deep in the hillside behind Mara's home in Northern California over a quarter of a century ago and forgotten all about the damn things. Then, about a month ago, Savanah had insisted on digging them up and bringing them here. She had never given him any explanation. To this day, he still didn't know why she hadn't left them where they were.

Dropping onto the sofa next to Savanah, he took her

hand in his. "I think you're right. Whoever that woman is who's been asking about us is probably looking for these books. Although I can't help wondering what she's searching for. The War's been over for years. Why the sudden interest in those old books now?"

"I don't know." Savanah worried her lower lip a moment. "I was thinking I should bring them up to date."

"What the hell for?"

"I've been dreaming about my mother. I'm not sure why. Maybe she's reminding me from beyond the grave that it's my responsibility to keep them updated. Something I've neglected for a lot of years."

"You do whatever you think is right," he said. "But I think you should get rid of them."

Savanah started to protest, but after a moment's thought, she changed her mind. The books had been handed down from hunter to hunter for generations, but Abbey wasn't a hunter and never would be. She had no fighting skills, no way to protect the precious volumes. "Maybe you're right. Maybe I'll just update them and give them back to Mara. They'll be safer with her and Logan than with either one of us." She paused a moment before saying, "Nick's name isn't listed in the book of vampires. Why do you suppose that is?"

"I have no idea."

"It seems odd, though, doesn't it?"

Rane grunted softly. Odd didn't begin to describe it. "Maybe you should go stay with Rafe and Kathy until we find out why that woman's looking for us."

"Excuse me, but why would I do that?"

"Because I don't want you in harm's way."

"Rane Cordova, in case you've forgotten, *I* used to be a vampire hunter. And a darn good one. I think I can still take care of myself."

He grinned sheepishly. "Sorry, sweetheart. It's in my nature to protect my mate."

She punched him in the shoulder, hard. "And mine, too."

"All right, I admit it. I'm just an old-fashioned chauvinist pig."

Savanah laughed softly. Whatever happened, they would face it together, just like always.

While Rane went to look in on Abbey, Savanah opened the black book. Pen in hand, she read over the names of known vampires. And suddenly it seemed wrong to add Derek's name, or Sheree's. Or Nick's, for that matter. If they were off the radar, so to speak, why not leave it that way? By the same token, why identify the vampires who had killed the McDonald sisters?

And what would be gained by adding Kyle Bowden's name to the list of werewolves? Kyle, who had once been married to Mara.

Savanah shook her head. She wasn't a hunter with an agenda anymore. She was a vampire with a family.

She turned the pages slowly, her finger tracing the names of people she knew and loved—Rane's brother, Rafe, and his wife, Kathy. Rane's parents, Vince and Cara Cordova. And Cara's parents, Roshan and Brenna DeLongpre.

Suddenly the mere idea of bringing her mother's books up to date felt like a betrayal of the worst kind.

Chapter Nineteen

Mara glanced around Rane's living room. She couldn't hide her surprise at finding Nick there, seated apart from the others.

"It's late," she remarked, taking a place on the sofa. "Even for vampires. I trust you have a good reason for summoning us?"

"I wouldn't have called if it wasn't important," Rane said. "Logan, good to see you."

Nodding, Logan sat beside his wife. "What's up?"

"Some woman's been asking questions about me and Savanah," Rane answered. "Savanah thinks it has to do with her mother's books, and I think she might be right."

"Books?" Nick asked. "What books?"

"Savanah comes from a long line of vampire hunters," Rane explained. "Her family kept two books. One contains a list of all known vampires, the other contains information about our kind—how to identify us, how to destroy us—things of that nature."

Nick leaned forward. "Where are these books?"

"In our bedroom, for now," Savanah said.

Rane regarded Nick thoughtfully a moment. "We were wondering why your name isn't listed."

"Maybe no one bothered to write it down."

"So, they kept a record of everyone but you?" Rane looked skeptical. "That seems unlikely, don't you think?"

Nick shrugged.

Logan studied Nick a moment before turning his attention to Rane. "What do you want us to do?"

"Savanah thinks we should return the books to Mara. She's the oldest and strongest of our kind. If anyone can protect them, she can."

"Why not just destroy the damn things?" Nick suggested.

"I thought of that," Savanah said. "But I just can't do it. They've been in my family for generations. They're part of my mother's legacy. A part of who I am. The information in those volumes can't be found anywhere else . . . it just doesn't seem right to burn them up like they were trash."

"If you don't mind, I'd like to see the one that lists the vampires," Nick said.

Savanah and Rane exchanged glances; then Savanah shrugged. "I guess it would be all right."

Rane left the room. He returned a short time later carrying a large black book.

He started to give it to Nick, then hesitated. "You're not to take it out of this room, or out of this house."

"He won't," Mara said, a note of warning obvious in her tone.

"I'll have *your* word, Desanto," Rane said.

"You've got it."

With a nod, Rane passed the book to Nick.

He opened it carefully. He had known such a book existed, but he had never expected to see it. He quickly scanned the names. Some, like Mara's, had been written so long ago they were almost illegible. Most were familiar to him—Joaquin Santiago, Roshan DeLongpre and his witch wife, Brenna. Alexi Kristov, Grigori Chiavari, Jason Rourke, Antonio Battista. Dominic St. John. Nick grunted softly. St. John was reputed to have killed quite a few of his own kind.

Nick read through the rest of the names, then closed the volume and returned it to Rane.

"I'll take the books home with me," Mara said. "I know a place where no one will ever find them."

Rane nodded. "Thanks. I knew we could count on you."

"Even without the books here in the house, your lives could still be in danger," Logan remarked. "Whoever's hunting you isn't likely to take your word for it when you say you don't have them."

"I thought about that. I'm not worried about myself or Savanah."

"Just Abbey," Mara said.

"Right."

"The solution seems simple enough," Nick said. "Find the hunter and take her out. Problem solved."

"I'd like to avoid that, if possible," Rane said dryly. "Besides, we don't know if she's a hunter, or a vampire."

"Makes no difference," Nick said. "One's as easy to get rid of as the other."

Rane shook his head. "Killing isn't always the answer. In my experience, it only leads to more killing."

"Sometimes it's necessary."

"I have a better idea. I'm going into town tomorrow. If this woman's looking for me, I'll make it easy for her to find me."

"And then what?" Logan asked.

"That'll be up to her."

"Sounds simple enough," Logan said sardonically. "As long as she doesn't drive a stake through your heart."

"I'm not afraid of her," Rane retorted.

"No?" Nick sent a searing glance in Mara's direction. "You should be. In my experience, the female is always deadlier than the male."

Chapter Twenty

After taking his leave from the Cordova home, Nick went to the cottage to look in on Abbey. She was lying on her side, sleeping soundly. Rane had called his little meeting well after his daughter had gone to bed.

After making sure all the windows were closed and the cottage was locked up tight, Nick decided to go to Auburn and see if he could learn anything about the mysterious woman. Nick was certain she was a hunter. Either that, or a vampire old enough to walk in the sun.

Shielding his presence from mortal eyes, he went from hotel to hotel, checking the records for guests who had arrived in the last few days.

He sensed no hunters, and no vampires in any of the hotels, but he hit pay dirt at a disreputable-looking motel at the south end of town. F. Meloni, Room 216. Nick had never met either of the McDonald sisters, but he had kept track of hunters and vampires alike for a lot of years.

Every instinct he possessed told him F. Meloni was related to Lou's sister, Cindy Meloni. The only question was how, and that was something he intended to find out.

Room 216 was located in the back of a long, L-shaped building. A black SUV was parked in front. A deep breath told Nick she was inside. And she wasn't alone. He wondered if she was actually related to the McDonalds. If so, using her real name wasn't too smart. Unless it was some kind of trap, which was a definite possibility since she didn't seem to be making any effort to hide her identity. Maybe Meloni hoped Rane's curiosity would draw him in.

". . . meet there tomorrow night at the same time?" asked a deep male voice.

"Yes, inform the others." The voice was female. Meloni?

"What if she doesn't have the books?" another man asked.

"Then she'll know where they are," Meloni said. "We get the books. We take her head and his, and then . . ." Her voice trailed off. "Rivers, check out front."

"Why? Did you hear something?"

"Just a feeling."

Quietly cursing, Nick dissolved into mist. There always seemed to be a handful of hunters who had the ability to sense the presence of his kind. Apparently F. Meloni was one of them.

He hovered near the roof as the door opened and a tall blond man poked his head out. "There's no one here," the hunter said, glancing left and right. "You're imagining things."

Nick waited until the hunter closed the door before resuming his own shape.

For a moment, he considered breaking down the door and disposing of the lot of them. But this was Rane's fight, and Rane's territory.

Nick left the motel and strolled down the street. How many hunters were in town? How did they know about the books? Was this the same bunch hunting Pearl and Edna? If so, had the hunters somehow discovered that the old ladies had killed Lou McDonald and her sister? And if so, how? It was supposed to be a well-guarded secret.

Truthfully, he didn't care a whole hell of a lot what happened to any of them.

His only concern was keeping Abbey safe.

The lights were still on when Nick returned to the Cordova place. He paused outside the back door. Mara and Logan were still in the house. Judging from the heated conversation inside, no decision had been made regarding the elusive hunter.

Slipping through the door, Nick spent several minutes at Savanah's computer before sauntering into the living room.

"We didn't expect you back," Rane said.

"I can leave."

"Enough, you two!" Mara snapped. "Nick obviously came back for a reason. I suggest we listen to what he has to say. Nick?"

"I found your hunter." He glanced at Savanah. "I looked her up on your computer. I hope you don't mind."

"Of course not," Savanah said, with a wave of her hand. "Who is she?"

"Turns out she's Cindy Meloni's daughter. Apparently she's decided to take up where her mother and her aunt left off. I don't know what she's planning, but from what I overheard, she's not alone. She's meeting with her cronies sometime tomorrow night." Nick glanced at Savanah. "She wants your books." He turned his attention to Rane. "And she wants your head. Savanah's, too."

"Looks like you've got two choices," Logan said to Rane. "Stay and fight, or get the hell out of Dodge until this blows over."

"I'm not leaving my home or my horses!" Savanah declared. "I left Oregon without a word, but I'm not moving again until I'm good and ready. If this Meloni woman wants a fight, let her bring it on."

"What about Abbey?" Nick asked quietly. "If you're determined to go toe-to-toe with Meloni and her followers, I don't think Abbey should be here."

"Abbey." Savanah's shoulders slumped. "Rane, Nick's right. She can't be here if there's a fight. It's too dangerous."

"I can protect my daughter," Rane said, bristling.

"What if you're wrong, Cordova? Are you willing to take that chance?"

"What are you suggesting?"

"No one asked me, but I've got an idea," Mara said. "Why don't I take Abbey home with me? It's been a long time since we spent any time together. And I am her godmother, after all."

Rane rubbed his jaw thoughtfully. "What do you think, Savanah?"

"I think it's a great idea. We'll discuss it with her in the morning."

"Now that you've got that settled," Nick drawled, "there's just one more thing you all need to know. Wherever Abbey goes, I go."

Abbey stood inside a circle of vampires. She turned slowly, glancing at each one—her godmother, Logan,

Nick, her mother and father—and wondered what the heck was going on.

She paused in front of her father. "I just got here a few days ago. Why do I have to leave?"

"Because I'm your father and I think it's for the best. We don't know how many hunters there are, or what they're planning to do. But your mom and I will feel a lot better if you're out of harm's way. Hopefully, it will only be for a day or two."

Abbey looked at Mara. "It isn't that I don't want to spend time with you," she said. "But I just got settled here, and . . ." Her gaze drifted to Nick.

"It'll be all right, love," he said, taking her hand in his. "I'll be there to keep you company."

"You're coming with me?"

"Damn straight."

"I guess that makes all the difference, doesn't it?" Rane muttered.

"You should be glad I'm here," Nick replied. "She'll be with the two oldest vampires on the planet. If Mara and I can't keep her safe, I don't know who can."

Chapter Twenty-One

It was two hours after sunset when Abbey, Nick, Mara, and Logan arrived at their destination, luggage in hand.

Abbey stared at the gray stone castle looming above them like some prehistoric monster. "Where are we? I thought we were going to your place in California."

"Transylvania," Mara said cheerfully. "I decided the books—and you—would be safer here."

"Transylvania!" Abbey stared at Nick. "Did you know we were coming here?"

"Nope. Hell of a place, though." Nick shook his head. The castle had to be over a thousand years old. He chuckled softly. It didn't take much of an imagination to picture Dracula peering out of one of the narrow, leaded windows on the second floor.

A wave of Mara's hand opened the massive oak door. A fire sparked to life in the enormous hearth. Added light came from a number of fat white candles in wrought-iron sconces.

Abbey followed Mara and Logan inside, stopped when she realized Nick was still outside. "Aren't you coming in?"

"I guess that's up to her." Nick jerked his chin toward

Mara, who stood in the foyer, a faint smile twitching her lips. "Well?"

"Niccola, you may enter."

"Thank you. Sire." Sarcasm dripped off the last word.

He stopped just inside the door, brow furrowed, nostrils flaring.

Mara and Logan had also gone still.

Logan took a deep breath, then muttered, "What the hell are *they* doing here?"

Abbey dropped her suitcase beside the door, then glanced around, wondering who he was talking about. There was no one else in the room but the four of them.

Or so she'd thought, until a tall, angular woman with shoulder-length, snow-white hair stepped out from behind a half-open door on the far side of the room.

"We . . . we're sorry," she stammered, "but we had nowhere else to go." Reaching behind her, she tugged another woman into view.

Abbey glanced at the newcomer. She was shorter than her companion, a trifle plump, with curly red hair that was obviously dyed. Both wore jeans and sneakers and fake flowers in their hair; the tall one wore a bright green shirt, the short one sported a multicolored sweater. Abbey guessed the women to be in their mid-seventies. They could only be Edna and Pearl, she thought, the women her uncle Rafe had turned during the War.

Heaving a sigh of exasperation, Mara moved into the living room. Dropping her suitcase beside the sofa, she sat down, crossed her legs, and glared at the elderly women, who remained on the far side of the room.

As if that would protect them, Abbey thought.

Nick stood near the hearth, his suitcase at his feet, his arms folded over his chest.

Logan dropped his luggage beside Abbey's. Abbey

fidgeted beside him. "Pearl's the tall one," he whispered. "Edna's the redhead."

Abbey nodded, her attention on Mara, who looked none too happy with the intruders.

"I take it you've heard that you're being hunted," Mara said, tapping her fingers on the arm of the sofa.

"Yes," Edna answered. "Derek told us. He said we could stay here."

"Derek? When did you see my son?"

"He saved our lives not long ago when a hunter captured us. The man wanted our cure for his daughter."

"Did you give it to him?"

"Of course."

"Did it work?" Nick asked.

"We didn't wait around to find out, dear," Pearl said.

"You two are very popular all of a sudden," Logan mused. "Why is that?"

Edna slid a glance at Pearl. "I have no idea."

"Are you two hiding something?" Mara asked sharply.

"What makes you think that?" Pearl asked.

"Because you both look guilty as hell."

The two elderly vampires exchanged glances.

"They've got two men here in the castle somewhere," Nick said. "Can't you smell them?"

Mara lifted her head, her eyes widening as she caught their scent. "You brought two mortals here? Without my permission? And locked them in the dungeon?"

"We were bored," Edna said sheepishly.

Nick laughed.

Logan shook his head.

Mara glared at the two women. "Get your boy toys out of my house. Now!"

As Abbey watched Edna and Pearl hurry out of the room, she wondered if her life could get any more bizarre.

* * *

Later, while Mara, Logan, Nick, and the old ladies went hunting, Abbey explored the castle. She wandered slowly around the great hall, running her fingers over the ancient gray stones. The windows, set high in the walls, were mere slits.

The biggest fireplace she had ever seen took up most of one wall, the mantel so high over her head, she couldn't reach it. Several medieval weapons hung above the fireplace—a mace, a lance, a long bow. A pair of sofas and several overstuffed chairs—all covered in dark red damask—were grouped in front of the hearth. A suit of armor stood in one corner. Large rugs covered the floor; tapestries hung from the walls.

Several doors led to other rooms. Some were vacant, one was a kitchen outfitted with another oversize fireplace. A cauldron hung from a tripod in the center of the hearth. A high wooden table she guessed was used for preparing food stood in the middle of the floor. A rack on the wall near the fireplace held a variety of odd-looking utensils and several large iron pots.

A narrow, winding staircase led from the great hall to the upper floors. The first room on the left at the top of the stairs was dominated by a bed with red velvet hangings. A rosewood wardrobe that was surely an antique stood against one wall. A matching four-drawer chest covered with a lace cloth flanked the bed.

The next three doors were open, the rooms unfurnished. A fourth room was locked. She found a good-sized storage closet between two of the bedrooms, but a bathroom was nowhere to be found.

Nick was waiting for her when she returned to the main floor. "Where are the others?" Abbey asked, glancing around.

He shrugged. "I don't know. Still hunting, I guess. I came back early because I was missing you."

"Are Edna and Pearl going to be staying here too?"

"For the time being."

"They're nothing like I expected."

"They're unique among our kind. No doubt about that. Mara said you should take the first room on the left at the top of the stairs."

The only furnished one, Abbey remembered. "What about you?"

"I haven't decided whether I want to rest here during the day."

"Oh. I assumed you would be staying here." *With me.*

"Come on," he said, picking up her suitcase. "Let's go get you settled."

Hand in hand, they climbed the narrow, stone steps to the second floor. Nick bowed her through the bedroom door, whistled softly as he followed her inside. "Nice." He held up her suitcase. "Where do you want this?"

"I don't know. I guess on the bed, for now."

"I've lived in houses smaller than this room," he remarked, strolling across the floor to glance out the window.

"It's very nice, except there's no bathroom," Abbey said. "Not in here. Nor anywhere in the castle."

He pointed at the chamber pot under the bed. "Medieval toilet."

She grimaced. "Seriously?"

"There's probably a garderobe around here somewhere."

"A what?"

"It's a small room with a hole in the floor. Sort of like

a toilet. It empties into a cesspit somewhere outside the castle."

"Sounds kind of crude."

"No worse than an outhouse," Nick said, shrugging. "And unlike a chamber pot, you don't have to empty it."

"What about showering?"

"No showers, but I imagine there's an old wooden tub somewhere."

"Talk about primitive," she muttered.

"I doubt if we'll be here more than a few days," Nick said, drawing her into his arms. "It shouldn't take your old man long to settle things with that hunter one way or the other."

"Do you really think killing the hunter is the only answer?"

He shrugged. "It's the easiest solution."

"So, if it was up to you, you would kill her?"

"If it was necessary to protect you? Damn straight."

Abbey gazed up at him, her expression solemn. "Have you killed a lot of people, Nick?"

"The truth?"

"Always."

"There were a lot of casualties in the beginning. I told you before that I didn't know I could feed without killing. But I had a lot of rage back then. Being a new vampire, high on blood and drunk on preternatural power, sometimes it was hard to hold back. You wouldn't have been safe with me back then."

"Am I now?"

"What do you think?"

"I don't want to think." Closing her eyes, she buried her face against his shoulder.

"Would you rather I lied to you?" he asked quietly.

"No." She blew out a deep breath. Somehow, she was going to have to come to terms with his past.

Nick took her sightseeing the next day. Transylvania was a town where myth and legend seemed to come together. Those who believed in vampires had long held Romania as the birthplace of the Undead; many were convinced that Vlad the Impaler had been a vampire.

They went to see Bran Castle, which was located in Brasov. Most people referred to it as Dracula's Castle. She thought it aptly named.

"There are a couple of other castles rumored to be the home of Bram Stoker's Dracula," Nick remarked as they toured the place.

Abbey nodded. The castle, a national monument and landmark, had been turned into a museum that displayed works of art and furniture that had once belonged to Queen Marie. Abbey especially enjoyed the displays of costumes, shields, and suits of armor.

A secret passageway connected the first and third floors. Finding themselves alone, Nick drew Abbey into his arms.

She grinned up at him. "I'll bet there aren't very many girls who can say they toured Dracula's Castle on the arm of a real vampire."

"I think you'd win that bet. You're probably the first girl about to get kissed here by a real vampire too," he murmured, and kissed her, there in the heart of Dracula's Castle.

Later that night, after giving Abbey one last kiss before tucking her into bed, Nick sought out Edna and Pearl. He found them downstairs in what had been the servant's quarters. It was a large room with four narrow cots, a small table, and a couple of chairs.

The two old ladies sat cross-legged on one of the cots, wineglasses in hand, watching a horror movie on a portable player.

Nick shook his head. They were a sight, clad in flannel pajama bottoms, gaudy shirts, and pink bunny slippers.

They regarded him warily when he entered the room.

"Evenin', ladies."

Edna smiled tentatively. "Mr. Desanto."

"Just Nick."

"Did you need something?" Pearl asked.

"That infamous cure of yours. Do you think it would work on me?"

"You!" Edna exclaimed. "You've got to be kidding!"

"No. You might say I'm dead serious."

"But, why?" Pearl asked.

"Because of Abbey," Edna surmised. "That's it, isn't it? She doesn't want to be a vampire, so you want to be human again." She sighed dramatically. "That's so romantic."

Nick fixed her with a hard stare. "Can you help me or not?"

"Of course," Edna said.

Head tilted to one side, Pearl regarded him a moment. "You know it might not work, you being so old, and all. We've really only had success with fledglings."

"I understand all that."

Edna fidgeted with the hem of her shirt with her free hand. "And if it doesn't work, there won't be any hard feelings, right?"

"Right. How long will it take to prepare?"

"About a week, dear. We need to gather the ingredients, and then it has to cook for at least forty-eight hours."

"We don't have any left from the last batch," Edna added. "Of course, even if we did, it wouldn't work on you. We'll need to triple the potency."

"Quadruple, maybe," Pearl said.

Nick braced his shoulder against the doorjamb. "Why are all those hunters after you?"

The women exchanged uneasy glances.

"I can always force you to tell me," he remarked.

Pearl shot him a disproving glance. "As far as we know, it's because of the McDonald sisters."

"It was self-defense!" Edna said with asperity.

Nick snorted softly. "It doesn't matter to me. Fewer hunters in the world is a good thing in my book. How did the coalition find out it was the two of you?"

Edna stared into her wineglass. "We've been asking ourselves that very question. No one else was there when it happened, except Derek. And he wouldn't have told anyone."

"Are you sure about that?"

"Of course! How could you even think he would . . . ?"

"All right, all right, forget it."

Pearl frowned. "You know, there is one other possibility."

"Let's hear it," Nick said curtly.

"McDonald and her sister found us in a bar." Pearl sipped her wine, her brow furrowed. "There's always a chance there was another hunter there. One we didn't see. . . ."

Nick shook his head. "And you just now thought of that?"

"It was a bad night," Edna exclaimed. "We were lucky to get away with our lives."

"You know, dear, I think there *was* another hunter there. . . ." Pearl's voice trailed off.

"What are you talking about?"

"Don't you remember? I told you that Rivers looked familiar. He was at the club that night." She nodded. "In fact, now that I think back, I'm sure of it."

Rivers, Nick thought. *He was one of the hunters with Meloni's crowd.*

"Well, you picked a fine time to remember that little detail!" Edna declared.

"We gave him our cure!" Pearl said indignantly. "Why would he tell his hunter friends that we killed the McDonalds?"

"Maybe he told them before his daughter was bitten," Edna suggested.

"Or maybe your cure killed her," Nick said dryly. "Whatever the reason, a lot of hunters are now after you."

"Life was a lot less complicated when *we* were the hunters," Edna muttered.

Pearl blew out a sigh. "I think you're right, dear."

"Forget the hunters," Nick growled. "And get to work on that cure."

Chapter Twenty-Two

Abbey called home as soon as she woke.

Her father answered on the first ring. "Are you all right?" he asked.

"I was going to ask you the same thing."

"We're fine. I went into town about an hour ago. There was no sign of the hunters anywhere. The clerk said Meloni checked out of the motel early this morning. Something must have spooked her."

"What do you think it was?"

"I don't know. How are things in Transylvania?"

"Fine. Nick took me sightseeing yesterday. It's a lovely country, at least what I've seen of it."

"What's Mara's castle like? I've always wanted to see the place."

"Other than the fact that it's woefully lacking in electricity, running water, flush toilets, and showers, I guess it's all right. Oh, I left out really big and drafty."

"Roughing it, huh?" her father asked, chuckling.

"Guess who else is here?"

"I don't know. Who?"

"Edna and Pearl."

"What are they doing there?"

"Hiding out, I guess. They really are something, aren't they?"

"Something else," her father muttered dryly.

"They had two men locked up in the dungeon when we got here. Can you believe it? Stop laughing, it isn't funny."

Rane cleared his throat. "Sorry, but it is funny. I'll bet Mara was fit to be tied."

"You could say that."

"Well, they couldn't have picked a safer place," Rane mused. "No one's going to look for them there."

"I guess not. Since the hunters are gone, can I come home now?"

"Wait a few days."

"Do I have to?"

"Humor me, okay?"

"Is there something you aren't telling me?"

"No, I just want to be sure it's safe, that's all."

"Okay. Give my love to Mom. And be careful."

"You too."

Abbey disconnected the call and tossed her phone on the bed. So, the hunters were gone. Why had they given up so easily? And where were they now?

Rising, she stepped into her slippers, then filled the basin on the dresser with water from the ewer and washed her face and hands. Tonight, come hell or high water, she was having a bath!

Her stomach growled loudly as she dried her hands. Only then did it occur to her that she was the only mortal in the house and that she wasn't likely to find anything to eat in the place.

She was wondering how far it was to the village when she saw the note tacked to the bedroom door.

There's food and drink in the kitchen. Mara

Making her way downstairs, Abbey thought it surprising that her godmother would have thought of providing for her. After all, it had been over a quarter of a century since Mara had eaten mortal food.

In the kitchen, Abbey found a box of groceries on the table and an ice chest on the floor. A peanut butter and jelly sandwich and a glass of milk served as breakfast.

After carrying her meal into the great hall, she curled up on the sofa. Nibbling on her sandwich, she thought about Nick. Why had he been reluctant to spend the night in the castle? And if he hadn't stayed here, where had he gone?

And when would she see him again?

Nick stirred, wondering what had roused him. And then he knew. He smiled with the knowledge that Abbey was thinking of him. Funny, he thought, how strong their bond was, considering he had only tasted a small amount of her blood.

And had hungered for more ever since.

Last night, he had decided to take his rest inside the castle. To that end, he had gone into the city, awakened one of the merchants, and procured a twin bed, which he had set up in the empty bedroom next to Abbey's.

Now, lacing his hands behind his head, he stared up at the frescoed ceiling, which depicted chubby, fresh-faced angels and laughing fairies frolicking amid rainbow-colored clouds. No doubt the room had once been a nursery. He grinned, thinking the artist would likely be horrified to discover an ancient vampire sleeping beneath his masterpiece.

Nick's thoughts turned to Edna and Pearl. He doubted their so-called cure would work, but for Abbey's sake, he was willing to give it a try. Although she hadn't said as much, he knew she had no desire to become a vampire. It seemed odd to him that, having been raised by a family of vampires, she had no wish to join them.

On the other hand, given a choice, he wasn't sure he would have chosen such a life for himself either. He had grown to accept what he was, but there remained an emptiness inside, a sense of not being a part of the world around him, that had never disappeared. At times, he felt as if he was viewing the world from the outside, like a spectator watching a play. The actors changed, the scenery changed, but he remained forever the same.

Perhaps human life was precious because it was so short. Mortals never knew, from one day to the next, whether they would survive to see another sunrise. Most vampires—knowing that they had hundreds of years ahead of them—became indifferent to matters of life and death. The majority of vampires forgot all too quickly what it had been like to be human. In time, men and women became nothing more than a source of nourishment. Or a form of idle amusement. Humans were such fragile creatures, so easily frightened, so easily manipulated. A thought could turn them into little more than zombies, compelled to do a vampire's bidding.

And yet the Cordova family had managed to retain a portion of their humanity. They shared territory with one another. They had successful marriages. They didn't kill their prey. They didn't see mortals as nothing more than a food source. Truly, they were unique among their kind.

His thoughts turned to Abbey. Always Abbey. She was a sweet, gentle, caring young woman, an earthly angel who deserved far better than someone like him. He knew a moment of regret for having entangled her in his life.

But she was his now, and only death would part them.

Abbey smiled when she looked up and saw Nick coming down the winding staircase. "Were you looking for me?" she asked.

"Of course not," he said, sweeping her off the sofa and into his arms. "I can always find you. But FYI, I took the room next to yours so *you* can find *me*."

Before she could reply to this unexpected news, his mouth closed over hers in a searing kiss that told her he had missed her as much as she had missed him.

Nick felt all his desires spring to vibrant life as she kissed him back. Fighting the temptation to take her there, on the floor, he lifted his head and drew a deep breath. She stared up at him through half-glazed eyes. The rapid beat of her heart called to him, the whisper of the red tide flowing through her veins fired his hunger.

Raining kisses across the top of her head, he backed toward the sofa and sat down. After settling her on his lap, he kissed her again. And again.

She was practically gasping for air when he lifted his head. "Abbey, I need a favor."

She blinked at him. "A favor?"

He nodded, wondering how to ask for what he so desperately desired without freaking her out.

"What do you need?" she asked quietly, and then,

apparently seeing the hunger burning in his eyes, she gasped, one hand going protectively to her throat.

"I'm sorry," he said gruffly. "Forget it."

"Why are you asking me?"

"What do you mean?"

"Last time you took what you wanted without my even being aware of it."

"As I recall, you weren't too happy about that."

She didn't deny it. "Will it hurt?"

"No." His finger traced the curve of her throat. "You'll enjoy it."

She looked skeptical.

"Trust me?"

"You'll stop if I don't like it?"

"I promise."

She worried her lower lip between her teeth a moment, then turned her head to the side, offering him her throat.

He took a deep breath, inhaling the scent of her skin, her blood, hearing the sudden uptick in the beat of her heart, the unmistakable smell of fear on her skin.

Drawing her into his arms, he kissed her, his hands stroking her back, gentling her to his touch as if she was a skittish mare. He murmured to her as he scattered feather-light kisses along the length of her neck and when she was relaxed, pliant, he took what he wanted, what he needed. He took only a little, knowing the only way to truly satisfy his hunger would be to take it all.

She moaned softly, her hands clutching his shoulders, when he lifted his head. A lick of his tongue sealed the wounds.

"Abbey?"

"Mmm?"

"Are you all right?"

"What? Oh, yes, I'm fine." She sighed, her lips

curving in a smile. "That was wonderful." She looked up at him, her brow furrowing as her fingertips stroked his neck. "What does vampire blood taste like?"

He lifted one brow. "Why?"

"I'm just curious. Does it taste the same as mine?"

"No. It's thicker. Darker. Curious, Pandora? Ready to open the box?"

"Maybe."

Still watching her, he bit into his wrist, then held out his arm. "Go ahead."

"Don't I get to bite you?"

"No." He jerked his chin toward the blood oozing from his wrist. "Change your mind?"

She stared at the dark red blood, a faint look of revulsion in her eyes, and then she lowered her head and licked several drops from his skin. "Oh!" Her head jerked up, her eyes filled with wonder. "It's . . . It's . . . I don't know how to describe it! I mean, it's like swallowing lightning!"

Nick laughed softly, then hugged her close as the bond between them grew deeper, stronger.

"You enjoyed it, too, didn't you?"

"Yes, love, though not as much as you did. There is a vast difference between taking a lick to satisfy a moment's curiosity and drinking to satisfy a craving that can't be denied."

"I'll have to take your word for that," she said primly.

He laughed again. "You never fail to delight me, my sweet. Curious as a cat one moment, and uncertain the next."

She snuggled against him, wondering at the subtle change in her feelings toward him, her heightened awareness of him beside her. Almost it seemed as though her heart had slowed to beat in time with his, but that was just her imagination, of course.

She lifted a hand to her throat. Her skin was slightly warm where he had bitten her. He had taken her blood. She had tasted his. The mere idea should have repulsed her. Instead, it filled her with an unexpected sense of satisfaction. Of belonging. "Do vampires drink from each other?"

"Occasionally."

"Do mortals ever drink from you?"

"Not from me. But there are vampires who will allow mortals—mostly Goths—to drink their blood. Why? Do you want some more?"

"Not right now."

Nick laughed softly. "Too much probably wouldn't be good for you." He stroked her cheek. His blood was very old, very powerful. The blood of the ancients, when taken too often, had been known to drive men insane. But small amounts had cured the sick, healed or prolonged the life of the dying. "Enough talk about blood. What would you like to do today?"

"I don't care, as long as we're together."

"I've always wanted to visit Sighisoara. Are you game?"

"Let's go!"

Hand in hand, Nick and Abbey toured the historic center. Abbey was thrilled to find a renaissance festival in full swing. Everywhere she looked, there were people in medieval costumes—knights and peasants, musicians and craftsmen, farmers and clerics. She loved the old-world charm of the place—the buildings in pastel shades of gold and green and pink and blue, the cobbled streets, the ornate churches, the medieval architecture, the turrets and towers.

They walked along narrow alleyways and hilly streets, and up steep flights of stairs. Later, they rested in a secluded square. Referring to a guidebook she had picked up along the way, Abbey learned that the city had a population of over thirty-two thousand and had been inhabited since the sixth century BC.

Not surprisingly, there was a page devoted to Vlad Dracula, also known as Vlad Tepes and Vlad the Impaler.

"He was born here in Sighisoara," Nick remarked, reading over her shoulder.

"Do you think he was really a vampire?"

"Not to my knowledge. But anything is possible. Most rumors carry a grain of truth."

"That's no answer."

"In spite of all the hype, I don't think he was a vampire," Nick said, chuckling. "But if he was, I'd like to meet him."

They spent the rest of the day wandering through the city. Abbey sampled a variety of food offered at some of the medieval booths; they stopped at a café where she ate a late lunch, then strolled through a gift shop where Nick bought her a delicate scarf in muted shades of mauve, blue, and lavender.

At dusk, she was ready to go home.

Gathering her into his arms, Nick whispered, "Hang on," and whisked them back to Mara's castle.

After seeing Abbey safely home, Nick left to go hunting.

Mara and Logan left shortly after he did. Apparently Edna and Pearl had also gone hunting.

Sitting on the sofa, her bare feet propped on a low table, Abbey spent several minutes contemplating the whole predator-prey scenario. Was it better to be the hunter, ever in search of prey? Or the hunted, always in danger? The lion or the lamb? If she had a choice, which would she rather be?

She thought about the nature films she had seen in school—brutal scenes of lions bringing down deer, sharks hunting seals, foxes chasing rabbits.

"Much better to be the hunter," she decided. And then she smiled. "Unless it's Nick hunting me."

Of course, in her case, there was no hunting involved. He asked and she acquiesced.

She sat up straight, her gaze darting left and right when she heard a noise from upstairs. She chided herself for being so jumpy when the noise came again. It was just the wind. Of course, who could blame her for being a little on edge? She had spent the day in the heart of Dracula country. And it was more than a little spooky, being in Mara's drafty old castle all alone. It was exactly like the setting used for all those old Dracula movies. And carried the same scary atmosphere prevalent in those silly teen flicks where the heroine—alone and unarmed—went haring off to explore the dungeon.

Determined to have a bath and wash her hair, Abbey filled several large cast-iron pots with water and set them to warm in the hearth in the kitchen while she went looking for a bathtub. She found one in a room off the kitchen. She had intended to carry it up to her bedchamber. Looking at it now, she wondered what she'd been thinking. There was no way she could carry the thing into the kitchen, let alone up the stairs.

When the water was hot, she dumped it in the tub, added a bit of cold, then rummaged in the box of supplies, wondering if Mara had thought to include soap.

She found a lavender-scented bar in the bottom, along with a washcloth, a bath towel, a toothbrush, and a tube of toothpaste. Silently thanking Mara for her thoughtfulness, Abbey undressed and stepped into the tub. She sighed with pleasure as the warm water closed over her.

Did Mara and the others bathe in this old tub? Or did they just whisk themselves back home where they could soak in a real bathtub with hot and cold running water?

Lying there, she found herself thinking about her housemates—out hunting in the shadows for prey. Nick had told her he no longer killed when feeding, but what about Mara and Logan and the old ladies? Somehow, she just couldn't imagine Edna and Pearl sinking their fangs into some unwary mortal. The pair looked more like bingo-playing grandmothers than blood-sucking vampires. Abbey grimaced as she imagined Pearl hypnotizing some old man and drinking his blood. Or did she prefer someone younger?

She thrust the unsettling thought from her mind. Better to think about Nick. And even as his image rose in her mind, he appeared in the doorway.

Startled, she grabbed the towel from the chair beside the tub and covered herself as best she could. "What are you doing here?" she sputtered. "Can't you see I'm taking a bath?"

"Yes, ma'am," he drawled with a wicked grin. "And a lovely sight it is."

She glared at him. "Now my towel is all wet and it's the only one I have."

"Not to worry. I'll get you another."

"Nick Desanto, you get out of here right this minute!"

Laughing, he vanished from her sight, only to return moments later bearing an armful of fluffy white bath towels, a bottle of French perfume, and a bouquet of red roses.

He placed the perfume and the flowers on the chair,

dropped the towels on the floor within easy reach, then bowed from the waist. "Enjoy your ablutions, my lady. I'll be in the Great Hall, should you need someone to wash your back."

Abbey stared after him as he sauntered out of the room and quietly closed the door. An image of Nick taking the soap from her hand and running it over her back and other, more intimate parts of her body almost tempted her to take him up on his offer.

"I'm still here if you've changed your mind."

With a huff of annoyance, she wadded up the wet towel and threw it at the door.

A wave of masculine laughter was his only response.

Dry and clean and wearing a pair of pj's, a robe, and slippers, Abbey scuffed into the Great Hall. If she hadn't known the occupants were vampires, it would have looked like an ordinary gathering of friends. A fire crackled cheerfully in the hearth. Mara, Logan, and Nick were playing poker; Edna was painting her nails; Pearl was engrossed in a battered paperback copy of *Frankenstein*.

"Good evening, dear," Pearl said, smiling over the top of her book.

"Hi."

"Have you ever read Shelley?" Pearl asked.

Abbey shook her head as she crossed the room and took a place on the sofa near the hearth. "Too scary for me."

"Scary?" Edna shook her head. "What's scarier than vampires?"

"Hunters?" Pearl suggested.

Abbey grinned. She didn't know the old ladies very well, but she couldn't help liking them. There was an innocence about them that was totally out of character for vampires.

A shout of victory from the poker table had Abbey looking that way.

"Four queens!" Mara crowed, fanning her cards on the table. "I win again."

"I don't know how you do it," Logan groused. "That's five hands in a row."

"Didn't you know?" Mara said, raking in a sizeable pot. "I used to deal in Monte Carlo."

Logan shuffled the deck. "You never told me that."

She shrugged. "I wasn't there very long."

"Bite the pit boss, did you?" Nick asked, stifling a grin.

Mara's face reflected her surprise. "How did you know?"

"I didn't. But I know you." Nick glanced at his hand, then tossed a handful of chips in the pot.

"Just how well did you know her?" Logan's voice was rough, like sandpaper over steel.

Mara's shoulders tensed.

The two men glowered at each other across the table.

Edna and Pearl exchanged nervous glances.

Abbey bit down on her lower lip. The tension between Logan and Nick was unmistakable, as was the fine edge of jealousy in Logan's voice. She glanced from Nick to Logan and back again. Would they fight? Nick was older, presumably stronger. Would he win? Or would Mara defend her husband against a former lover?

And just how well *did* Nick know Mara? Had he lied to her when he said there was no love between himself and his sire?

Logan pushed away from the table and gained his feet, his body rigid.

Nick also stood, hands tightly clenched at his sides.

"Oh, for goodness' sake!" Mara exclaimed. "Stop acting like idiots, you two! Logan, I met Nick first. We have a past together, brief as it was. Get over it. You're my husband. It's you I love. Now, sit down and deal."

Abbey held her breath. And then, as if a brisk wind had swept through the room, the tension vanished.

Logan and Nick resumed their seats.

Edna picked up her nail polish. Pearl went back to her book.

Abbey sighed with relief, but she couldn't dismiss the nagging voice in the back of her mind, the one that wondered if Nick had told her the whole truth.

Chapter Twenty-Three

Mara glared at Nick. "Haven't you caused enough trouble for one night? What's so important that we have to meet in secret? All I need is for Logan to find the two of us up here in the tower, all alone."

"What do you know about Abbey?"

"Everything there is to know, I guess. Why?"

"She got into my head the other night. Saw glimpses of my past. There's no way she should have been able to do that."

Brow furrowed, Mara moved to the window and stared out into the darkness. "That is odd."

"Do you think it's possible she has some psychic power that's been dormant until now?"

"I suppose anything is possible."

"What do you know about Savanah's sperm donor?"

"Nothing. I never thought to ask her about it."

"Do you think Savanah knows who it was?"

With a shrug, Mara turned to face him. "She might. Why? What are you thinking?"

Nick raked his fingers through his hair. "I'm not sure, but Abbey's either psychic or she has some other sort of preternatural power. There's no other explanation."

"Well, if you really want to know, I guess you'll have to ask Savanah."

"Yeah."

"Are we done here?"

He nodded, but made no move to leave.

Neither did she. Taking a step closer, Mara cupped his cheek in her palm. "It wasn't all so bad, was it?"

"No." Standing so close, he was reminded of the first night they had met. Then, as now, he had been aware of her incomparable beauty, her innate allure. He had told Abbey he had never loved Mara.

He had told himself the same lie the night Mara had abandoned him so many centuries ago.

Nick stood outside, his hands shoved deep into his pockets as he gazed into the darkness beyond the castle. It was almost four A.M. Mara and Logan were in their room. They had been arguing for the last twenty minutes, and though they kept their voices pitched low, Nick heard every word. It all boiled down to one thing: Logan Blackwood was suffering from a bad bout of jealousy, combined with a sense of betrayal because his wife had never told him about Nick, among other things.

For his part, Nick failed to understand why Blackwood was so upset. It was no secret that Mara had had countless lovers over the course of her long existence. Surely Logan knew it as well as everyone else. Or was Blackwood just upset because one of those lovers was now under his roof?

Nick shook his head as the sound of their argument

ended abruptly, followed by the whisper of clothing hastily being flung aside, the faint sigh of the mattress as the lovers ended their quarrel.

Logan Blackwood was a lucky man.

Nick smiled faintly. He had been smitten by Mara the moment he first saw her. They had enjoyed a brief, explosive few months together—nights of hunting, followed by hours of insatiable lovemaking. If there was one thing he loved about being a vampire, it was the incredible amount of stamina that came with it. No mortal man or woman could have survived.

Thoughts of intimacy immediately brought Abbey to mind. He had seen her face when Logan lost his temper earlier. In spite of what he had told her, she suspected he had cared for Mara more than he'd said, wondered if he still cared.

He had been certain he was telling Abbey the truth when he'd told her there had been no love between himself and Mara. Tonight, in the tower room, he realized he had been kidding himself for years. But what he felt for Mara was nothing compared to his feelings for Abbey. Mara was his sire. There would always be a bond between them, one that could only be broken by his death, or hers. But comparing his affection for Mara to what he felt for Abbey was like comparing the faint glow of a single candle to the blinding brightness of the sun. There was simply no comparison. His love for Abbey was richer, deeper, stronger.

Tuning out the soft cries and moans of the happy couple, Nick went up to the room where Abbey slept.

She lay on her side, one hand beneath her cheek. Her hair, spread across the pillowcase like a splash of dark chocolate, tempted his touch.

She stirred, murmuring his name, and he knew she

was dreaming of him. Needing to hold her, he shucked his boots and stretched out beside her. How beautiful she was. Her skin smooth and soft. Her lips pink and perfect and slightly parted.

Her breath mingled with his as she murmured his name again.

He caressed her cheek, ever so lightly, traced the contours of her lips with his fingertip, pressed a kiss to her brow.

"Nick?" Her eyelids fluttered open. "Nick!"

"Shh."

"Is something wrong?"

"No. I was just missing you."

Sleepy-eyed, she smiled at him. "Are you really here?"

"If you want me to be."

"I was dreaming of you."

"I know. I can make it come true, if you're willing."

"Nick . . ."

"I know. I promised to court you." Drawing her into his arms, he kissed her cheeks, her brow, her eyelids, before claiming her lips with his. His body reacted to her nearness, as his hunger responded to the siren call of her blood.

He reminded himself that they had only known each other a short time, that even though she cared for him, was undeniably attracted to him, she still had doubts about their relationship. He needed to slow down, for both their sakes.

Cupping her face in his palms, he kissed her one more time, then eased away from her and sat up. Brushing a wisp of hair from her cheek, he said, "Go back to sleep, love. I'll see you in the morning."

"Good night, Nick," she whispered. And then she said the words he had longed to hear. "I love you."

* * *

Abbey woke with a smile on her lips and the sun in her face. Nick had come to her last night. Or had that been a part of her dream? And what a dream it had been!

They had been walking in the woods behind the castle beneath a full moon. He had pulled her into his arms and the next thing she knew, they had been stretched out on an enormous bed floating in the middle of the ocean. He had undressed her, tossing her clothing into the water. His kisses, his caresses, his words, had carried her away until she was aching for him with every fiber of her being. And then, at the moment of fulfillment, she had felt the prick of his fangs at her throat.

And the next thing she knew, she was in the midst of the ocean, drowning in a sea of crimson ecstasy. It had been exhilarating and frightening in equal measure.

With a shake of her head, Abbey tossed the covers aside. Rising, she washed her hands and face in the basin on the dresser. She glanced out the window as dark clouds shrouded the sun. After donning a pair of jeans and a sweater, she headed downstairs.

She had just finished breakfast when her father called.

"How's it going?" he asked. "Everything okay there?"

"Yes. Nick took me sightseeing again yesterday. It was fun, but I'm missing Freckles. And you and Mom, of course," she added quickly. "When can I come home?"

"Soon, I'd say. Roshan and your uncle Rafe spent the last two nights in town, but there's still no sign of the hunters, and no explanation for their sudden departure. If nothing happens in the next few days, I'll tell Mara to bring you home."

"Another few days," she said, groaning dramatically. "Dad, you have no idea what it's like here. I mean, it wouldn't be so bad if the place had a few modern conveniences. Wouldn't you think Mara would at least install some plumbing?"

Rane chuckled. "It would probably cost a fortune to modernize that old place."

"I guess."

"What are Pearl and Edna up to?"

"Nothing that I know of. I really don't see very much of them. Why?"

"Just curious. You might let them know the coalition raised the bounty on their heads."

"I will."

"I'll call you tomorrow, honey."

"Okay. Give my love to Mom."

"Will do."

Abbey disconnected the call and slipped her phone back into her pocket. All that talk of hunters, combined with the information about the increased reward for Edna and Pearl, reminded her once again how different her life was from that of her family, and how truly uninvolved she had been in their lives over the last five years.

Now she was home again, dating a vampire, and there was no ignoring the fact that there was no longer anything remotely normal about her life. The thing that bothered her the most was her sudden ability to read Nick's mind. She had never wondered who her biological father was, but she was wondering now. Had he been a college graduate? Was he married? Had he liked art and music? Of course, she had no idea if that kind of information had been made available, but as

soon as she got home, she was going to have a long talk
with her mother.

Kneeling in front of the fireplace in one of the
upstairs bedrooms, Pearl stirred the liquid bubbling in
the heavy cast-iron pot hanging from a tripod over a
small fire.

"Do you think that's enough monkshood?" Edna
asked, peering over her shoulder.

"As sure as I can be, dear," Pearl replied, adding a
dash of hawthorn, a few drops of rose oil, and several
cloves of garlic.

Wrinkling her nose against the smell, Edna took
several steps backward. "What do you think he'll do to
us if it doesn't work?"

"I don't want to think about it. Hand me that vial of
blood, will you, dear?"

Edna passed her the vial, watched the liquid in the
pot turn crimson as Pearl stirred it into the mix. "I
wonder if the hunter's child regained her humanity."

"We'll probably never know, but I hope so." Pearl
stirred the mixture again, then stood. "Forty-eight hours
from now, Nick might be human again, although I can't
imagine why he'd want to be. All it will get him is sickness, old age, and death."

Sighing, Edna pressed her hand over her heart. "I
think it's romantic. Imagine having a man who loved
you that much."

"If Abbey was smart, she'd let him bring her across.
Then they could have hundreds of years together instead of one, short, mortal lifetime."

"Hmm. Maybe you're right," Edna allowed.

"Of course I'm right, but it isn't our choice to make,
is it, dear?" Pearl covered the pot, then tucked a stray

lock of hair behind her ear. "All this cooking is making me hungry. How about you?"

Looking up from a book she'd found in the library, Abbey frowned as a strange odor stung her nostrils. What on earth was that horrid smell? Since she was the only one in the place who did any cooking—and darn little of that since she'd been here—she couldn't imagine what it was. Or why the smell wasn't coming from the kitchen.

She glanced at the time on her phone. Just after six in the evening. Abbey frowned, wondering where her housemates were. She hadn't seen any of them all day and she was bored, bored, bored.

She laid the book aside, then followed the awful smell up the stairs and down the corridor to one of the bedrooms. The door was closed, but the smell was definitely coming from that room.

"Hello? Is anyone in there?"

When there was no answer, she reached for the knob, then hesitated. This wasn't her house. At home, a closed door meant "keep out."

But what if the house was on fire? It certainly smelled as if something was burning.

She pressed her ear to the door and when she didn't hear anything, she turned the handle and stepped into the room. It was empty save for a small round table that held a brown leather case. The stink came from a pot suspended from a tripod in the fireplace.

Ignoring the little voice in the back of her head that told her she had no business snooping around, she used the hem of her sweater to lift the lid, felt the bile rise in her throat when she saw the thick red liquid bubbling inside the pot. What on earth was it?

After quickly replacing the lid, she stumbled away from the fireplace, then turned and hurried out the door.

And ran smack into Nick.

"Whoa, girl," he said, catching her by the shoulders. "Where's the fire?"

Pointing behind her, she said, "In there."

"What? Wait a minute. Are you saying the castle's on fire?"

"No! No." She shook her head. "Something's cooking in there." She shuddered. "Something disgusting."

Nick couldn't argue with that. The scent of blood and herbs had disturbed his rest. He had hoped the smell came from something else, but he had a terrible suspicion that he knew what it was. He swore under his breath. He had credited Edna and Pearl with more sense than to brew their magical elixir here, inside the castle.

Blocking his thoughts, Nick forced a laugh as he guided Abbey toward the stairway. "I'm sure it's nothing."

"It doesn't smell like nothing," she muttered, wrinkling her nose. "It reeks!"

He couldn't argue with that.

If what they were cooking was his desired cure, he sure as hell hoped it tasted better than it smelled!

Nick confronted the two elderly vampires later that night. "What the hell were you thinking? Cooking that crap in here?"

Pearl looked up from the hearth, where she had been stirring the pot. "Where else did you think we'd make it? We can't go home."

"You could have taken it down to the dungeon."

"Edna saw a rat there."

"A rat?" Nick glanced from one woman to the other. "A rat? You're vampires, for crying out loud. Our kind has been known to dine on rats when there was nothing else."

Edna grimaced. "I'd rather starve!"

Nick jerked his chin toward the hearth. "Is that my cure you've got cooking in there?"

"Yes." Pearl set her spoon aside and covered the pot. "It's coming along nicely."

"It stinks to high heaven."

"That's the wormwood. And the garlic, of course."

"Wormwood," Nick muttered. "And garlic." He took a deep breath. "Whose blood is in there?"

Pearl and Edna exchanged glances.

"I asked you a question."

"It's blood from an infant."

Nick's eyes narrowed. "Don't tell me . . ."

"Oh, no!" Pearl exclaimed. "The babe passed away. Killed in a car accident, he was."

Edna nodded. "We thought blood that was pure would work better than anything else."

Nick stared at the pot. He had never tasted the blood of children. The thought of doing it now was repugnant. But he was willing to try anything to restore his humanity.

"Keep this door locked from now on." He fixed each woman with a hard stare as he stepped into the hall. "And remember, no one's to know this is for me."

After leaving Edna and Pearl, Nick went hunting in the city. He preyed on the first female he saw, then sent her on her way.

He was contemplating whether to stop by the local pub for a glass of wine or return to the castle when he heard Abbey's voice in his mind.

Nick? Come home. I miss you.

Her request stopped him in his tracks. No one, save Mara, had ever been inside his head. It was disconcerting, knowing a mortal—even when that mortal was Abbey—was walking around inside his mind.

A thought took him to Abbey's room. She smelled of soap and shampoo, leading him to believe she had bathed and washed her hair before climbing into bed.

Abbey grinned when Nick materialized in her room. The first time she had read his thoughts had been a little disturbing, but now she decided it was a pretty neat trick, being able to contact him even when he was miles away.

"You look like the cat that swallowed the canary," Nick muttered, closing the door behind him.

"I'm sorry." She made a vague gesture with her hand. "I couldn't help trying out my new . . . ah . . . spooky psychic power or whatever it is. Do you mind?"

"No."

"I can't believe it worked. That is why you're here, isn't it? Because I sent my thoughts to you?"

"I got your message loud and clear." His gaze moved over her. "What now?"

She frowned. And then her cheeks flooded with color. She had called him home and when he arrived, she was waiting for him in bed. It didn't take a genius to know what he must be thinking.

Nick laughed softly as he sat on the edge of the mattress and pulled her into his arms. "I'm pretty sure you didn't bring me here to seduce me, although I'm more than willing to let you have your way with me."

She looked away, her cheeks feeling like they were on fire. "You're making fun of me."

"Never." He placed a finger under her chin and lifted her head. "Now that I'm here, I can tuck you into bed and kiss you good night."

"Stay with me for a little while?"

"I'm not sure that's a good idea."

"Please?"

"All right, love." He toed off his boots, removed his shirt. "But I'm warning you, I've only got so much self-control."

Abbey lifted the covers, admiring his broad shoulders and flat stomach as he slid in beside her and drew her into his arms.

Nick held her for several minutes, dusting feather-light kisses on her brow, her cheeks, the tip of her nose, the corners of her lips. Her response was less enthusiastic than usual, causing him to ask, "Is something wrong?"

She shook her head and then sighed. "I guess I'm a little homesick. I'm fond of Mara and Logan, and the castle's lovely in an old-world way, but . . ."

"It isn't home." He had a number of houses, Nick mused, but none of them were home.

"I don't know why I'm feeling so blue. Dad says I can come back in a day or two. I guess . . ."

"Go on."

"Well, my life has been kind of hectic lately, what with meeting you and moving back to Auburn and then, just when I thought things were settling down, my dad decided I should stay with Mara." She paused to take a breath. "And then Mara decided we should come to Romania, of all places, and . . ."

Nick kissed her, slowly, deeply, until he felt her relax

in his arms. "I'll take you home day after tomorrow. If not to your place, then to mine."

"Oh, Nick!" Throwing her arms around him, she kissed him, then drew back, her eyes wide. "Are you out of your mind?"

"What are you talking about?"

"Don't deny it. I read your thoughts. I can't believe that on top of everything else that's happening, you're actually thinking about taking that crazy cure!"

Sitting up, Nick raked his fingers through his hair. Dammit. He hadn't intended to tell Abbey about the cure until it was a done deal, but he had let his guard down when she kissed him, and now the proverbial cat was out of the bag.

"That's what's cooking in their room, isn't it?" She scooted into a sitting position. "They're brewing one of their so-called cures."

"Calm down, love. I'm doing it for you."

"For me? Why?" She plucked at the edge of the blanket. "I've never asked you to change."

"I know, but relationships between vampires and mortals rarely end well."

"That's not true! Look at my family."

"Do you think those relationships would have endured this long if the women had remained mortal?"

"I'd like to think so."

"I know you don't want to be what I am," Nick said. "And I don't blame you. It isn't a life I would have chosen for myself."

"But . . . ?"

"I want to try the old ladies' cure," he said. "Not just for you. But for myself. I told you before that I was tired of living, that I had intended to ask Mara to end my existence. This way is better."

Abbey stared at him a moment. He was right. She

had never wanted to be a vampire. But she couldn't help thinking he was making a huge sacrifice, giving up his powers, his strength, and an endless future for a few short years with her.

"If the cure works, will you marry me, Abbey?"

"Oh, Nick!" she cried, throwing her arms around his neck. "I'll marry you even if it doesn't."

Chapter Twenty-Four

Rane tossed his cell phone on the table. "Well, shit."

Savanah looked at her husband, still stunned by Abbey's news. Her daughter was going to marry Nick Desanto and Abbey expected them to be happy about it? "She hardly knows the man."

"He's not a man," Rane growled. "He's a vampire that's over two thousand years old."

"Well, you have to admit, he seems to love Abbey and he's treated her, and us, with respect."

"Don't tell me you're on her side?" he asked incredulously.

"No, of course not. But she's very much in love with him. I could hear it in her voice. She's happy, Rane. Really happy."

"She can be happy with someone else."

Savanah placed her hand on his arm. "If we make this hard for her, or let her know we don't approve, it will only drive her away. You don't want that, do you?"

"Of course not. But . . ."

"There's always a chance she'll change her mind.

They haven't set a date yet. And she'll be coming home soon."

"I should have driven a stake in his heart the first time I saw him."

"You might want to keep those thoughts to yourself when they come home," Savanah suggested with a wry grin. "What are you really worried about? You must have known that, growing up in our family, there was always a good possibility she would marry a vampire."

"What am I afraid of?" Hands balled into fists, Rane paced the living room floor. "I'm afraid that he might turn her against her will. Abbey doesn't want to be a vampire. She never has. He wouldn't be the first of us to turn a woman against her will." He slammed his fist against the wall. "If he hurts her . . . if he mistreats her . . . I swear I'll destroy him if it's the last thing I ever do!"

Chapter Twenty-Five

Abbey stood in the middle of the bedroom floor, her hands fisted on her hips. "But I want to be there!"

"No. I don't know what effect, if any, it will have on me."

"Nick . . ."

"Abbey, please don't fight me on this."

A sigh of resignation slipped past her lips. "All right. But you'll come to me as soon as you can. You promise?"

"Of course."

"Does Mara know you're doing this?"

"No. And neither should you." Drawing her into his arms, he hugged her tightly. "I've got to go."

Abbey clung to him a moment, wishing she could talk him out of taking the cure. What if it didn't work? What if it did? What if it killed him?

"I'll be fine, Abbey. Stop worrying about me."

"I love you, Nick."

"I know." His gaze moved over her, as if to memorize her face, before he left the room.

* * *

"The dungeon?" Nick asked, one brow raised in wry amusement. "What about the rats?"

"We have no idea how our serum will affect you," Pearl explained, ignoring his attempt at humor. "We've never tried it on anyone as ancient as you. It's for your own protection, as well as ours."

With a shake of his head, Nick stepped into the cell, which held a wooden cot covered by a patchwork quilt, and nothing else. He could have told them that the cell wouldn't hold him if he wanted to get out, but what the hell. Locking him up seemed to make them feel safer.

Pearl closed and locked the door, then pulled a small brown bottle from her skirt pocket and handed it through the bars.

Nick stared at it. "What now?"

"You drink it, of course," Edna said. "And then . . . who knows?"

"You don't inspire a lot of confidence," Nick muttered. He uncapped the bottle, grimaced at the liquid's foul odor.

"If it works, you'll wake up mortal in the morning," Pearl said.

"And if it doesn't?"

"You could wake up dead," Edna replied matter-of-factly. "As in, really, really dead."

Pearl sent Edna a quelling glance. "I doubt that will happen. If it doesn't work, you'll be no worse off than you are now."

Nick regarded the bottle through narrowed eyes. "Like I said, you don't inspire a lot of confidence."

"Good night," Pearl said.

"And good luck," Edna added.

Nick waited until he was alone. Then, taking a deep

breath, he downed the contents of the bottle in one long swallow.

As he'd feared, the stuff tasted even worse than it smelled.

The ache in his gut started an hour later. Nothing more than a twinge at first, and then, little by little, the twinge grew stronger, until what began as minor discomfort quickly accelerated to unbearable pain and then to unspeakable agony. His blood burned like molten lava in his veins.

Minutes turned to hours. As the pain grew worse, he writhed helplessly on the floor. Time lost all meaning. He was trapped in the fires of hell, at the mercy of the bottle's vile contents.

He choked back the screams that clawed at his throat.

And prayed for death.

And she came.

Ever so gently, she lifted his head onto her lap. Her hand stroked his brow, cool against his heated skin, soft and oh, so gentle. Her words made no sense, but the sound of her voice soothed him. She massaged his throat and when he opened his mouth, something warm and salty trickled over his tongue.

"Abbey?"

"Sorry, no."

"Mara." Her name emerged from his throat in a growl of denial.

"Niccola, what the hell were you thinking?"

"How did you know?"

She continued to stroke his brow. "I'm your sire, you fool. How are you feeling?"

He groaned. "How do you think?"

"I think you look like hell."

"Yeah? Well, that's how I feel."

"You did this for Abbey, didn't you?"

He grunted in reply.

"Does she know?"

"Yeah."

"You really are in love with her, aren't you?"

"I asked her to marry me." He struggled to sit up. "And yes, she said yes. And yes, I'm going to try this again."

With a rueful shake of her head, Mara stood and helped him to his feet. "Are you doing this because she wants you to?"

"No." He leaned against the back wall, his arms wrapped around his stomach.

"You're either in love or out of your mind," Mara declared. "I'm not sure which."

Abbey had been pacing the floor for what seemed like an eternity when Nick materialized in her room.

"Good Lord!" she exclaimed, hurrying to his side. "Are you all right?" Her gaze moved over him. She had often heard the expression "like death warmed over." Now she knew what it looked like. Grabbing his hand, she tugged him toward the bed. "Sit down before you fall down."

"I'm all right."

"Uh-huh. And I'm the Queen of England."

Muttering an oath, he fell back on the mattress and closed his eyes.

Abbey stared at him. His face was drawn and pale. There were dark shadows under his eyes; lines of pain bracketed his mouth. She wasn't sure, but it seemed as if he was having trouble breathing. "Nick?" She shook his shoulder. "Nick!"

"You don't have to shout."

She sank down on the bed beside him. "You scared me. I thought . . ."

"Stop worrying. I'm fine." It wasn't quite the truth. His insides were still on fire, but, thanks to Mara's blood, the pain was no longer intolerable.

"So," Abbey said, brushing the hair from his brow. "I guess it didn't work."

"I'll try again in a few days."

"Please don't." She took his hand in hers and pressed it to her heart. "I love you just the way you are." Bending down, she kissed his cheek. "Forget the cure, and let's go back home tomorrow like we planned."

Home, he thought. If he tried the cure a second time with the same results, would Mara come to his rescue again?

And what would be his fate if she didn't?

It was near dawn before Abbey fell asleep. Easing out from beside her, Nick went into town. He preyed upon the first person he saw—an old drunk huddled in an alley. The man's clothes reeked of cheap wine and tobacco, his blood was vile, but it restored much of Nick's strength. He didn't bother to wipe his memory from the derelict's mind. Even if the old guy remembered what had happened, no one was likely to believe he'd seen a vampire.

After sealing the wounds in the old man's neck, Nick left the alley. A short time later, he checked into a hotel where he took a long, hot shower before returning to the castle.

He found Edna and Pearl in the great hall bent over a chessboard.

Edna's eyes widened when she looked up and saw him. "Remember what you said! No hard feelings."

"I want another go at that cure."

"Are you sure, dear?"

"I wouldn't be here if I wasn't."

"But . . . I think it's only fair to tell you that it's not likely to work this time either. The next step would be to increase the dose." Pearl shook her head. "But I'm afraid that might kill you."

"I agree," Edna said. "And after seeing the results this time . . . well, I can't imagine a new batch would be any more effective. We can't work magic, you know."

"I'm willing to take my chances. I'm taking Abbey home tomorrow. When the cure's ready, let me know. Have you got a cell phone?" He had bought one on a whim a few years ago. He rarely used it.

"Of course, dear. Doesn't everyone?"

Nick gave Pearl his number. "All right, don't just sit there like bumps on a log," he growled. "Go figure out a way to make that cure work, or I'll hand the two of you over to those hunters myself."

"Very well," Edna said. "It's your funeral. Come along, Pearl. We've got work to do."

Abbey had her bag packed and was ready to go when Nick rose the following evening. She met him in the Great Hall, where he was talking to Logan and Mara.

They all looked her way when she entered the room.

"So," Mara said, "you're leaving us."

Abbey nodded. "I'm afraid I'm homesick."

Mara smiled. "Of course. We'll be returning to California in a day or two. I confess, I miss the creature comforts so sorely lacking here. Logan thinks we should either renovate this old place or sell it." She glanced around, then sighed. "It's going to cost a fortune to fix it up, but I can't part with it."

"What about Edna and Pearl?" Nick asked.

"Since it isn't safe for them to return to the States, I've decided to let them stay here to look after things."

"Thank you for everything," Abbey said.

Mara nodded. "Give my love to your mom and dad. And tell your mother the books are hidden where no one will ever find them."

"I will."

Abbey hugged Mara and Logan, then picked up her suitcase.

"Ready?" Nick asked.

When she nodded, he tucked his suitcase under one arm and wrapped his other arm around her waist. "Here we go."

The next thing she knew, they were standing in the middle of the living room in the cottage.

Abbey dropped her suitcase on the floor beside Nick's. She clung to him for several moments, until the world stopped spinning. They had left Mara's place at six P.M., Romanian time. Here in California, it was ten hours earlier and the sun was shining brightly.

She was about to ask Nick if he wanted to go riding when he turned sharply toward the door, his eyes showing red, nostrils flaring.

"What is it?" Abbey whispered.

"Hunters. A lot of them."

"Here?" She glanced nervously around the room.

"No. Up at the house." He drew in a deep breath. Blood had been spilled. Copious amounts of it.

"My parents!" Abbey exclaimed, the color draining from her face. "I've got to go up there!"

She ran toward the door, skidded to a stop when she almost ran into Nick.

"Not so fast," he said. "Not until I check it out."

"Nick, they could be hurt. Or . . ." She blinked back her tears. They couldn't be dead!

"There's nothing you can do up there. You need to stay here until I find out what's going on."

"I can't just sit here and wait, not knowing."

"Abbey, listen to me. I don't know what happened up there, but I smell blood, and I'm not sure whose it is. I'm going to take you to my lair in New Jersey. When we get there, I want you to call your uncle Rafe and ask him to come and stay with you. Got it?"

"But . . ."

"Don't argue with me. You can't do any good here."

He didn't wait for her answer. Wrapping her in his arms, he transported the two of them to his lair in New Jersey. "I'll let you know what's going on as soon as I find out." He scribbled his address and phone number on a scrap of paper and thrust it into her hand. "Call your uncle. Promise me?"

She nodded. Nick was right. There was nothing she could do at home. "Be careful!"

"Don't worry about me. Make that call. And keep the doors and windows locked."

Nick dissolved into mist as he approached the Cordova house. He could hear voices inside—a lot of voices. He hadn't told Abbey, but the blood he'd smelled was mostly vampire blood. And overlying it, the unmistakable smell of death.

Hovering outside a downstairs window, he quickly took in the scene before him. The living room was a shambles. Sofa pillows were scattered on the floor, drawers had been emptied. Pictures hung askew, leading Nick to believe the intruders had been searching for a wall safe. No doubt the rest of the house had also been turned upside down.

Eleven hunters formed a loose circle around Rane and Savanah. A fire burned in the hearth; a poker rested on the coals, its tip glowing bright red. Both vampires were bound by heavy silver chains. Judging from the bloodstains on their tattered clothing, they had been tortured. It was hard to tell how long it had been going on, or how badly they had been hurt, since vampire wounds healed quickly.

"I grow weary of this." Meloni's voice, thick with anger and impatience. "Where are the books?"

"We've told you a hundred times," Rane said. "They aren't here and we don't know where they are."

"Liar!" Meloni raked a silver-bladed dagger down Rane's arm from his shoulder to his wrist. Blood oozed from the shallow gash. "I know you have them!"

"We did." Rane's voice was tight, laced with pain as the silver burned through him. "We gave them away."

Meloni snorted. "You expect us to believe that?"

"It's the truth!" Savanah cried. "Leave him alone!"

"Truth!" Meloni exclaimed with a sneer. "Vampires don't know the meaning of the word."

Having seen enough, Nick unleashed his preternatural power as he materialized in the midst of the hunters.

As one, the hunters reeled backward, their faces going slack, weapons clattering to the floor.

A thought held them immobile. They all glared at him, their combined hatred a tangible presence in the room.

"Nice party," Nick muttered. Holding Meloni's gaze with his, he said, "Release my friends."

Moving robotlike, she did as she was told though her eyes blazed with impotent fury.

Rane helped Savanah to her feet. "Where's Abbey?"

"She's safe," Nick said curtly. "What the hell's going on? How'd they get past your wards?"

"A couple of them caught Savanah outside, alone. They shot her with darts laced with silver. I heard her cry out and when I went to see what was wrong, a bunch of them sprayed me in the face with holy water. It rendered me helpless just long enough for them to overpower the two of us."

"Why didn't you just tell them where the books are?" Nick asked.

"They would have just killed us that much sooner. Besides, we don't know."

Nick grunted softly. Rane could have told the hunters that Mara had the books. They might have believed him. Or maybe not. Either way, he was pretty sure the hunters wouldn't have left them alive.

"What do we do now?" Savanah asked.

"If it was up to me, I'd have a big lunch and bury the remains," Nick said. "But it's your house, so . . ." He shrugged, then frowned when another vampire materialized in the room. Though he had never met Rafe Cordova, there was no mistaking the man's resemblance to Rane. They could only be brothers. "What are you doing here? You're supposed to be with Abbey."

"Kathy's looking after her," Rafe explained. "I thought I might be needed here." His gaze moved over Rane. "How you doing, brother?"

"I've been better."

"Rafe." Savanah smiled warmly. "It's good to see you."

"You too," he said, giving her a hug.

Rane jerked his head toward the hunters. "Shouldn't we get back to the matter at hand?"

"Wipe their memories and let them go," Rafe said.

Nick snorted. "Seriously?"

"You can't be thinking of killing all eleven of them," Rafe said incredulously. "Someone's bound to know this bunch was coming here. We'll have every hunter in the country breathing down our necks."

Nick glanced at Meloni and the others. "Looks to me like they already are."

"Rafe's always been a softie," Rane said, "but I think in this case, he's right. I don't know about the rest of you, but I'm not in the mood to dispose of eleven bodies."

"I think you're making a big mistake by leaving them alive," Nick said. "But you do what you have to do. Abbey's waiting for me at my place."

"Is she living with you now?" There was no mistaking the disapproval in Rane's voice.

"No, I took her there to get her out of harm's way. I'll bring her home tomorrow."

Savanah stepped between Desanto and her husband. "Thank you, Nick."

He gave her a curt nod of acknowledgment, and then left the house.

Nick found Abbey asleep on the sofa, her cheeks stained with tears. He stood there looking at her for a long time. She was, he thought, the most beautiful being he had ever seen. Just being near her made him ache inside in a way he didn't understand. He loved her with all his heart, and yet it went deeper than that.

He glanced up as a woman entered the room. "You must be Kathy," he said. "I'm Nick. Thanks for coming."

She nodded. "Everything okay at Rane's place?"

He nodded. "Nothing we couldn't handle."

"You love her, don't you?" Kathy asked, nodding in Abbey's direction.

"More than my own life. Thanks again for keeping an eye on her."

"Happy to help. Now, if you don't need me for anything else, I'll be going home."

"We're good. Let me know if I can ever return the favor."

Nick walked Kathy to the door and then, moving to the window, he stared into the distance, his thoughts turned inward. He loved Abbey with his whole heart, but what did he have to offer her? He was ancient; she was little more than a child. He had seen things, done things, that would sicken her if she knew.

She deserved a normal life, with a man who shared similar interests, one who had grown up in the same era she had, shared similar memories.

A man who could give her children, and grow old at her side.

A man who wouldn't look at eleven helpless humans and think of them as lunch.

Chapter Twenty-Six

Brow furrowed, Mara stared at the computer screen. Several days ago, she had hired a rather disreputable Internet detective to search for the man whose sperm Savanah had chosen.

The findings were interesting, to say the least.

She glanced over her shoulder as Logan came up behind her.

"What's up, wife?"

"My man came through. The information given on the donor card lists his name as Miles Jay Cunningham, age twenty-nine, born in Loch Lynn Heights, Maryland, unmarried. He listed his profession as accountant."

"Seems harmless enough."

"Ah, but when my man dug a little deeper, he discovered that Miles Jay Cunningham, also known as Miles Novotny, was a warlock aligned with a well-known coven in New Orleans."

"The plot thickens."

"That's not all. In Boston, he was known as Miles Lightner, a self-proclaimed psychic and healer. In Santa Fe, he went by the name of Ace Lightner. For a time, he worked as a dealer in Atlantic City. Until they caught him dealing from the bottom."

"Where is he now?"

"He died in prison two years ago while he was serving a fifteen-year sentence for stealing uncut diamonds worth a cool half million from one of his clients."

Logan clucked softly. "End of the trail."

"Yes, but it might explain why Abbey was able to read Nick's mind. I think her abilities are negligible at best, but Nick's preternatural powers have somehow enhanced hers."

"So, what are you going to do with this info?"

"I don't know. Give it to Abbey, I suppose, although I'm not sure she will appreciate knowing her biological father was a crook."

"She might like to know he was a warlock."

"I wonder if Savanah knew?"

Logan shrugged. "Where are the lovebirds now?"

"Abbey's at home with her parents." Mara cocked her head to the side, a distant look in her eyes. "I can't find Nick."

"Isn't he with Abbey?"

"No. He's stronger than I thought," she murmured, looking troubled. "He's blocking me."

"What the hell is he up to?"

Mara shook her head, her expression troubled. "I don't know for sure, but I have a pretty good idea."

Chapter Twenty-Seven

Abbey woke in her own bed in the cottage with no recollection of how she had gotten there. The last thing she remembered was lying on the sofa at Nick's house, praying that Nick and her parents and her uncle Rafe were all right.

Rising, she showered and dressed, then went up to the main house, thinking Nick was probably there, waiting for her.

She found her parents in the living room, putting things to right. "Hunters did this?" Abbey glanced at the overturned furniture, the torn pillow cushions, the papers and books scattered on the floor. The wooden stakes, clubs, and silver chains stacked in one corner. The blood stains on the carpet.

"Yes," her mother said succinctly. "Hunters."

The word, spoken with loathing, echoed inside Abbey's head. She had heard the word most of her life. She knew what it meant. But never before had the reality of the danger vampire hunters presented hit home quite so forcefully. Hunters had invaded her home. Had they prevailed, her parents would now be dead.

Abbey looked at her mother and father. She could

see no visible wounds, but vampires healed quickly. Her gaze drifted to the blood on the rug. Was it theirs? Or . . . ? "Where are the hunters?"

"They're gone."

Gone. What did that mean, exactly? And did she really want to know? Visions of her parents fighting, killing to defend their lives, filled her mind with grotesque images.

"But you're both all right?"

"We're fine," her father said. "Where's Nick?"

"I thought he was here."

Rane shook his head. "He helped us out yesterday. We haven't seen him since."

Refusing to consider what that meant, Abbey spent the next few hours helping her parents clean up the mess. The hunters had searched every room, every closet, every nook and cranny. Tables were overturned, mattresses ripped, drawers emptied. Clothes had been tossed out of closets.

By nightfall, the clutter had been cleaned up. The ruined mattresses were stacked outside the back door, along with the living-room carpet, and the broken furniture. Few pieces had been left intact or unscarred. After looking it over, her father decided to scrap the lot of it.

"You've been wanting to redecorate," Rane said, draping his arm around Savanah's shoulders. "I guess now's the time."

Where was Nick? That was the question that haunted Abbey throughout the night. She tried several times to contact him telepathically, but either she had lost the ability to do so, or he was blocking her.

She told herself not to worry, that everything was

tine. But try as she might, she couldn't make herself believe it.

In bed that night, she cried herself to sleep. In the morning, her cheeks were still damp with tears.

Her parents came by late that afternoon to see if she wanted to go furniture shopping with them, but Abbey declined, saying she needed to look after the stock.

"You really should come with us," her mother coaxed. "After all, we need to refurbish your old room, too."

"There's no hurry," Abbey said. "I'm happy in the cottage. Mom, could I talk to you a minute before you go?"

Savanah glanced at Rane.

"No problem," he said. "I'll wait outside."

"What's on your mind?" Savanah asked when she and Abbey were alone.

"I was wondering who . . ." Abbey bit down on her lower lip. "When you went to the sperm bank, did they tell you anything about my biological father?"

Savanah frowned. "Just his age and that he was a healthy white male. Why? What brought this up all of a sudden?"

"Sometimes I can read Nick's mind."

"I see. Have you and Nick exchanged blood?"

Abbey hesitated, then said, "I tasted a little, but I could read his thoughts before that."

"I suppose I could look into it, if it's important to you. Of course, it's been so long . . . I don't know if they'd still have that information, or even if the office is still there. But I'll check into it tomorrow evening and if I find out anything, I'll let you know."

"Thanks, Mom."

"Are you sure you don't want to come with us?"

"Not this time."

"All right. We won't be long," her mother said, giving her a hug.

After her parents left, Abbey quickly changed into her work clothes and tugged on her boots. She hurried down to the barn where she fed and watered the stock, mucked out the stalls, checked the cinches on all the saddles, noting that the one on her father's favorite saddle needed to be replaced. But no matter how busy her hands, her mind replayed one question over and over again.

Where was Nick?

Had he changed his mind about marrying her?

Was he hurt? Dying? Dead?

Why couldn't she contact him?

Why hadn't he contacted her?

Try as she might, she couldn't stop worrying. Couldn't stop wondering if his last kiss good night had really been good-bye.

Chapter Twenty-Eight

If you were a vampire, there was no better place to be than in the heart of New Orleans during Mardi Gras. It was one big, never-ending party. A veritable smorgasbord for a hungry vampire as people from all over the country—all over the world—came to eat, drink, and be scared out of their minds.

The city was rife with haunted houses and voodoo churches, with stories of ghosts and zombies who prowled the city's graveyards by night, and with witches and fortune-tellers who plied their trade by day.

You never knew who lurked behind an elaborate feather mask. Was it merely a human out for a good time, or a creature of the night looking for prey? People let down their hair and their morals. Whiskey and wine flowed like water.

And so did the blood.

Nick had been in town less than an hour and had already counted at least thirty vampires roaming the streets, mingling with the tourists, luring them into dark corners and darker alleys.

He wasn't sure what had drawn him to the city. A need to indulge his vampire nature, perhaps? Or to remind himself yet again that he was no fit companion for the woman he loved.

He knew Abbey was trying to contact him but he ruthlessly blocked her thoughts.

He needed time alone. Time to decide what was best for the two of them. His two biggest fears were that if the cure didn't work, he might, in a moment of weakness, drain her dry, or worse, force her to accept the Dark Gift, something that would surely make her hate him. And no doubt bring the wrath of the entire Cordova clan down on his head. Yet, loving her as he did, how could he watch her wither away and die when he could so easily prevent it?

Nick let the crowd on the street carry him along, though he was oblivious to the noise and the excitement.

He had convinced himself that Abbey was safe with him, that he was in total control of his hunger, but deep inside, he was afraid he was lying to himself. It took all his self-control to be with her and not drink from her, to hold her in his arms and not seduce her, to kiss her good night when what he wanted with every fiber of his being was to carry her to bed and make love to her hour after hour.

Eventually he wound up in front of a two-hundred-year-old, two-story house at the end of a dark street. The exterior needed a coat of paint, the wraparound porch was missing a few posts, the chimney leaned precariously to the left.

Opening his preternatural senses, Nick probed the interior. Aside from the witch, the only other living creatures were a cat and a bird.

Hoping the porch stairs were sturdier than they looked, Nick made his way to the door.

It opened before he knocked, revealing a petite

woman clad in a gauzy, low-cut white blouse and a long, flowered skirt. Premature gray hair fell over her shoulders in lush waves. Her feet were bare. She stared up at him through slanted black eyes, a beguiling smile curving her lips.

"Nick," she murmured. "It has been too long."

She stepped back, allowing him entrance into her home.

It had changed little since he had seen it last. A cat, different from the one she'd had before, hissed at him, then turned and fled the room.

The witch laughed softly. "None of my familiars have been fond of you. Why is that, do you suppose?"

Nick shrugged. "Predators always recognize each other. How have you been, Zendeya?"

"The same as always." She waved him toward the sofa while she took a seat in her favorite rocker. "What brings you here?"

"I'm not sure."

"Lies do not become you." She tilted her head to the side. "I see you surrounded by blood and death."

Nick barked a short laugh. "Does that surprise you?"

Her voice dropped an octave. "You are seeking something that does not exist. Beware, Niccola Desanto, the path you are traveling will not lead where you wish to go."

"What the hell does that mean?"

"Only you can know."

"Have you ever heard of a vampire being cured?"

Her brows rose in surprise. "Is that what you are seeking?"

"Yeah. Can you do it?"

She shook her head. "Zara might have been able to work such magic, but it is beyond my ability. And I know of no other witch who holds such power."

Zara. He remembered her well. She was a distant relative of Zendeya's. It had been Zara who had magically removed his name from Savanah's book many centuries ago. Of course, the book had belonged to one of Savanah's ancestors at the time.

Zendeya rose in a single sinuous movement. Hips swaying provocatively, she crossed the floor to take the seat beside him. She leaned toward him, revealing the deep V of her cleavage. The scent of her perfume reminded him of the nights he had spent in her bed.

She trailed her fingertips along his arm. "I have thought of you often since last we met."

"Have you?"

"We had some good times together."

"That we did."

She gazed into his eyes, her hand stroking his thigh. "I have missed you." She tilted her head back and to the side, offering him her throat.

Most vampires did not find witch blood to their liking. It lacked the sweetness of mortal blood, but that had never been a turn-off for Nick. Sweet or sour, blood was blood.

Zendeya drew his head down. He inhaled the musky scent of her skin, her blood, the incense that burned in one of the other rooms.

His hands curled over her shoulders—predator capturing his prey—as he lowered his head to drink. Her blood carried a sharpness, an edge of bitterness, missing in mortal blood. It gave an added kick to the taste.

He lifted his head as an odd sense of guilt rose within him, though he could think of no reason for such an emotion. He was a vampire, doing what vampires did. And yet, somehow, he felt as though he were cheating on Abbey, which was the height of foolishness.

"Stay the night," Zendeya whispered.

It was a tempting offer. It had been a long time since he had bedded a woman. He had experienced the pleasures of the witch's bed before. She was a lusty wench, completely uninhibited, willing to try anything once.

"Sorry, *ma petite,* but I can't stay."

"Do I no longer please you?"

"It's not that." He caressed her cheek. "But I'm afraid my heart belongs to another."

She shrugged. "It isn't your heart I want."

Nick laughed softly, sealed the tiny wounds in her slender throat, then stood. "Always a pleasure, Zendeya."

Rising, she followed him to the door. "When you tire of your current lady love, I'll be here, waiting."

"I'll remember."

Nick had no sooner left Zendeya's place than his phone rang. It was Pearl.

"Nick? It's ready."

"So soon?"

"Edna thought we might be cooking it too long. After thinking it over, I decided she could be right. When shall we expect you?"

"I'm on my way."

Edna and Pearl were waiting for him in the Great Hall when he arrived. Edna was pacing the floor, her long multicolored skirt swishing around her ankles. Pearl sat in one of the chairs, idly drumming her fingertips on the overstuffed arm. They were both as nervous as hens.

Nick blew out a breath. He was feeling a little edgy himself.

Pearl stood. "Are you sure about this? Really sure?"

He dragged his hand over his jaw. "Let's get on with it."

He followed the old ladies down the winding staircase to the dungeon, obligingly entered the cell Pearl indicated, waited patiently while she locked the door and pocketed the key before offering him a small green bottle.

Nick held it up to the light, wondering if he should ask what was inside. Uncapping the bottle, he decided he didn't want to know. Muttering, "This one smells worse than the last one," he downed the contents in one quick swallow. It burned all the way down.

"If this doesn't work . . ." Pearl made a vague gesture with her hand.

"Nothing else will. I understand."

"We'll come check on you in a little while," Edna said.

Alone in the cell, Nick paced the floor. Back and forth. Back and forth. If this didn't work, he would have to decide what to do about Abbey. Not long ago, he had been determined to make her his no matter what. But now, knowing her as he did, loving her more than he would have thought possible, he needed to put his selfish desires aside and do what was best for her. And that wasn't marrying a two-thousand-year-old vampire. He knew what would happen if they stayed together. Knew, deep in his heart, that sooner or later, regardless of the consequences, he would force the Dark Gift on her. It was the only way to keep her safe from his insatiable hunger.

Minutes stretched into an hour. Two. And nothing happened. Other than the lingering rawness in his throat, there was no pain as there had been the first time, no discomfort at all.

Discouraged, he stretched out on the cot, his arms folded behind his head, and closed his eyes.

Tomorrow, he would see Abbey one more time.

And then never again.

Nick woke with no sense of the time. Sitting up, he raked his fingers through his hair, scrubbed his hand over his jaw.

What the hell!

Frowning, he ran his fingers over his chin. Was that stubble he felt? As in whiskers? Impossible. He hadn't needed to shave since becoming a vampire.

Rising, he tried to open his preternatural senses, knew a moment of gut-wrenching fear when nothing happened. He wrapped his hands around the bars. Where were Edna and Pearl? They had the key. What if they'd left the castle? He fought down a rush of panic. They wouldn't go off and leave him here alone. Would they?

His stomach growled. The uniquely human sound startled him, as did the realization that he was hungry.

Not for blood.

But for food.

It took him a moment to acknowledge what that meant, and then he murmured, "It worked. God bless those two old bats, it worked!" Suddenly restless, he tugged on the bars. Yesterday, he could have ripped them out of the stone floor. Today, nothing. "Pearl! Edna! Where the hell are you?"

They materialized outside the cell moments later.

Pearl stared at him. "It worked! I don't believe it, but it worked."

"It's a miracle," Edna said. "I have no sense of him as a vampire." She licked her lips. "He smells so tasty."

"Don't try it," Nick warned.

She snorted. "As if you could stop me now."

"Just get me the hell out of here."

Pearl reached into her skirt pocket and withdrew the key. "Edna, behave yourself now," she warned as she unlocked the door. "Mara won't take it kindly if you hurt him."

"How do you feel?" Edna asked.

"Fine."

"See, I was right," Edna said, looking smug. "You were cooking it too long."

"Yes, dear."

"That's enough, you two. I need one of you to take me to Auburn."

"I'll do it," Pearl said quickly. "Edna, you stay here. I won't be gone long."

Nick tensed as Pearl put her arms around him. It was an odd sensation, being whisked through time and space. As a vampire, it had been normal, natural. As a human, it left him feeling disoriented, dizzy, and a trifle queasy.

When his head cleared, he saw they were on the outskirts of the Cordova ranch. Force of habit had him trying to sense Abbey's whereabouts. Nothing happened. He grunted softly. The absence of his preternatural powers was going to take some getting used to. "Where's Abbey?"

Pearl lifted her head, nostrils flaring. "She's in her cottage, watching TV."

"Is she alone?"

"Yes. Rane and Savanah aren't home. How do you feel, Nick? Really?"

"A little strange, I admit, but good otherwise." He took Pearl's hands in his. "Thank you for everything."

"You're welcome, dear. I hope you'll be happy together."

"We will be. Thanks, again. If there's ever anything I can do for you . . ."

Pearl nodded. A smile and a wave and she was gone.

Nick stood there a moment, suddenly uncertain of what to do. Abbey had never known him as anything but a vampire. What if she didn't find the human side of him as attractive as his vampire side? As a vampire, he had been strong, confident, afraid of nothing. He had little memory of being human. No doubt it would all come back to him.

Too late for second thoughts. What was done was done. There was no going back. Shaking off his doubts, he hurried across the field to the cottage. Took a deep breath. And knocked on the front door.

Frowning, Abbey wondered who had come calling. Her parents had gone into town to see a movie. Nick wouldn't knock. Nick. Just thinking about him made her heart ache. Where was he?

Aware that it was dark out and she was alone in the house, she called, "Who's there?"

"Your fiancé."

"Nick!" She flung open the door and hurled herself into his arms. "Where have you been? I've been so worried!"

"I'm here now." He hugged her close, inhaling the scent of her perfume, aware that, for the first time since he had met her, he couldn't hear the beat of her heart, couldn't smell the blood flowing in her veins. Couldn't read her thoughts.

"What is it?" she asked, drawing back a little. "What's wrong?"

"Nothing's wrong. Let's go inside. We have a lot to talk about."

Abbey stared at Nick, unable to believe her ears. He wasn't a vampire anymore. He wanted to marry her right away. "I don't know what to say."

"Not exactly the response I was hoping for."

"Oh, don't get me wrong!" she said quickly. "I'll marry you tonight if you want. It's just that . . . the cure . . . I can't believe it worked. Who would have thought those silly old ladies actually knew what they were doing." Her gaze moved over him. "How do you feel?"

"I'm not sure. It'll take some getting used to, I guess."

Laughing, she threw her arms around him. "This is so amazing!"

"So, you still love me?"

"Of course I do. Why wouldn't I?"

He shrugged. "Vampires have an inherent allure that human males lack."

"Well, I still find you incredibly handsome and sexy, if that's what you're worried about. Ohmigosh! I can't wait to tell Mom and Dad."

Nick grunted softly. He wasn't looking forward to that.

Abbey sat on the sofa and pulled him down beside her. "You said you wanted to get married right away. How soon is 'right away'?" she asked, snuggling against him. "I mean, I'll need a few days to find a dress. And a church . . ." She looked up at him, her brow furrowed. "Do you have any preference? I mean, are you Catholic or Protestant or . . . ?"

Nick shook his head. "I haven't been to church in centuries, love. Wherever you want to get married is fine with me."

"All right. Is there anyone you want to invite?"

"Just Edna and Pearl. If it wasn't for them, we wouldn't be getting married."

"What do you mean?" She sat up, her gaze searching his face.

"It doesn't matter now."

"You were going to leave me, weren't you? If the cure didn't work, you were just going to walk away without so much as a good-bye and I would never have seen you again."

He nodded. "It wasn't an easy decision, but I realized there could be no future for us as long as I was a vampire. I knew that sooner or later, I'd turn you and you'd hate me for it. Or one night I'd drain you dry, and I couldn't live with that." He cupped her face in his hands. "I never told you what a temptation you were, or how hard it was to resist the urge to feed on you. But once I put some distance between us, I knew I'd been lying to myself and that as long as I was a vampire, your life would always be in danger."

"I never knew . . . you should have told me." She squeezed his hand. "I guess it doesn't matter now. So, a small wedding, with Edna and Pearl and my family." She smiled up at him. "I love you, Nick."

"Not half as much as I love you."

"You're not sorry, are you? That you're not a vampire anymore?"

"No." Drawing her into his arms, he kissed her. It was different, somehow, he mused. Not worse, not better, just different. Always before, his hunger and his desire had been tightly interwoven. Now, there was only a man's normal desire for the woman he loved. Lifting his head, he whispered, "Buy the first dress you like, love. I can't wait much longer."

Chapter Twenty-Nine

"Married?" Savanah leaned forward on the sofa, her brow furrowing as she glanced from Nick to her daughter. "So soon?"

"Hold on a minute." Rane lifted his head slightly, nostrils flaring. "What's going on here?"

"I took Pearl's cure," Nick said, squeezing Abbey's hand. "And it worked. I'm not a vampire anymore."

Rane snorted. "I don't believe it."

"Sure you do."

"And now you want to get married?"

"You said I was too old for her before. I guess, in a way, I still am. But now, for all intents and purposes, I'm a twenty-nine-year-old man in love with your daughter, and asking for your permission to marry her."

Savanah shook her head, and then she smiled. "I think that's the most selfless, romantic thing I've ever heard of. You have my blessing."

Rane glowered at his wife, who glowered right back.

"And your father's blessing, as well," Savanah said firmly, leaving no room for argument.

Rising, Abbey embraced her mother. "Thanks, Mom."

"I know he makes you happy, darling, and that's good enough for me. Well!" she said briskly. "We have a lot of planning to do. You'll need a dress and a church and . . ." She blew out a breath, her eyes filling with tears. "I can't believe it. My little girl is getting married."

"That went well," Nick muttered as he and Abbey walked back to her cottage.

"They'll get used to the idea. Mom and I are going shopping tomorrow. I promise to find a dress at the first store."

"You'll be a beautiful bride."

"I still can't believe you're not a vampire anymore."

"Are you sorry?"

"No, of course not. Let's sit outside," Abbey suggested when they reached the cottage. "It's such a pretty night."

"It is that," Nick agreed. He held Abbey's hand as they sat on the swing, his thumb stroking her knuckles. He missed the blood bond between them, though he would never tell her that. "What were you and your mom talking about in the kitchen?"

"Oh. She was wondering if we wanted to get married in the church where she married my father. And where Uncle Rafe married Aunt Kathy." Abbey grinned. "And where my grandpa married Grandma. I guess you could say it's tradition for the vampires in our family to be married by Father Lanzoni."

"Lanzoni," Nick said thoughtfully. "I've heard of him." Lanzoni was one of the ancient vampires.

"It seems odd, don't you think? A vampire being a priest?"

"He was a priest before he was turned. From what I've heard, he doesn't have a church or a congregation."

Nick grinned at her. "I guess you could say he's a freelance priest."

"We don't have to be married in the church my mother suggested, or by Father Lanzoni, if you'd rather not. It doesn't really matter to me."

"I don't mind. I've always wanted to meet the famous vampire priest." Nick slipped his arm around Abbey's shoulders and drew her close. "Whatever you want is fine with me, love. While you're shopping for a dress, I'll pick up a tux."

"Where do you want to live, after we're married?"

"Wherever you want. I have several houses you can choose from, or we can buy something new."

"Were you really a computer programmer?"

He shrugged. "For a while."

"Have you had a lot of jobs?"

"So many, I've forgotten most of them." It had been easy to pick up this skill or that when he was a vampire. He had been able to accomplish anything he set his mind to. Learning had come easily to him then.

Nick swore under his breath. He had made his choice and he had no regrets. Why was he now thinking about what he had so willingly given up?

"Nick?"

"Hmm?"

"Is something wrong?"

"No, why?"

"We've been sitting here for ten minutes and you haven't kissed me yet."

Drawing her into his arms, he claimed her lips with his. And everything else faded into insignificance. There was only Abbey kissing him in return, the warmth of her love filling all the cold, empty corners in his heart and soul.

* * *

Mara stood on the balcony of her Northern California home, her senses reaching out to touch—one by one—those she considered her family, something she did from time to time. She frowned as the bond she and Nick had shared for centuries eluded her.

She uttered a short, pithy oath when she finally made a connection. She homed in on the ancient blood bond that allowed her to find him. Once, the link between them had run both ways. Now his bond to her was gone as if it had never existed.

Which could only mean . . .

Mara shook her head in disbelief. "Oh, Nicky," she whispered. "What have you done?"

Chapter Thirty

Abbey could scarcely contain her excitement as she looked at her reflection in the full-length mirror. The girl staring back at her looked radiant—cheeks flushed, eyes glowing. Her gown was long and white, with a sweetheart neckline, a full skirt, and short, poufy sleeves. It made her feel like a princess in a fairy tale.

"Oh, Abbey," Savanah murmured. "You look like Cinderella going to the ball!"

"I feel that way too!" Arms outstretched, she twirled around. "What do you think, Aunt Kathy?"

"It looks like it was made for you."

"Do you think Nick will like it?"

"He'll love it," Kathy said. "I can't wait to get to know him better." She shook her head. "I've never heard of a vampire being cured. Well, except for Mara, of course. But she wasn't cured, exactly."

"Which of these veils do you like? The short one?" Savanah asked, holding up the veil in question, "or the long one?"

"Definitely the long one," Abbey replied. She smiled as her mother set it in place. The headpiece was adorned with lustrous pearls and brilliants; the gauzy veil fell to the floor in graceful folds. "Oh, Mom! It's perfect!"

"It is indeed," Savanah agreed, wiping the tears from her eyes.

Everything was perfect, Abbey thought. Her dress. Her husband-to-be. Life itself.

Tomorrow was her wedding day!

At home, Abbey hung her gown in the closet, then called, "Nick? Where are you?"

"In the kitchen, love. So, how'd it go?" he asked, taking Abbey in his arms.

"We had the best time, and I found the most beautiful dress! I can't wait for you to see it!"

"Well, don't just stand there, girl. Go put it on."

"Not now, silly. Don't you know it's bad luck for the groom to see the bride in her dress before the wedding?" She glanced past him to the counter, which was covered with sandwich makings—mustard, ketchup, mayonnaise, three kinds of lunch meat, two kinds of cheese, pickles, tomatoes, onions, lettuce, and two loaves of bread—potato and whole wheat. "I know vampires don't gain weight, but you're not a vampire anymore, and if you keep eating the way you have the last couple of days, you're going to be as fat as a pig."

"I can't help it," he said, chuckling. "Everything tastes so good. You want a sandwich?"

"Sure. I haven't eaten since lunch. Mom and Aunt Kathy offered to take me to dinner, but . . ." She shrugged. "It's not much fun when you're the only one eating."

"Or the only one *not* eating," he muttered.

They moved to the counter and worked side by side.

"This is fun," Abbey remarked, piling several slices of roast beef on a piece of potato bread. "We've never cooked together before."

"This isn't exactly cooking," Nick remarked, adding several slices of cheese to his own sandwich. "What are we having for dinner?"

"Dinner?" Abbey glanced at the containers of potato salad and baked beans, then shook her head. "Isn't this dinner?"

Nick shrugged. Since he hadn't eaten in centuries, he had a lot of lost time to make up for.

"Oh, well," Abbey said with mock resignation. "I guess we'll just get fat together."

Nick added a few pickles to his sandwich, then licked his fingers. "I'll love you fat or thin."

"I tried to contact you telepathically today," Abbey remarked, carrying her sandwich and a glass of milk to the table. "I couldn't do it."

"I'm pretty sure part of your ability to read my mind had to do with my being a vampire," he said, taking the chair across from hers. "I'm not sure why that made a difference, unless it had something to do with the fact that I'd tasted your blood."

"Maybe, but . . ."

"But what?"

She hesitated, then said, "Well, I kind of miss it."

Nick grunted softly. His being mortal again would take some getting used to for both of them.

Abbey's wedding day dawned bright and clear. Lying in bed, she stared up at the ceiling. "Mrs. Abbey Marie Desanto. Abbey Desanto. Mrs. Nick Desanto." She giggled, thinking she sounded like a schoolgirl with her first crush.

She was getting married. To Nick. The sweetest, sexiest, most handsome man in the whole world.

She loved it that he hadn't wanted to wait and yet there were so many things they hadn't discussed. Mainly, they needed to decide where they were going to live. She would be perfectly happy to stay here, in the cottage, although she doubted that Nick would think living in such close proximity to her father was a great idea. If he didn't mind, she would like to live near her parents. Maybe Nick owned a house close by. That would be perfect. If not . . . well, he had suggested buying something new.

Did he intend to work? He didn't need the money, so maybe they would travel, be vagabonds for a year or two.

She knew he wanted children, but not how many. Was it even possible for him to father a child after being a vampire for so long? If so, she thought two kids would be nice—a girl for her and a boy for Nick.

Kicking the covers aside, Abbey headed for the shower. She had a lot to do today. Her dad had volunteered to look after the stock this morning and while she was on her honeymoon. Bless the man! She just hoped that, in time, Nick and her father would become friends. But she couldn't worry about that now.

She giggled with excitement as she turned on the shower. Today was her wedding day!

Nick woke slowly. Locking his hands behind his head, he stared up at the hotel ceiling. Abbey had wanted him to stay at the cottage, but he had refused, telling her he wanted to spend his last night as a bachelor alone.

He stared at the tux hanging on the closet door.

He was getting married.

He sat up and swung his legs over the edge of the bed.

Married, after all this time.

He shook his head, thinking how bizarre it was that he was marrying into a vampire family when he was no longer a vampire. He wondered what Abbey's parents really thought about his return to humanity, whether Rane would ever accept him, and how Mara would react.

Mara. He had thought only death could break his link to her, but apparently becoming a mortal had the same effect. He could no longer sense the bond between them. It was an odd feeling, as if a vital part of himself had been cut away, leaving a great gaping hole that could never be filled. Of course, being a vampire and having tasted his blood, Mara would always be able to find him. He wasn't sure how he felt about that, but there was nothing he could do about it.

In the bathroom, he regarded his reflection in the mirror, shook his head when he saw the bristles on his chin. *Whiskers*, he thought, bemused. He hadn't shaved in centuries.

The hotel had thoughtfully provided a throwaway razor. He winced when he cut himself, stared at the bright red drop of blood that oozed from the tiny wound—so different from the thick, dark crimson of vampire blood. He dabbed at the cut with the washcloth, thinking that, if he was still a vampire, the cut would have already healed.

Funny, all the mundane things he had forgotten about being human.

He showered, dressed, and went down to the hotel dining room for breakfast. He had been forbidden to see his bride before the wedding. The day stretched before him. How was the groom supposed to spend his time while the bride primped?

Leaving the hotel, Nick strolled down the street, hands shoved into his pockets. The world looked different to him now—colors were less bright, sounds seemed muted. He no longer had the ability to read the minds of the people he passed, nor could he hear the beating of their hearts. He was keenly aware of gravity holding him down, binding him to the earth.

He was the one who had changed, he realized, not the world around him. His sense of himself had altered dramatically. He had lost a part of his identity and it had left a void inside, an emptiness where his vampire nature had been. The strength and power he had relied on for so many centuries was gone.

He was vulnerable now.

Mortal.

Subject to pain and sickness. Old age and death.

He told himself it didn't matter. Not so long ago, he had been seeking a release from immortality. *Be careful what you wish for,* he mused ruefully, then shook his head. None of it mattered anymore. All that mattered was Abbey. Tonight, she would finally be his.

Needing to hear her voice, he pulled out his phone and punched in her number.

She answered on the first ring. "Nick!"

"Hey, beautiful. How's the bride?"

"Hoping the groom is as nervous as I am."

"I passed nervous hours ago," Nick muttered. Right now, he was hovering perilously close to panic at the thought of being surrounded by a trio of powerful vampires—namely, Mara, Logan, and the vampire priest.

All things considered, he was especially nervous at the idea of being in Rane's company.

"How are you getting to the church?" Abbey asked.

"The old-fashioned way, love. By car."

"It's different, isn't it?" she asked quietly. "Being mortal again?"

"Yeah, but I'm not complaining. How are things on your end?"

"I'm not sure. On the surface, my parents seem okay with it. But it doesn't matter. I love you, Nick."

"I love you more."

"See you in church," she said, a smile in her voice. "I'll be the one in the long white dress."

Chuckling, Nick ended the call, thinking he was the luckiest man in the world.

Abbey was a nervous wreck by the time she and her parents arrived at the church.

She glanced around, awed by the towering oaks and the ancient house of worship set in a secluded glade. Moonlight filtered through the trees, a gentle breeze rustled the leaves, crickets and frogs lifted their voices in song. The setting might have been lifted from the pages of a fairy tale, Abbey thought. She wouldn't have been surprised to see Snow White and Prince Charming waiting for her inside.

"Ready?" her mother asked, coming to stand beside her.

Abbey nodded.

"If you're having second thoughts, it's not too late to change your mind," her father said.

"Dad, I'm not going to change my mind. I love Nick with all my heart. Can't you just be happy for me?"

After a moment's hesitation, Rane nodded. "Here we go, then."

He left Abbey inside the vestibule while he escorted

Savanah into the chapel and down the aisle to the front row.

Returning a moment later, he took Abbey's hand in his. "Be happy, honey," he said quietly. "And remember, your mother and I are always here for you if you need us."

"Thanks, Dad. I love you, too."

Clinging to her father's hand, she peered around the door. It was a lovely old church. The altar and the pews were carved from oak. Soft candlelight filled the chapel with a warm golden glow, illuminating the faces of the wooden statues along the walls. A shaft of bright silver moonlight filtered through the beautiful red, blue, and gold stained-glass window above the altar. Deep blue carpet runners covered the floor between the aisles.

Her family sat in the first two rows. They were all there—Kathy and Rafe, Mara and Logan, Roshan and Brenna, Vince and Cara, Derek and Sheree. And Edna and Pearl, looking like a pair of colorful butterflies in their gaudy, trademark floral shirts and long skirts. In honor of the occasion, they wore heels instead of tennis shoes.

Preternatural power hovered in the air like an unseen presence.

A moment later, the priest entered the chapel from a side door, followed by Nick.

Abbey's breath caught in her throat when she saw him. Though Nick no longer radiated power or possessed a vampire's innate allure, he was still the handsomest man she had ever met. His tux was the perfect foil for his dark good looks.

At a gesture from the priest, Abbey and her father walked down the aisle.

Father Lanzoni wore a black suit with a clerical collar. Of medium height, he had warm hazel eyes, olive skin, and wavy black hair heavily laced with silver at his temples.

He smiled at Abbey, winked at Nick, and then looked out at the wedding guests

"Welcome, my old friends. I am honored that you have invited me to officiate at this happy occasion.

"We are gathered here tonight to celebrate the joining together of these two young people. Who gives this woman in marriage?"

"Her mother and I do." Rane kissed his daughter's cheek, placed her hand in Nick's, then stepped back to sit beside Savanah.

"Marriage is an honorable institution," the priest said. "It is ordained of God for the blessing and happiness of His children here on earth. Only in the sacred bonds of matrimony can a man and a woman find true happiness and fulfillment. In the beginning, God joined Adam and Eve together and admonished them to cleave unto one another, to be fruitful and multiply. Niccola and Abbey, I would admonish you to do the same, to be ever faithful to one another, to treat your spouse as you would be treated. Never forget the love you have for each other, or the way you feel this night, filled with hope and expectations for a bright future.

"Abbey Marie Cordova, do you take Niccola Desanto, here present, to be your lawfully wedded husband, to have and to hold, to love and to cherish, in sickness and in health, for richer, for poorer, as long as you both shall live?"

Looking into Nick's eyes, she murmured a heartfelt "I do."

"Niccola Desanto, do you take Abbey Marie Cordova,

here present, to be your lawfully wedded wife, to have and to hold, to love and to cherish, in sickness and health, for richer, for poorer, as long as you both shall live?"

He nodded solemnly. "I do."

"Then by the power vested in me, I pronounce you, Niccola and Abbey, husband and wife, legally and lawfully wed. May the blessings of heaven rest upon you both," the priest said, smiling. "Nick, you may kiss your bride."

As Nick lifted her veil, he whispered, "I will love you for as long as I live."

"And I, you."

Cupping Abbey's face in his hands, Nick kissed her tenderly, keenly aware of Rane Cordova's dark gaze boring into his back.

Later, after everyone had kissed the bride and congratulated the groom, Abbey and Nick left the church, bound for the Madonna Inn in San Luis Obispo, where they had made plans to spend the night.

Abbey had decided to forgo a reception, since none of the guests could partake of food or cake, and Nick had agreed. The sooner he had his bride alone, the better.

Abbey couldn't stop looking at Nick, couldn't stop smiling.

He slid a glance in her direction. "What are you grinning at, Mrs. Desanto?"

"Nothing. I'm just happy. Aren't you?"

"You have no idea." Reaching for her hand, he gave it a squeeze.

"Was it hard for you, being surrounded by so many vampires? You looked a little stressed after the ceremony."

He considered a lie and opted for the truth. "Hard doesn't begin to describe it."

"Are you sorry you took the cure?"

"No, love. I knew what I was doing."

Nick pulled into the hotel parking lot two hours later. Abbey glanced out the side window while Nick looked for a parking place. The inn was lovely, with an old-world feel to it. There were plants and flowers everywhere, lots of balconies with white scrollwork.

She felt a rush of anticipation as Nick helped her out of the car. She had wanted him for so long. How often had she dreamed of this moment. Excitement fluttered in the pit of her stomach as they entered the hotel. Soon, the waiting would be over.

In the lobby, the first thing Abbey noticed was that, like the exterior, the interior boasted an abundance of pink in the decorations and the furniture. Everything was beautiful.

She glanced over Nick's shoulder while he registered, smiled when he signed in as *Mr. and Mrs. Desanto*. It gave her a little thrill to see her married name in writing for the first time.

Nick had reserved the Hearts and Flowers room. The beauty of it took her breath away. The walls were covered in red velvet flowered paper. The carpet, sofas, and chairs were also red, the tables of dark wood. A bottle of chilled champagne awaited their pleasure. Beyond the main room, she saw a king-size bed covered with a flowered spread.

"When I called for reservations, they told me this

room symbolizes love, joy, and celebration," Nick said, drawing Abbey into his arms. "And I've found all of them in you."

"And I, in you," Abbey murmured, deeply touched by his words and by the love shining in his eyes as he lowered his head and claimed her lips with his. Every kiss was like the first one, she thought, new and exciting.

She was breathless when he broke the kiss, breathless and aching for more. Her hands were eager as she slipped his jacket over his shoulders and tossed it on the sofa. His hands were equally eager as he removed her veil and laid it aside.

Smiling and feeling a little shy, Abbey unfastened his shirt and tossed it on top of his jacket. He didn't wear an undershirt. Her hands drifted over his shoulders and his chest, moving down, down, to unbuckle his belt. She caught her lower lip between her teeth while he kicked off his shoes and peeled off his socks, then stepped out of his trousers, revealing a pair of black bikini briefs.

She blushed when he slid them off.

"My turn," he murmured, his voice husky as he moved behind her to unfasten the long row of satin-covered buttons. He lifted the gown over her head, leaving her clad in a lacy white bra, bikini panties, and heels.

Whistling softly, Nick laid the gown aside, then went down on one knee. She gasped in surprise when he kissed her thigh, then kissed his way down her slender legs until he reached her ankles and removed her shoes.

She was a study in perfection, from the top of her head to the soles of her feet. Her skin was smooth and unblemished, her breasts a perfect fit for his hand, her belly flat, her hips nicely rounded, her legs long and shapely.

Standing, he lifted his bride into his arms, carried her swiftly to bed, and wrapped her in his embrace.

For a time, he was content to hold her, to rain kisses on her cheeks, her brow, the tip of her nose, her moist pink lips. It was odd to be so close to her and not be aware of the beating of her heart, not be tempted by the scent of her blood.

When the need to fully possess her grew overwhelming, he stripped away the last lacy barriers between them and rose over her.

Abbey twined her arms around his neck, her fingers delving into his hair. Was there anything in all the world as amazing as the feel of bare skin against bare skin? As incredibly arousing as Nick's hands moving over her body? She explored him with equal abandon, whispered his name as, with his hands and his kisses and his words, he brought her to the brink of fulfillment.

She moaned softly, then cried his name as his body melded with hers, the brief pain swallowed up in wave after wave of ecstasy.

Nick stroked Abbey's hair, ever so lightly. She slept beside him, her head pillowed on his shoulder, a faint smile on her lips. Everything he had given up had been worth this one night, he thought. In centuries as a vampire, he had never known such a sense of fulfillment, such feelings of love and acceptance, as he had found in Abbey's arms.

Perhaps in time her parents and the rest of the Cordova clan would accept him as one of the family. Rane and Savanah and the others had been cordial at the wedding, but there had been no mistaking the distrust in Rane Cordova's eyes. Not that Nick could blame him. Nick was, after all, still a stranger, a man who had, until recently, been an old and powerful vampire.

And now . . . ?

He stared out the window into the darkness beyond. What was he now?

Chapter Thirty-One

After a long lazy morning of lovemaking, followed by bathing together in the room's "rock" shower, Abbey and Nick decided to spend the afternoon at the pool, which entailed a trip to the gift shop so Abbey could find a bathing suit, something she had neglected to include in her trousseau. Nick had been in favor of a hot pink bikini that was little more than two scraps of cloth; Abbey had chosen a red two-piece that was a little more modest.

Now, she sat in the hot tub, shaded by an umbrella, content to watch Nick while he swam laps.

The sun glistened in his hair and on his shoulders as he cut cleanly through the water. He was hers, she thought, all hers, and she couldn't wait to hold him in her arms again, to feel his skin against her own, to experience again the wonder, the pleasure, of their lovemaking, his body sinking into hers . . .

She bit down on her lower lip. In spite of how wonderful last night had been, there had been something missing. She knew it was the sense of tightly leashed power that had once emanated from Nick. Odd, to think she missed it. More than that, she missed her ability to read his mind. Sitting there, she couldn't help wondering why she had been able to read his thoughts, to send hers to him, when he was a vampire, but not now, when he was human again. Had he been right? Had his vampire blood somehow enhanced her power and made it possible?

Not that she wasn't happy he was mortal, or that they could live a normal life together, maybe even have children, but . . .

Abbey shook her head, bewildered by her feelings. She loved him desperately. They were both young and healthy, with their whole lives ahead of them. . . .

She thrust her troubling thoughts aside when Nick climbed out of the water. She couldn't help noticing that every woman and every teenage girl in the area paused to watch him when he passed by. Well, she couldn't blame them. Tall, dark, handsome, and muscular, clad in a pair of navy blue trunks, he was a sight to stir any woman's heart.

"What are you grinning at?" he asked, dropping down on his haunches beside the hot tub.

"Look around. I'm the envy of every woman here."

"You think so?"

"Even without your vampire allure, they're all drooling over you and no doubt wishing I was dead."

"I think you're delusional, wife. Let's go stretch out on one of those deck chairs and order something cold to drink."

"All right." She took the hand he offered and stepped out of the water, conscious of every female eye in the place watching her.

They found two chairs close together. No sooner had they seated themselves when a waiter hurried over to see if there was anything they wished—a drink? Lunch? A light snack?

Nick ordered a bottle of beer. Abbey asked for a glass of iced tea, sugar, no lemon.

With a sigh, Nick stretched out, eyes closed, his hands locked behind his head. "The sun feels wonderful," he murmured.

"I don't understand why it feels any different today than at any other time. I mean, we've been out together during the day lots of times."

"But not like this. Sure, I could be up and around during the day, but I couldn't sit and bask in the sun's light." He gestured at their surroundings. "Not like this. And even though I could endure the sunlight, I was never really comfortable in it. Even Mara prefers the darkness. It's part of who we are." He paused. "Part of who I was."

Abbey chewed on her thumbnail. Had she heard a note of regret in his voice? He kept assuring her that he was happy to be mortal again. Did he mean it?

Or was he just trying to convince himself?

They ate dinner in the famed steakhouse—also decorated with lots of plants, flowers, and pink, Abbey noted. They ordered shrimp cocktails, prime rib with all the trimmings, and a bottle of champagne.

Abbey loved to watch Nick eat. He savored every bite and when she couldn't finish her steak, he ate that, too. For dessert, they had champagne cake—iced with pink frosting and flowers.

"I'm stuffed," Abbey said as they left the restaurant.

"Me too." Nick let out a sigh of satisfaction. "Let's drive into town and get an ice cream cone."

"Are you kidding me? After that meal you just wolfed down?"

"Come on, it'll be fun."

"Oh, all right. But just remember, you can't divorce me when I'm as big as a house."

Abbey bought a single scoop of fudge ripple. Nick decided on a hot fudge sundae, with extra hot fudge and double whipped cream.

"Let's go get an ice cream cone, the man said." Abbey shook her head. "All I've got to say is that's some cone!"

Later, while strolling down the sidewalk, Abbey paused now and then to peer into some of the store windows, admiring a pair of black heels, a red sweater, a coffee-colored skirt. Nick insisted on buying everything she admired.

"Think of them as wedding presents," he said, overriding her objections that he couldn't buy her everything she liked. "Besides, I can afford it."

"Are all vampires rich?" Abbey asked. "I mean, I know Mara and Logan have tons of money, and Roshan has a small fortune. My parents and Uncle Rafe are pretty well-off. And so is Vince."

Nick shrugged. "It's easy to acquire wealth if you survive long enough. New vampires generally take what they need from their prey."

"Oh." She wondered why that had never occurred to her. When you could hypnotize someone and steal their blood, stealing a few dollars while you were at it hardly seemed shocking. Turning to something more pleasant, she said, "We never decided where we're going to live."

"It doesn't matter to me. What about you?"

"Well, if you don't mind, I'd like to stay near my parents. I love looking after the horses and being able to ride every day."

He nodded. "All right, then. When we get back to Auburn, we'll look for a place. I don't mind being nearby, but I'm not living on your father's land."

Abbey smiled. "That works for me."

Abbey and Nick left the Inn the following morning. With no particular destination in mind, they traveled up the coast, stopping at various points of interest. Abbey thought each view of the ocean was more breathtaking than the last.

They spent the afternoon in Monterey, strolling along the beach, sitting in the sand watching the waves, kissing when they thought no one was looking. Abbey bought a camera at a gift shop and took so many photos of Nick that he threatened to toss the "blasted thing" into the bay. That evening, they ate dinner at an Italian restaurant, and then found a room at a quaint motel, where they spent the rest of the night making love.

In the morning, they drove to Big Sur. It was, Abbey thought, one of the most beautiful places she had ever seen. There were wildflowers everywhere. She clapped with delight as she watched a bunch of sea otters at play, gaped in amazement when a California condor flew by.

But the best thing was being with Nick. He was so relaxed, so enthusiastic, so willing to do whatever she wanted, whether it was window-shopping, lazing on the sand, or posing—with a great deal of reluctance—while she snapped one photo after another.

She let out a wordless cry of protest when he plucked the camera from her hand.

"Hey! You've taken hundreds of pictures of me," he said, holding the camera out of reach. "It's my turn. Smile, now."

"I hate having my picture taken."

"Tough."

Abbey acquiesced with a sigh. Fair was fair, she thought, striking pose after pose. "Okay, that's enough," she said when he'd taken about a million pictures.

"One more," he said. "Stand over there, by that big rock. Now, lick your lips and look sexy."

With a sigh of exasperation, Abbey suggested it was time for lunch.

Next thing she knew, they were in the car searching for a restaurant.

Later that night, Abbey reclined in the hotel bathtub. Eyes closed, she was half-asleep when Nick slid into the tub behind her.

"What are you doing?" she exclaimed.

"I was lonely in the other room without you," he said, his warm breath tickling her ear.

Abbey laughed softly. "Uh-huh."

She sighed with pleasure when his hands cupped her breasts. Until that night, she would have sworn it was impossible to make love in such a confined space, but Nick proved to be remarkably agile and inventive. Ever the gentleman, he even volunteered to mop up the water they splashed on the floor.

In the morning, they drove to San Jose. Abbey had always wanted to see the Winchester Mystery House, which boasted one hundred and sixty rooms.

It was everything Abbey had expected and more. Hand in hand, they took the Mansion Tour. Abbey was fascinated by everything she saw in the bizarre old home—the staircases that didn't go anywhere, the doors that opened onto blank walls, the window built into a floor. She learned that a Boston medium had told Sarah Winchester that her family was being haunted by the spirits of those who had been killed by the Winchester Rifle—manufactured by her late husband's father, Oliver Winchester—and that she should move West and build a house for herself and the spirits. Sarah moved to San Jose and bought an eight-room farmhouse. The medium also told Sarah that if she ever stopped adding to the house, she would die. With that thought in mind, Sarah kept carpenters working twenty-four hours a day, three hundred sixty-five days a year, for the next thirty-eight years. Since she had inherited twenty million dollars, she had plenty of cash to fuel her obsession.

"That was amazing," Abbey remarked over dinner that night. "Can you imagine anyone believing that medium's nonsense?" she asked, spearing a piece of lobster, "I wonder how Sarah Winchester ever got any sleep, what with all that sawing and hammering going on twenty-four-seven."

Nick shrugged. "I'm wondering why a medium in Boston would send Sarah out West."

"I don't know. Maybe the medium had a relative who was an out-of-work carpenter?"

"Right." Nick gestured at her plate with his fork. "Are you going to finish that?"

"No, help yourself." She shook her head as he transferred what was left of her lobster to his plate. "One thing about being married to you, we'll probably never have any leftovers."

"Very funny," Nick muttered. "What shall we do tomorrow?"

"I think I'm ready to go back to Auburn and go house hunting," Abbey said, folding her napkin and placing it on the table. "How about you?"

He nodded. "Sounds good to me. How big a place do you want?"

"I don't know. Something big, but not too big. With a wraparound porch, and a balcony on the second floor. And a sunny kitchen with a pantry. And a fireplace in the master bedroom. And his-and-hers walk-in closets."

"Anything else?"

"Hmm. I don't think so."

"All right, wife. Tomorrow we'll see if we can find your dream house."

As it turned out, they found exactly what they were looking for the next afternoon while browsing real estate websites on Abbey's phone. It was a two-story, four-bedroom house, with fireplaces in the living room, the den, and the master bedroom; a large kitchen; a dining room paneled in oak; three bathrooms; and a laundry room.

"And it's only twenty minutes from my dad's place," Abbey exclaimed, then grimaced when she saw the asking price. "Can we afford that much?"

"Not to worry, love. It'll be yours before the sun sets."

They drove to the real estate office as soon as they returned to Auburn. The Realtor was more than willing to show them the property, which sat on a large, fenced lot.

Abbey fell in love with the house the minute she walked in the door. "This is it!" she exclaimed. "We'll take it!"

Nick shot the Realtor a wry grin. "Not much point in trying to talk you down on the price, is there?"

"Not much," the Realtor said, smiling from ear to ear. "I think she just closed the deal."

* * *

Abbey was surprised at how quickly married life settled into a routine. She spent the morning at the ranch, feeding the stock, mucking the stalls, grooming and exercising the horses. Nick often accompanied her. He seemed to enjoy working outdoors. She certainly enjoyed watching him, since he usually took his shirt off. Three or four times a week, they went riding together.

One afternoon, after picking up a load of hay and straw, Nick called her up to the loft.

Curious, she climbed the ladder, her mouth falling open when she saw Nick stretched out on an old blanket, buck naked.

"Ever made love in a hayloft?" he asked, waggling his eyebrows.

"No, but I have a feeling I'm about to."

He patted the blanket beside him. "Come here, darlin'."

Feeling suddenly bold, Abbey tugged her T-shirt over her head and tossed it aside. Then, with Nick providing the proper background music, she did a slow striptease.

She let out a shriek when he sprang to his feet and carried her to the blanket where he made slow, wicked love to her until the sun went down.

Rane continued to pay Abbey for looking after the stock. She enjoyed having a little money of her own, even though Nick had given her a credit card and told her to buy whatever she liked.

Several afternoons a week, Nick took her shopping for furniture for the new house. Once again, he gave her carte blanche, telling her to buy whatever she wanted.

"Don't you have any preferences?" she asked one

afternoon. "Modern or country? Italian or French? Oak or walnut?"

"Not really. Furniture is furniture. Just buy something comfortable to sit on. And a great big bed," he added with a wink, "and I'll leave the colors and the style to you."

Evenings were the best times. After dinner, they often sat on the swing on the porch of the cottage, discussing the news or the weather, or simply holding hands and enjoying the beauty of the night before going to bed.

Some nights, they didn't make it as far as the bedroom. But Abbey didn't mind. In the living room, in the kitchen, in the bathtub, on the floor, on the sofa, it didn't matter as long as she was in Nick's arms. She never tired of looking at him, holding him, learning every inch of his body from head to toe and back up again.

"Good thing we got a thirty-day escrow," Nick remarked as Abbey signed the final papers that made the house theirs. "I'm not sure you could have waited another hour, let alone another thirty days."

Abbey stuck her tongue out at him. "I'm sure this is old hat to you. You have lots of houses. But this is my first."

He kissed her cheek. "It's the first one I've ever bought for a woman I loved."

"You've bought houses for other women?"

Nick cleared his throat. "Not lately."

Abbey experienced a sudden, unexpected twinge of jealousy. No matter what she and Nick did together, he would have done it with some other woman first. She told herself that it didn't matter, that it was all in the past, that there was no point in dwelling on things that had happened before she had even been born. But it didn't work.

"Why did you put the house in my name and not in both of our names?" she asked as they left the real estate office.

"I wanted you to have a place of your own, just in case."

She looked up at him, her brow furrowed. "In case of what?"

"You never know," he said, giving her hand a squeeze. "Just humor me, okay?"

"Okay." Her husband might have purchased many houses for many women, but he had never given one to a wife, she thought with a smile of satisfaction, because he had never been a husband before.

Marriage was a first for them both.

With the deed tucked in Abbey's purse, they drove to their new home. Hand in hand, they climbed the steps to the front porch.

Abbey grinned when Nick swung her into his arms and carried her across the threshold.

After closing and locking the door, he brushed a kiss across her lips.

Abbey moaned a soft protest when he set her on her feet. But he wasn't through with her. Taking her in his arms, he drew her down on the braided rug in front of the fireplace.

"Welcome to your new home, Mrs. Desanto," he whispered, and kissed her again, more deeply this time.

It took only moments to shed their clothing and

soon they were locked in each other's arms. He aroused her quickly, almost desperately, covering her body with kisses, his hands boldly caressing her as he whispered that he loved her, would always love her.

She welcomed his caresses, kissing him in return as her own hands roamed over his back and shoulders. She loved the feel of his bare skin against hers, the silk of his hair brushing her cheek, his low groan of pleasure as he carried her to paradise and back again.

Much later, after a long shower that ended in more lovemaking, Nick left Abbey sitting on the floor of their bedroom in her nightgown, making diagrams of where to put the living-room furniture that was to arrive in the morning.

While dressing, he had told her he needed to go buy a good razor, now that he was shaving on a regular basis. It wasn't exactly a lie. He needed the razor. But the real truth was that he had felt a sudden, undeniable urge to be alone in the darkness of the night.

Nick drove to the city, parked behind the bank, and started walking. The darkness wrapped around him, welcoming him home like an old friend. Hands shoved into his pockets, he strolled down the street, acutely aware of each man and woman he passed. He was pretty much the same as other men, he thought. He smelled like they did. Why did he feel so distant? So different? Like an alien lost among humans?

Gradually, he became aware of a low throbbing emanating from the people he passed. It was a sound that had once been all too familiar, a sound that awakened an old, familiar hunger.

After entering the store, Nick blinked against the bright lights as he searched for a razor. He plucked one

from the rack, then paused in front of a display of
sunglasses. He tried on several, selected a pair, and
headed toward the door. There were several bunches of
flowers in a display near the checkout stand. He chose
a bouquet of blood-red roses, paid the clerk, and left
the building, refusing to acknowledge what he feared
was true.

Nick's fears were reinforced in the course of the next
few days. Food began to sit heavily on his stomach, and
no matter how much he consumed, he was always
hungry. He developed a craving for steak, blood rare.
The sun hurt his eyes. He avoided Abbey during the
day, making one excuse after another for why he no
longer accompanied her when she worked with the
horses, why he slept late in the mornings, stayed awake
later at night.

His hellish thirst was growing stronger, harder to
resist. Soon the pain would grow unbearable and he
would have to feed before it became excruciating,
before he buried his fangs in the curve of Abbey's
throat and drained her dry.

If Abbey was aware of the changes taking place, she
never said a word, but she had to know, he thought.

She had to realize the cure was failing.

The big question now was, would it make a difference?

Chapter Thirty-Two

Edna sighed, and when Pearl didn't respond, she sighed again, more loudly this time.

"Oh, for heaven's sake, what's the matter?" Pearl asked irritably. "Can't you see I'm trying to read this stupid book?"

"I'm tired of reading," Edna snapped. "I'm tired of playing chess. I'm tired of being cooped up in this drafty old castle!"

Pearl laid her book aside and blew out a sigh of her own. "I know, dear."

"What are we supposed to do, now that Mara has hired all these contractors to come in and modernize this place? We won't have a moment's peace, with men knocking out walls and hammering all day and all night. It wouldn't be so bad if we could feed off them, but of course she's forbidden it."

"I think we had best find a new hideout ASAP," Pearl remarked. "Although we'll never find a place as safe and secure as this one."

"Do you think Mara would let us stay with her and Logan?"

Pearl snorted. "I doubt it."

"I don't know why not. We don't take up much room."

"You know how she and Logan value their privacy," Pearl said. "She barely tolerates us as it is."

"What about Nick? He said if there was ever *anything* he could do for us, to let him know. Besides, I don't know about you, but I'm sick and tired of Transylvania."

"I suppose it wouldn't hurt to ask. If he's like most vampires, he probably has a lot of different lairs. And now that he's human again, he really doesn't need them." Pearl nodded as she made a decision. "Pack your things, dear. We're off to California again."

"We should have just stayed in the state while we were there for the wedding," Edna declared. "I don't know how we'll find Nick, now that he's mortal."

Pearl frowned a moment, then smiled. "We'll go to Rane's place. He'll know where to find him."

Chapter Thirty-Three

Sitting up in bed, Abbey studied Nick while he slept. Hard to believe they had already been married for three months. The days and nights had flown by. She had never been happier, and yet something wasn't right. She had asked Nick several times what was wrong. Each time, he had assured her she was imagining things.

But she wasn't. The last few weeks, he had been sleeping later and later every day. He had taken to wearing sunglasses when he went outside, even when the day was overcast. He ate less and didn't seem to enjoy it as much. Last night, he had skipped dinner. When they made love, she knew he was holding back. Most disturbing of all was the fact that he continually made excuses to go off alone at night.

Was he having an affair? She thrust the thought aside as soon as it crossed her mind. Nick loved her. If she was sure of nothing else, she was sure of that.

She wished she had someone to talk to, someone she could confide in. Time and again she had started to go to her parents' house, only to turn back. She couldn't discuss her fears with her mom and dad, couldn't let them know how worried she was.

The most troublesome thing of all had happened last night while they were making love. On the brink of climax, she had felt the scrape of Nick's teeth against her neck. It hadn't felt like a love bite, though she adamantly refused to think it could have been anything else.

Frowning, Abbey ran her fingertips lightly over his jaw. For the first time since they had been married, there were no prickly morning bristles on his chin.

She had been blind, she thought. For the last few weeks, the evidence had been staring her in the face and she had refused to acknowledge it.

A sudden coldness started in the pit of her stomach and slowly spread to her limbs, leaving her feeling numb inside and out.

It couldn't be true!

Stifling a cry of denial, she grabbed a change of clothes and fled the room. In the den, she quickly changed out of her nightgown and into a pair of jeans and a sweatshirt. Her work boots were waiting by the back door. She jammed her feet into her boots, grabbed her cell phone and her car keys, and ran out of the house.

Outside, she took several deep breaths.

What was she so afraid of? Mortal or vampire, she knew in her heart that Nick would never hurt her.

But what if she was wrong? What if he was no longer the Nick she had fallen in love with? What if reverting was like becoming a fledgling all over again? What if he couldn't control his hunger or his need to feed? What if . . . ?

She unlocked the car door and slid behind the

wheel. After backing out of the driveway, she stomped on the gas. She needed time alone to sort out her disquieting feelings, and she could think of no better place to do that than on the back of a horse.

Abbey was weary but relaxed when she drove home that evening. After pulling into the driveway, she shut off the engine, then frowned as a bright red sports car pulled in behind her. She felt a sudden panic as she recalled that hunters had been in the area not long ago.

She blew out a sigh of relief when the doors opened and two women stepped out. Only Edna and Pearl would be caught wearing those gaudy blouses, long skirts, and tennis shoes.

Abbey frowned as she climbed out of the car. What were they doing here?

"Hello, dear," Pearl said.

"Hi."

"Is Nick home?"

"I don't know. I guess so." Abbey bit down on her lower lip. The polite thing to do would be to invite them in. And still she hesitated. It was one thing to entertain her immediate family, but Edna and Pearl? She really didn't know them very well. They seemed friendly enough, but they *were* vampires.

The decision was taken out of her hands when Nick came striding toward them.

Edna stared at him, a murmured "uh-oh," escaping her lips as he drew closer.

"Ladies," he said, inclining his head to Pearl and then Edna. "What brings you here?"

Edna grabbed Pearl's hand. "We need to go."

"What's wrong with you? We just—" Pearl glanced at Nick, her eyes widening with understanding. "Oh, my."

"It's all right, Pearl," Nick said, taking Abbey's hand. "No hard feelings. Come on in, you two."

Heads together, Edna and Pearl followed their hosts into the house.

After inviting their guests to sit down, Nick and Abbey sat on the other sofa. "So," Nick asked again, "what brings the two of you here?"

"Well, you see," Pearl began, "we got tired of living in Transylvania, and I thought, that is, *we* thought, that since you said if there was ever *anything* you could do . . . but maybe you're not feeling all that grateful anymore."

"Why don't we cut to the chase," Nick said. "Just tell me what you want."

"Well," Edna said, "we know you have a lot of houses and we were wondering if we could stay in one of them for a while. We can't go home to Texas, and the wards on your houses are sure to be stronger than anything we could come up with."

"I've got places all around the world. You can use any one you want."

Edna and Pearl looked at him, their expressions of astonishment almost comical.

"You mean it?" Edna asked.

"I said it, didn't I?"

Pearl leaned forward, her gaze intense. "If you don't mind my asking, what happened?"

Nick glanced at Abbey, sitting silently beside him. One look at her face and he knew what he was about to say wouldn't come as a surprise. "I don't know what went wrong. It's your serum. What I do know is that a part of me—the mortal part—is dying a little at a time.

The sun bothers me now. Food makes me sick to my stomach." He glanced at Abbey again, watched the color drain from her face. "The lust for blood is growing stronger."

"I'm sorry, dear," Pearl said quietly.

He nodded. "You said there were no guarantees. It was fun while it lasted. Where are you staying?"

"With Rafe and Kathy for the time being," Edna replied.

"I'll text you a list of my houses," Nick said. "Pick the one you want and let me know."

"Thank you, dear."

Edna leaned forward, her brow furrowed. "Rafe told us that Rane and Savanah were attacked by hunters a while back. Is that true?"

"Yeah. They were looking for Savanah's books."

"We should be going," Edna said, obviously disturbed by the thought of hunters in the area. "I'm sure you newlyweds want to be alone."

Nick walked Edna and Pearl to the door. He stood there a moment, watching them drive away. Abbey had been unusually quiet during their visit with the old ladies. Never a good sign.

He raked his fingers through his hair, thinking that the upcoming conversation with his bride was not one he wanted to have.

Abbey was sitting on the sofa where he had left her.

She looked up when he entered the room. "Why didn't you tell me?"

"I wasn't sure, until last night." He shoved his hands into his pants pockets, then went to stand in front of the fireplace. "Where does this leave us?"

"What do you mean?"

He lifted one brow. "You married a mortal, not a vampire."

"You seem to forget that when you proposed to me, I told you I'd marry you whether you were mortal or not."

"Do you still feel that way?"

Rising, she closed the distance between them. Folding her hands over his shoulders, she went up on her tiptoes and kissed him. "What do you think?"

He blew out a breath. "To tell you the truth, I was a little worried about how you'd react. You were so happy that the cure seemed to be working."

"So were you."

"I was, at first."

"At first?"

Taking her by the hand, Nick led her back to the sofa and drew her down beside him. "I was a vampire for a very long time. I thought I was tired of that way of life, tired of living, but being human made me realize just how wrong I was. Being a vampire is what I am, *who* I am. I don't know *how* to be human anymore. Being mortal again made me feel like I was wearing clothes that weren't mine. Do you know what I mean?"

"I think so."

"I missed the power being a vampire gave me. The strength." He gave her hand a squeeze. "I missed the blood bond between us."

"I did, too. And . . ."

"Go on."

"I don't know how to explain it." She traced his lips with her fingertips. "I didn't love you any less, but you weren't really you."

"I didn't feel like me, either."

"And now? Is it like being turned the first time?" she

asked, unable to keep a little tremor of fear out of her voice.

"No. It's nothing like that." If he started to lose control . . . he couldn't let that happen.

She looked up at him, her eyes luminous. "We're all right, then?"

He nodded. "I'm not looking forward to telling your parents, though," he said, then muttered, "Oh, hell, they're here."

You had to hand it to Rane Cordova, Nick thought as he ushered Abbey's parents into the living room. The man cut right to the chase. "What the hell's going on?"

"Dad, why don't you sit down?" Abbey said. "You too, Mom. We have a lot to talk about."

Looking worried, Savanah took a place on the sofa next to Abbey.

Rane continued to stand.

As did Nick.

"Pearl's serum worked," Nick said curtly. "But only briefly." He swore under his breath. Shit, half the family was about to show up. "Abbey, why don't you get the door?"

Abbey welcomed Rafe and Kathy, politely asked after Vince and Cara and Roshan and Brenna.

Mara and Logan followed Kathy and Rafe into the house. As always, Mara entered the room like a queen granting favors. Clad in a long crimson gown, her hair trailing down her back like a river of ebony, she looked every inch the part.

Appearing more than a little frightened, Edna and Pearl trailed behind Mara. They sat in the chairs she indicated, their hands tightly clasped in their laps.

Nick frowned when he saw the elderly vampires. "Why did you bring them here?"

Mara shrugged. "They're part of this. I'm sure Rane has questions. I know I do."

Moving to Nick's side, Abbey took his hand in hers in a clear gesture of support.

Mara sat down with a sigh. "Nicky, why didn't you get in touch with me before you tried that ridiculous cure? I could have told you it wouldn't work."

"How could you know that?"

"It only works on fledglings, and then only because they still have a small amount of human fluids left in their system. It's how Vince was able to father children. Ancient vampires can't be cured. Pearl's serum might have dampened your powers and your instincts temporarily, but you were always a vampire."

"You married my daughter under false pretenses," Rane muttered.

"Daddy, I would have married him anyway," Abbey said. "Vampire or mortal or . . . or zombie, I love Nick. Nothing will change that and the sooner you accept it, the better."

With a huff of resignation, Rane went to sit beside his wife.

"Well, now that that's settled," Mara said, turning her attention to Rafe, "perhaps you can tell me why Edna and Pearl are living in your lair on Park Avenue?"

"You don't have to talk about us like we're not here!" Pearl said, bristling.

"Be quiet. Rafe?"

He sent an apologetic glance at Pearl. "They said they were tired of living in that drafty old wreck of a castle and asked if they could stay with us in New York for a while and I said yes. It's my understanding that they plan to move into one of Nick's lairs."

Mara's gaze swung in Nick's direction. "Is that true?"

Nick dropped into one of the easy chairs beside the fireplace and drew Abbey down on his lap. "Yes, not that it's any business of yours. Why? You got a problem with that?"

"Not if you don't."

"They did their best." Nick took a deep breath, his nostrils filling with Abbey's scent. The steady beat of her heart, the whisper of the crimson tide flowing through her veins, rumbled in his ears like thunder.

He lifted Abbey from his lap and stood abruptly, his breath coming in short, hard gasps.

Abbey called his name, but he was past hearing. A thought took him out of the house, away from the growing temptation of her blood, and into the city.

He needed to feed, he thought desperately.

Before it was too late.

He should have known Mara would follow him. She caught up with him as soon as he reached the city. With a smile that was decidedly smug, she linked her arm through his.

"It's been a while since we hunted together," she purred. "What are you in the mood for? Chinese? Italian? Mexican?"

"Very funny," he growled. "Does Logan know where you are?"

She waved a hand in the air, as if to dismiss his question.

"He won't like it, you following me."

"He'll understand. I'm your sire. You need me right now."

"Like hell."

"Stop it. You're hurting and on the edge of desperation. In your current condition, you're liable to do something you'll regret later, like drain a family of five or something."

Nick growled again. It was the sound of a hungry predator.

"This way," Mara said, tugging on his arm.

He followed her blindly, the hunger blazing through his veins like liquid fire, stealing the breath from his body. He burned with need, with the urge to hunt, to kill.

His head went up as he caught the scent of prey.

Mara smiled. "Almost there."

They ghosted along a narrow, winding pathway through a park toward an outdoor amphitheater. Hundreds of people, maybe as many as a thousand, sat in a wide semicircle around the stage, some clapping and singing along with the band, others dancing or swaying to the music. Several couples were making out in the darkness beyond the floodlights.

"Smorgasbord," Mara whispered. "Drink your fill."

Nick inhaled deeply. The air smelled of perspiration and pot, excitement and lust. And blood. So much blood. Enough to satisfy every craving clawing at his vitals, every need.

His fangs brushed his tongue as he called his first victim to him. He wrapped the young woman in his arms, like a spider cocooning a fly, before he sank his fangs into her throat. He closed his eyes in ecstasy as the first crimson drops fell on his tongue, groaned deep in his throat as warmth spread through every nerve and cell, filling him, reviving him.

He hissed, felt his eyes turn to flame when Mara laid a restraining hand on his arm.

"Enough!"

It was a command from his sire, one he was compelled to obey. Teeth bared, he glowered at her over the top of the woman's head.

"Abbey will be upset if you take a life," Mara reminded him. "Look around, Nicky. There is more than enough prey to quench even your thirst."

With a curt nod, Nick released the woman from his thrall and called another to his side.

Chapter Thirty-Four

Abbey glanced around the living room, which had fallen uncomfortably quiet after Mara's departure. She wanted to ask what was going on, but hesitated to break the taut silence. The air was charged with emotions, one of which—rampant jealousy—was clearly written on Logan's face.

Edna and Pearl looked uneasy, as if they expected everyone to blame them for what had just happened.

"Well, that tears it," Rane muttered.

Savanah laid her hand on his arm. "Rane, please," she said quietly. "You're not helping."

Shaking off her hand, Rane focused his gaze on Pearl. "Did you know this would happen?"

"Of course not. There's no way to predict how the serum will work, or how the recipient will react."

"But you knew there was a chance?"

"I didn't expect it to work at all," she snapped. "Nick is a grown man. He knew what he was getting into. I told him it probably wouldn't work, that it was as likely to destroy him as not. He decided to take his chances."

"This isn't getting us anywhere," Abbey said, rising. "I made my choice, and Nick made his. We're the ones who have to live with it. Dad, I know you don't like Nick. I know you're worried about me. But I knew what I was getting into. I would have married Nick no matter what. I wish you'd accept my decision and give us your blessing."

"She's right," Rafe said. "You can't live your daughter's life for her."

Rane glared at his brother. "And when he turns her against her will, am I supposed to accept that, too?"

"You don't know that will happen," Rafe said. "And if it does . . . what the hell. We're all vampires here. She'll have all the love and support she needs to transition."

With an aggrieved sigh, Rane sat back, his arms crossed over his chest.

"Where's Logan?" Kathy asked, glancing around the room.

Rane snorted. "Where do you think?"

Nick spoke quietly to the woman in his arms, wiping the memory of what had happened from her mind before releasing her from his thrall.

Mara stared at him, one brow lifted. "You have a prodigious thirst. Any chance of filling it tonight?"

He flashed her a wry grin, then shrugged. "It's been several months since I fed, you know. Lots of lost time to make up for."

She laughed softly. The husky sound sank deep into Nick's memory, reminding him of the nights he had spent wrapped in her embrace. Long nights of unbridled passion punctuated by an overpowering lust for blood. They had hunted together, sometimes sharing their prey. There had been no guilt back then, only a need that couldn't be denied, and Mara, more beautiful than any woman he had ever known, urging him on.

So many memories shared in such a short time. Nights of passion and pleasure he would never forget. It was only later, after she had abandoned him, that he had started to hate her.

"There were more good times than bad," she murmured.

"Do you think so?"

"Don't you?" Leaning forward, she licked a bit of blood from his lower lip. "Sometimes I think that . . . Logan! What are you doing here?"

"Looks like I'm interrupting a love scene," he said, his voice raw. "Too bad I left my camera at home."

"Stop it."

"I won't stop it! I've seen the way you look at him. The way he looks at you."

Mara fisted her hands on her hips, her jaw jutting forward, her eyes flashing fire. "I thought we settled this."

"So did I. Obviously I was wrong." Eyes red, fangs extended, Logan glared at Nick. "Stay away from my wife, or fight me for her, here and now."

Nick shook his head. "You damn fool. Calm down. There's nothing going on here. Mara loves you, not me. And I'm in love with Abbey."

"That's not what it looks like," Logan growled. "To hell with both of you. I'm outta here."

He was gone amid a swirl of glittering black motes.

"Sorry," Nick muttered, although he wasn't sure what he was apologizing for. She had followed him, not the other way around.

"It's not your fault." Mara blew out a sigh. "Are you going to be okay?"

"I'm fine. You'd better go after him." Before she could leave, he placed his hand on her arm. "Wait. Can I ask a favor?"

"Of course."

He hesitated, reluctant to tell her what he wanted.

There was no need to tell her. She knew him better than he knew himself. Biting into her left wrist, she held it out to him. "Go on."

He cradled her arm in his hands and lowered his head. Her blood was like no other, thick and rich. Her power flowed into him and through him. He could feel it cleansing him, destroying the last of Pearl's serum.

Mara touched his cheek and when he lifted his head, she kissed him. She tasted of blood and midnight and eternal darkness.

Taking a step back, she gazed deeply into his eyes, into the very depths of his soul.

And then she was gone.

Nick stood in the shadows on the front porch. An indrawn breath told him Abbey was alone in the house.

Hands clenched, he stared into the distance, wondering if he would be welcome. Had her father turned her against him?

A wave of his hand opened the door, but when he tried to enter the house, he couldn't cross the threshold. It told Nick more clearly than anything else that the transformation from human to vampire was complete.

The house belonged to Abbey. He could no longer enter without an invitation.

"Abbey?"

"I'm in here."

He bit back an oath. Should he ask for an invite, or

just get the hell out of her life now, before it was too late?

"Nick?"

"I've got a bit of a problem."

"What do you mean?"

He heard the frown in her voice, the sound of her footsteps as she padded toward the door. "I can't come in."

She stared at him blankly for a moment, then murmured, "Oh, of course. Nick Desanto, you will always be welcome in this house. Please come in."

He followed her into the living room. "Why were you sitting in the dark?" When he turned on the lights, she looked away, but not before he saw the tears shining in her eyes. Muttering an oath, he closed the distance between them. "I'm sorry, love."

"Where did you go?"

"Where do you think?"

She nodded. "Hunting."

"I had to get out of the house. Away from you before . . . before I did something we'd both regret."

"You were with Mara, weren't you?" When he hesitated, she said, "Don't lie to me, Nick. I can smell her perfume on you."

"She knew I was in no condition to be left alone. If it wasn't for her, I don't know what I would have done."

"Is that why you kissed her?"

"I didn't."

She lifted one brow. "That's her lipstick, isn't it?"

Shit! "*She* kissed *me*. It didn't mean anything."

"Isn't that what men always say when they've been unfaithful?" Fighting tears, she sank down on the sofa.

"Dammit, Abbey, nothing happened between us. She kept me from killing when that was all I wanted to do.

She gave me some of her blood to strengthen me. And she kissed me good-bye. That's all there was to it."

Abbey clasped her hands tightly in her lap. Right or wrong, justified or not, she was jealous of every moment Nick spent with Mara. If he needed blood, she wanted him to take hers. She wanted to be the one he turned to, no matter what the problem, even though she realized that there would be times when only another vampire could provide the help he needed. She would just have to get used to it.

"You've got to believe me," Nick said quietly. "By the love I have for you, I swear I'm telling you the truth."

"I believe you, Nick. I'm sorry I was so upset. I should have trusted you." She bit down on her lip. "Did Logan find the two of you together?"

"Yeah, he found us. It wasn't pretty."

"He's jealous, too, but then, who can blame him?"

Murmuring her name, Nick pulled her into his arms. She resisted a moment, then relaxed against him. She could feel the subtle differences in him, the latent strength, the tightly leashed power. The faint hum of preternatural energy brushed her cheek, as warm as a spring breeze.

She looked up, meeting his gaze, and felt that incredible power flow over her, raising the hairs along her arms, making her stomach curl with anticipation.

He lowered his head slowly, giving her time to pull away. When she didn't, he covered her mouth with his, his tongue sweeping across her lips, darting inside to tangle with hers.

Abbey moaned softly as Nick deepened the kiss. She slid her hands under his shirt, her nails raking his back and shoulders.

A moment later, the lights went out and a fire sprang to life in the hearth. Nick's mouth never left hers as he drew her down onto the rug in front of the fireplace and stretched out beside her.

"You're wearing too many clothes," he muttered, and in moments, they were undressing each other until they lay naked in each other's arms.

He drew her body close to his, his eyes blazing with desire as hot as the flames crackling in the hearth as he kissed and caressed every inch of her, until, desperate for release, she cried out for him to take her. Only then did he rise over her, a mystical, preternatural being with fire in his eyes and magic in his hands.

His fangs pricked her throat, quickly and gently, and his power flowed into her, reestablishing the blood bond between them, giving her access to his thoughts, as he had access to hers. As their bodies came together, she felt everything he felt, knew what he was thinking, just as he was aware of her thoughts and feelings. He knew what she wanted almost before she did. She writhed beneath him, wanting to be closer, closer.

"Now, darlin'," he murmured huskily, and swept her over the edge of passion into ecstasy.

Nick held Abbey close, one hand lightly stroking her hair. Exhausted and fulfilled, she had quickly fallen asleep in his arms.

He lay there, his eyes closed, relishing the weight of his preternatural power. He knew then that, had the cure worked, sooner or later he would have asked Mara to turn him again. He had been a vampire too long to ever truly be happy as a mortal. He had missed the preternatural strength at his fingertips, the sense of invincibility, the ability to move faster than the eye could follow. The blood.

Nick listened to the slow steady beat of Abbey's

heart, the quiet flow of blood in her veins. It was like music to his ears. He wasn't sorry he had tried Pearl's cure. It had made him realize how much he had enjoyed being a vampire, something he had lost sight of somewhere along the way. Nor did he regret the few short weeks he'd had to sample mortal food and drink. So many flavors and textures, such variety, and yet, on some level he hadn't recognized at the time, it hadn't really satisfied him, no doubt because as Mara had pointed out, he had never been truly human.

Cradling Abbey against his chest, he stood and carried her up the stairs to their bedroom. Even in sleep, she snuggled against him. She stirred but didn't wake when he tucked her into bed.

He stood there a moment, listening to the night. She called to him like a jealous lover, her voice soft and enticing as she whispered to him, reminding him of the myriad pleasures to be found in her darkness.

Nick stared out the window. The lure of the hunt was tempting, he thought, glancing at Abbey again, but not so tempting as the woman sleeping in his bed.

Chapter Thirty-Five

Logan Blackwood prowled the timbered hills behind Mara's house in Northern California, his gut churning, his thoughts chaotic. He had acted like a lovesick fool. The knowledge made his stomach muscles clench. And yet, who the hell could blame him? He wasn't blind or stupid. He had seen the way Mara looked at Nick, the way Nick looked at her. She had flown to Nick's side the first time he had tried that blasted cure.

She had gone to him again tonight.

Logan slammed his fist into a tree, splitting the trunk in half. What was he supposed to do? Just sit idly by while she played nursemaid to another man? Dammit, he loved her. He had loved her from the moment he first saw her, gliding toward him through the dark of night, a vision in a long white gown, her hair falling over her shoulders like black silk, her skin translucent. One smile and he had been lost. He had loved her then. He loved her now and for always. Even when he should have hated her, he loved her. But this time she'd gone too far. He might be a vampire, but he was still a man, and a man had his pride. He wasn't her lap dog or her consort. He was her husband.

"A little jealousy is a healthy thing in a husband."

He didn't turn to face her. "Is it?"

"Hektor . . ." His ancient name, whispered softly, weakened his anger, as she had surely known it would. But he refused to face her.

He heard her sigh and then she was standing in front of him—beautiful, ethereal, a goddess come to earth, an enchantress who had stolen his heart and his soul centuries ago.

"Don't be angry," she murmured, her fingertips trailing down his cheek. "You know it's you I love. You and no one else."

"You love him, too. Admit it."

"In a way, yes, I do." Rising on her tiptoes, she nipped his earlobe, hard enough to draw blood. "But only you have my heart."

"Do I?"

Annoyance flickered in the depths of her deep green eyes. "You doubt me?"

He shrugged.

Lifting her chin, she stepped out of her heels and began to undress, slowly, provocatively. She unzipped her long red gown and let it fall. Holding his gaze with hers, she removed her lacy black bra, the matching panties—until she stood naked before him, her skin glowing in the light of the moon. Perfect. Eternally flawless.

Determined to hold on to his anger, he started to turn away, only to discover that he couldn't move. Trapped by her gaze, he stood there as she slowly stripped him of his clothing, her fingers trailing fire wherever she touched him.

He glared at her, helpless, naked.

And blatantly aroused.

A faint smile curved her lips as she cocooned him in her arms and sank down on the ground. The grass was damp, the air cool, but she was like a living flame as she moved over him, torturing him with her kisses, arousing him until his need grew painful. When he was burning for her, she released him from her spell.

Growling low in his throat, he flipped her onto her back, straddled her hips, and trapped both of her hands in one of his. "Mine," he hissed. "Only mine."

"Always, Hektor, my most beloved. As you will forever be mine."

And then she was on top, showering him with kisses, and there was no more need for talk.

Chapter Thirty-Six

Pearl's hand trembled as she set her wineglass aside. "I thought the crap was going to hit the fan when Rane found out Nick was a vampire again."

Edna nodded, her own hands none too steady as she refilled her glass.

"I think we should get out of town right away," Pearl said urgently. "In fact, I think we should get out of the state and away from everyone who knows us. Find a place where we've never been before. Where we don't have ties to anyone else."

"You could be right," Edna agreed. "Were you thinking of any place in particular?"

"Not really. Just some part of the country where no one would think to look for vampires. We need to alter our appearances, too. Maybe dye our hair and change the way we dress, and . . . and . . . I don't know. Get colored contacts or start wearing glasses . . ." Pearl snapped her fingers. "I've got it! I know just the place!"

"You do?"

Pearl nodded. "I was looking for something online the other night, I don't remember what," she said, her voice rising with excitement. "And I found this cute little motel/café/bar for sale in Dunc, New Mexico. . . ."

Edna frowned. "I've never even heard of the place."

"My point exactly. And listen to this, there's a two bedroom apartment over the bar. I remember thinking if we were ever in the market to buy a place, it would be perfect."

"New Mexico?" Edna said dubiously. "Seriously?"

"Think about it, dear. From what I hear, the vampire population is practically zero, which means there probably aren't a lot of hunters there, either. If we change our appearance . . . and our names . . . what do you think?"

"A lot of wealthy men retire to New Mexico."

"Boy crazy, I tell you," Pearl muttered, grinning broadly. "I'm going to call the Realtor tomorrow and make an offer."

"But . . . what about our old homes in Texas?"

"I think we should sell them. Cut all of our ties to people and places we've known."

Edna frowned thoughtfully, then nodded. "Maybe you're right. We haven't been home in years. It's going to be hard to part with my house, though. So many memories there."

"I know, dear. But I'm sure this is the right thing to do."

Edna nodded absently. "I think I'll become a blonde. And change my name to Brittany."

Pearl nodded. "And I'll dye my hair brown and change my name to . . . hmm . . . Pamela. Or maybe Anita."

Brittany—formerly Edna—now sporting shoulder-length golden-blond hair and wearing a beige designer

pantsuit, signed her name on the deed, then passed
the pen to Anita—formerly Pearl—who wore a brown
dress and matching heels. She signed her name with a
flourish.

"Welcome to town," the Realtor said, smiling broadly.
"I hope you'll be happy here."

"I'm sure we will be," Edna said, batting her eyelashes at him. And who could blame her, she thought.
She had always loved fair-haired men and James Harkness was tall and lean, with dark blond hair and vivid
blue eyes beneath his black cowboy hat. And best of all,
he appeared to be in his early to mid-sixties.

James smiled at her. "Forgive my impertinence, Miss
Brittany, but are you married or anything?"

"Why, no, I'm not."

"Then, begging your pardon if I'm out of line, but
would you care to go out with me some night?"

"Why, I would love it."

"If your business partner isn't opposed to blind
dates, I have a friend for her."

Edna glanced at Pearl, one brow raised.

"I'm not opposed to blind dates," Pearl said, "as long
as my date isn't blind."

James threw back his head and laughed. "How about
if we pick you ladies up tomorrow night at, say, eight?"

"That would be wonderful," Edna said, rising.

James stood and came around the desk. "Are you
staying at the hotel in town?"

"Yes, for now."

"Until tomorrow night, then." He shook hands with
Pearl, then took Edna's hand in his and kissed her
palm. "Until tomorrow night, sweet lady."

Edna was all aflutter as they left the office. "I must
say, this is the best idea you've ever had!" she exclaimed

as they drove to the hotel. "That man is positively dreamy!"

"Yes, he is, dear. But please, try not to devour him on your first date."

"Devour him?" Edna said, aghast. "Girlfriend, I'm going to marry him!"

"I'm as nervous as a cat," Edna said. "Do I really look all right as a blonde?"

"You're lovely, dear."

"Are you sure this dress is me? It's so . . . so . . ." Her shoulders slumped. "Ordinary."

"It's very attractive. We agreed, no bold colors, nothing to draw attention. How do I look?" Pearl asked, turning this way and that.

"Black is very slimming, you know."

Pearl fisted her hands on her hips. "Are you saying I'm fat?"

"Of course not! You've never been fat! And I've always hated you for it," Edna said, and burst into giggles.

"I hope my date is as handsome as yours," Pearl remarked, smoothing her hand over her hair. "And speaking of your date, did you notice anything strange about him?"

"Strange? What kind of strange?"

"For a moment I could have sworn I detected a hint of vampire."

Edna's eyes widened. "Really?"

Pearl nodded. "Really."

"Well, wouldn't that be something! Maybe we should spray ourselves with that awful stuff that masks our scent."

"I think you're right," Pearl said, stepping into a pair

of low-heeled black shoes. "Better safe than sorry, I always say."

James Harkness arrived at eight sharp, looking quite handsome in a blue plaid cowboy shirt, jeans with a crease sharp enough to cut steel, and black boots polished to within an inch of their life.

He winked at Edna, smiled at Pearl as he introduced her to his friend, Monroe Taylor.

"I'm mighty pleased to make your acquaintance, Miss Anita."

"Thank you." Monroe was a little taller than James. He wore his light brown hair cut short. His dark brown eyes twinkled as he bowed over her hand. "It's a pleasure to meet you, too. Mr. Taylor."

"Just Monroe, darlin'."

"So, what would you ladies like to do this evening?" James asked.

"Why don't you decide?" Pearl suggested. "After all, we're new in town."

"Well, there's the movies, or bowling, or we could go rowing on the lake."

"Rowing sounds like fun," Pearl said.

"And romantic, too," Edna said, locking arms with James. "As long as Jimmy and I get our own boat."

Pearl sat with her hands folded in her lap as Monroe picked up the oars and rowed out toward the center of the lake. It was a beautiful, star-studded night presided over by a bright yellow moon. A faint breeze chilled the air. Of course, being a vampire, the cold didn't bother her.

It had been decades since she had been on a blind date. She scarcely remembered what it had been like to be young and insecure, hoping a boy would like her, wondering if he would kiss her good night. But it all came back to her as Monroe made small talk, asking about her past, if she had children . . . children. They were all gone now, she thought sadly. Most likely her grandchildren, too. She had great grandchildren somewhere in West Texas, but she had lost touch with them years ago.

"Anita?"

She stared at Monroe blankly. *Who is Anita?* she wondered, and then realized he meant her. "I'm sorry, I guess I was daydreaming."

He smiled, revealing a dimple in his cheek. "Remembering something pleasant, I hope."

She shook her head. "Just an old memory, best forgotten."

"I have a few of those myself," he remarked. "I guess, when you get to be our age, there are bound to be some things you wish you could change, or do over."

Pearl nodded. She didn't regret becoming a vampire, but she was sorry she'd lost touch with her children. At least they had all been grown and married with children of their own when she was turned. She didn't know what she would have done if she'd been a young mother at the time. It was all water under the bridge now, she thought. If not for Edna, she didn't know how she would have endured becoming a vampire.

"I was wondering if you'd like to go dancing?" Monroe asked. "I know a little after-hours place not too far from here."

"That sounds like fun. I just hope I remember how. I haven't been dancing in years." She glanced around. "I don't see Ed . . . er, Brittany anywhere."

"They went ashore a few minutes ago."

"Oh." She really had been lost in thought, Pearl mused, if she hadn't even noticed. Leave it to Edna to want to spend time alone with James. She just hoped her friend was looking for a kiss in the moonlight and not a midnight snack.

"Is that a problem, if it's just you and me?"

"No, not at all." The problem was that she really liked Monroe. It surprised her to realize that without much effort, she could easily find herself falling in love with him.

Monroe rowed swiftly to shore. After returning the boat to the rental place, they drove a few miles out of town. The Midnight Blue Tavern was located on the side of a dirt road. A green neon sign blinked OPEN ALL NIGHT. Perhaps a dozen cars and trucks were parked in the empty field across the way.

The unmistakable scent of vampire reached Pearl's nostrils as soon as she stepped out of the car. All her senses went on high alert. "Do you come here often?"

"Probably a couple times a week," Monroe replied, taking her by the hand.

Pearl nodded. There was nothing to worry about, she thought, her gaze darting right and left to probe the shadows. She was quite capable of taking care of herself. Or so she thought. Until she stepped into the dimly lit nightclub. Inside, the scent of vampire was overpowering.

Monroe guided her to a table for two in the back. After holding her chair for her, he took his own seat, then reached for her hand again. "So, tell me," he said, his thumb lightly stroking her palm, "how long have you been one of us?"

Pearl stared at him. How could he possibly know? She had sprayed herself liberally with Sophie's Scent-

Be-Gone, which should have made it impossible for hunters—or vampires—to recognize her for what she was.

And then she realized he must have used a similar spray. "How did you know?"

"I recognized your brand of scent-be-gone."

She tensed, ready to defend herself if need be, her mind whirling. Had she and Edna fallen into some kind of trap? Did Monroe know who she was? Was he planning to collect the reward being offered by the coalition? Closing her eyes, she took a deep breath. She was just being paranoid.

"Relax, Anita," he said, squeezing her hand. "You're perfectly safe with me. How long have you been a vampire?"

"A woman never tells," she said, lips twitching. "You?"

"About eighty-five years."

"Is James one, too?"

"Uh-huh. Brittany?"

"Yes."

"What brought the two of you to New Mexico?"

"We heard there were only a few vampires here."

"Yeah," he said with a wry grin. "That's what most people think. Pretty much everybody in here tonight is a vampire, including Al, the bartender."

"I don't believe this." She shook her head. They had come to New Mexico in hopes of getting away from the vampire community. If there were vampires here . . . "Are you troubled by hunters?"

"We get one now and then."

She nodded. From the way he said it, she knew any hunter who found his way into this sleepy little town never left. "Where did James take Brittany?"

"Probably bowling. That man loves to bowl." He

looked up when a waitress came to take their order. "Hey, Diane, bring us two of the house specials, will ya?"

"Sure, Monroe," the waitress said with a wink. "Just got a fresh batch in tonight."

"What's the house special?" Pearl asked.

"Pinot Noir with a dash of AB negative." Sitting back, he regarded her a moment. "You don't meet many vampires who were turned late in life," he remarked. "Who brought you across?"

"An old enemy turned me for spite. You?"

"My son, Clayton."

Pearl stared at him, unable to comprehend such a thing. "I . . . I don't know what to say."

"It's not what you're thinking. I asked him to do it."

"Why?"

He shrugged. "I was dying and I wasn't ready to go."

Pearl nodded. She could understand that. At first, she had hated Rafe for turning her, but now, years later, she was grateful.

The waitress returned carrying two crystal goblets on a wooden tray. The liquid inside was dark red and smelled divine.

"Just put it on my tab," Monroe said. "And give yourself a generous tip."

"Will do, honey. Ya'll have a great night."

"Have you known James a long time?" Pearl asked.

"You could say that. I brought him across a week after I was turned. At his request," Monroe added quickly.

"What happened to your son?"

Sadness flickered in Monroe's eyes. "He was killed. Some hunter named Lou McDonald took him out not long ago."

Pearl leaned forward and placed her hand over his. "I'm so sorry."

"I vowed to kill McDonald, but someone beat me to it."

"Oh?" Pearl went very still. Did he know the truth?

"Yeah, some vampire named Pearl Jackson. If I ever meet her, I'll pat her on the back and buy her a drink."

For a moment, she could only stare at him, and then she burst out laughing.

Monroe frowned at her. "What's so funny?"

Taking a deep breath, Pearl said, "Maybe someday, when I know you better, I'll tell you."

Chapter Thirty-Seven

Nick hit the mute on the remote. "You seem upset about something," he remarked. "Do you want to tell me what it is?"

Abbey shrugged. "It's nothing, really. Turn the sound back on. This is the best part."

"You can tell me what's bothering you," Nick said, barely holding on to his patience. "Or I can slip inside your head and root around in there until I find it."

"Oh! That sounds so gross!" Scooting to the other side of the sofa, she folded her arms over her chest and glared at him. "I told you, it's nothing."

"Then tell me."

With a huff of annoyance, she said, "Oh, all right! If you must know, I asked my mom a while back if she had any information about my biological father."

Nick frowned. "And that's why you're so upset?"

"Well, she never got back to me." Abbey held up one hand to stay his next question. "She said she'd let me know if she found anything, so I guess she didn't, but . . . I don't know. I just can't believe she made a decision like that when all she knew about the man was his age and that he was a healthy white male. Not about something so important."

"What are you afraid of?"

"I'm not afraid. I just . . ." She spread her hands in a gesture of futility. "I just want to know who he was. I mean, think about it. Maybe he had some kind of preternatural power and that's why I could sometimes read your thoughts when we first met."

Nick grunted softly. It made sense. And he couldn't blame her for being curious. "I'll see what I can find out, love."

Abbey scooted closer and kissed him on the cheek. "Thank you, Nick."

He nodded. "We friends again?"

She made a face at him. "I wasn't mad at you. Just . . . just frustrated. You'll let me know if you discover anything, won't you? No matter what it is?"

"I promise." If anyone knew anything about Abbey's parentage, it would be Mara. After hitting the mute button again, Nick handed Abbey the remote. "I need to go out for a while. I won't be long."

"All right." He went out to hunt every night about this time. It was a part of him and she accepted it as such, although it was difficult to think of him going into the city, searching for prey, drinking from another woman.

He kissed her lightly and vanished from her sight.

Nick found his prey quickly, took what he needed, and sent the woman on her way. Moving quicker than the human eye could follow, he headed for a local hangout. Inside, he ordered two glasses of red wine, then focused his thoughts on Mara.

Moments later, she entered the tavern. As always,

he was taken aback by her incomparable beauty, as was every other man in the place. As if pulled by the same string, they all followed her progress toward him. Their combined envy when she slid sinuously into his booth was a palpable presence in the room.

"Nicky," she murmured with a wry grin. "We've got to stop meeting like this."

"Very funny."

"Is something wrong?" She picked up the wineglass in front of her and took a sip. "Ah, my favorite chardonnay. How sweet of you to remember."

"Turn it off, Cleopatra. I didn't come here to flirt with you."

"Another hope crushed. So, what do you want?"

"Abbey's been fretting over who her biological father is. I figured if anyone knew anything about him, it would be you."

"Has she asked her mother?"

"Yeah. Savanah said all she knew about the man was his age and that he was healthy."

"I see."

Nick tilted his head to one side. "You know more than that, don't you?"

"Perhaps. How are things between the two of you now that you're no longer human?"

"Same as they were before. Abbey never had a problem with my being a vampire."

Obviously skeptical, Mara lifted one brow. "And when she grows old and you don't?"

"I don't know. I'll worry about it when it happens." He swirled the wine in his glass. "So, are you going to tell me what you know about Abbey's biological father?"

"He appears to have been quite an interesting character. His name was Miles Cunningham. He was twenty-nine when he donated his sperm. Born in Maryland, never married. He listed his profession as an accountant." Mara ran her finger around the rim of her wineglass. "In the course of his lifetime, he went by several aliases, none that I have ever heard of. He was also rumored to be a formidable warlock who was allied with a powerful coven in New Orleans. He died in prison two years ago while serving a fifteen-year sentence for grand larceny, among other things."

"He couldn't have been much of a warlock if he couldn't magic his way out of prison," Nick muttered. "Still, I can understand why Savanah never told Abbey about him."

"I'm not sure Savanah ever knew. Are you going to tell Abbey?"

"She deserves to know the truth."

"Are you sure that's a good idea?"

"Probably not. But I promised Abbey I'd let her know whatever I found out." Of course, he hadn't expected to find out the man in question was a warlock and a crook. He frowned thoughtfully. "How'd you come by all this information?"

She shrugged. "I have my sources."

"Uh-huh. And what were you planning to do with it?"

"I hadn't decided, but it's up to you now. Do what you wish."

"Thanks," he said dryly.

"Always glad to help," she said, smirking. "Does Abbey know we're meeting on the sly?"

"What do you think? Did you tell Logan?"

"What do you think?"

"It's good to see you, Mara, as always."

"And you." She finished her wine and set the glass aside. Leaning across the table, she cupped his cheek in her hand and kissed him lightly. Then, with a wink and a little extra swagger in her walk, she made her way to the exit.

Nick grinned as every male eye in the tavern focused on Mara's swaying hips as she sauntered out the door.

Abbey was watching the end of the movie when Nick returned home. "You were gone a long time tonight."

"Sorry." Sitting beside her, he drew her close, his fingers caressing her cheek, sliding up into her hair. Cupping the back of her head, he covered her mouth with his. "Did you miss me?"

"Maybe." She tugged his shirt from inside his jeans and slipped her hand underneath.

"Maybe?"

She leaned forward to kiss him, only to draw back, her brow furrowed. "Where were you?"

Shit.

"You were with Mara again, weren't you?"

"Reading my mind, love?"

"No. Smelling her perfume," she replied tartly. Scooting to the other end of the sofa, she crossed her arms over her chest. "Why did you go sneaking off to see her?"

"I didn't go *sneaking* off."

"No?" She lifted one brow. "Didn't you tell me you were going hunting?"

"Do you want to listen to what I have to say, or not?"

She nodded curtly.

"You've been upset because you don't know anything about your biological father. I figured if anybody would know about him, it would be Mara."

Abbey leaned forward, her eyes sparkling with curiosity. "Did she know him?"

"No, but she had some information."

"Tell me!"

"Are you sure you want to hear this? It isn't all good."

"Nick, you promised! What did she tell you?"

"For starters, it seems he was a warlock, with ties to a coven in New Orleans."

Abbey sat back, stunned. "He was a witch?" She didn't know what she had expected, but this wasn't it.

"So it seems."

"Is that the good news or the bad?"

"I guess it depends on how you feel about witches. I'm pretty sure it's his preternatural power that let you read my thoughts. You probably have some latent power of your own that you haven't tapped into."

"Me?" She blinked at him. "I'm not a witch."

"How do you know?"

Abbey fell back against the sofa cushions. If she was a witch, wouldn't she know it? Except for being able to read Nick's mind, she had never done anything the least bit supernatural. "What else did Mara tell you?"

"It seems he used several aliases over the years. He was sent to prison for fleecing a man out of a fortune in uncut diamonds."

"Is he still alive?"

"No. He died in prison two years ago."

Abbey stared blankly into the distance. Not only was her biological father a warlock, he was a thief, as well. Surely her mother hadn't known what kind of man he was. "Did Mara know his real name?"

"He listed his name as Miles Cunningham on the donor card. Are you all right?"

"Why wouldn't I be all right? Just because the blood of a warlock who was also a thief and who knows what else runs through my veins?" She blinked rapidly in an effort to stay her tears.

Nick closed the distance between them and drew her into his arms. "It doesn't matter who fathered you," he said, stroking her hair. "What matters is who you are. Rane and your mother have had more influence on you than some man you've never met. And they did a hell of a good job."

Abbey buried her face in the hollow of his shoulder, grateful for his nearness, his words of comfort. Maybe he was right. For decades, scientists had been trying to determine which factor played a stronger role in a child's development—heredity or environment. Nature versus nurture. To date, there was no decision as to which played a more important part. So even though her biological father had been a thief, she had been taught that stealing was wrong, so it was unlikely that she would become a thief. But being able to read Nick's mind hadn't been taught. "Do you think my mother knew he was a warlock?"

"I doubt it."

"Do you think I should tell her?"

"After all this time?" He shrugged. "I guess that's up to you."

Abbey sighed. On the one hand, if her mother didn't already know, there was nothing to be gained by telling her at this late date. What was done was done and couldn't be undone. Besides, if her mother didn't know and discovered that Miles Cunningham's character had been less than sterling, she might start feeling guilty. And there was nothing to be gained by that, either.

Sitting up, Abbey shook her head. "What do you think I should do?"

"If it was me, I'd let it go."

She nodded. For now, that seemed like the best

thing to do. "How do I find out if I have any witchy powers?"

"Witchy?" Nick chuckled. "What are you thinking? That you can twitch your nose and make things disappear?"

"Can I?"

"How should I know? I'm a vampire, not a witch. Give it a try and see what happens."

"Yeah, right. I love you, Nick."

"That's magic all by itself."

"Why do you say that?"

"You're a young, beautiful, talented woman, and I'm an ancient vampire. You don't think there's magic involved?"

Murmuring, "Just love," she wrapped her arms around his neck. "Can I taste you?"

"Sure. As long as I can taste you in return."

"Deal."

She sat back while he bit into his wrist, then held it out to her. She regarded the blood a moment, then lowered her head and lapped it up like a kitten with a bowl of cream. It sizzled through her, making her feel vibrant and alive, as if she could climb Everest or leap tall buildings in a single bound.

"That's enough, love. My turn now." He sealed the shallow wound in his wrist, then drew her gently into his arms. After brushing the hair away from her neck, he laved the skin beneath her ear with his tongue before lowering his head to her throat.

Abbey sighed as she felt the prick of his fangs, wondering again why it didn't hurt, and how anything so bizarre could feel so wonderful.

She knew a moment of regret when he drew back. His tongue was warm against her neck as he sealed the tiny wounds left by his fangs.

Feeling deliciously content, she snuggled against him, her head resting against his chest, one arm wrapped around his waist. Soon, he would carry her to bed. Just the thought made her heart skip a beat.

Making love to Nick was an incredible experience. Poets always talked about two people becoming one. She had always assumed it was just a figure of speech, but in their case, it was true. It wasn't just their bodies that came together, but their hearts and minds, as well. He knew her better than she knew herself, knew what she wanted before she did.

Nick stroked her cheek. "You seem very introspective. What are you thinking about?"

"Do you think I'd like being a vampire?"

"What brought that up?"

"Oh . . . um . . . I just wondered if it would enhance our lovemaking."

Nick drew back a little so he could see her face. "Are you complaining?"

"No, never. I mean, it's wonderful. I love that I know what you're feeling and everything, but . . . well, you've got all these amazing preternatural senses and . . ."

Nick chuckled. "I've never heard of anyone wanting to be a vampire to improve their sex life."

Punching him on the arm, she said, "It sounds awful when you put it like that!"

"Ow!"

"Oh, please, that didn't hurt and you know it."

"If you want to be a vampire, honey, I'm your go-to guy."

"I didn't say I want to be turned. I just wanted to know if you thought I'd like it."

He shook his head, his expression pensive as his hand idly stroked up and down her back. "I honestly don't know. On the plus side, my blood is ancient, which means you'd be powerful from the get-go. After a month or so, you'd be able to be awake during the day, although you might have to stay out of direct sunlight for a time. It would definitely heighten your senses," he said, waggling his eyebrows suggestively. "All of them."

She scowled at him. "Pervert."

"Hey, you're the one who brought it up."

"But the blood . . ." She grimaced. "How do you ever get used to that?" A few sips of Nick's blood was one thing, but to drink enough to survive . . . yuck!

Nick shook his head. "I can't believe you never discussed any of this with your folks. Weren't you curious when you were a little girl?"

"Well, no, not really. My mom was human then and she made excuses for why my dad slept late and why he didn't eat with us. And when I was old enough to understand . . ." She shrugged. "I don't know. The blood. Tell me about the blood."

"When you're a vampire, drinking blood is normal. Natural."

"Hmm. I don't know. Giving up chocolate and pasta and bread and ice cream for a warm-liquid diet . . ." Abbey shook her head. "I just don't think I'd want to do that."

"It's up to you, love."

"Remember when you told me there wasn't any future for us as long as you were a vampire? That you were afraid you'd turn me against my will, or that you'd drain me dry?"

Nick went still. "I remember." Those possibilities worried him on a daily basis.

She looked up at him, her gaze searching his. "Do you still feel that way?"

He nodded. "I won't lie to you, Abbey my love.

You're a constant temptation. If I ever do anything to make you afraid of me, or put you in fear for your life, all you have to do is tell me to leave and I'll have to go. You know that, don't you?"

"That's the real reason you put the house in my name, isn't it? So I could revoke your invitation?"

He nodded.

"Nick, promise you won't ever leave me."

"Abbey . . ."

"No. You're thinking it would be for the best if you just left and never came back, aren't you?"

He didn't deny it.

"Promise me, Nick. I can stand anything as long as you're with me."

"All right, love, I promise I won't leave you."

He just hoped it was a promise he could keep.

During the next few days, whenever she was alone, Abbey tried to discover whether she possessed any supernatural powers. She tried opening doors by willing them to open. She stared at a candle, trying to light it with the power of her mind, the way Nick lit a fire in the hearth. Nothing happened.

She tried to levitate.

She tried to pick the ace of spades out of a deck of cards.

She bought a book of spells and read it from cover to cover, hoping to find the secret to unleashing whatever power she had. Nothing happened.

"Some witch," she muttered when she tried to conjure fire, and failed again. According to the book, it was supposed to be one of the easiest spells to master.

There were all kinds of magic—mud magic, rain magic, herb magic. Cauldron magic. Cauldrons had long been associated with witches, along with brooms, pointy hats, warts, and black cats. Cauldrons had also been considered a potent magical tool since before recorded history because they utilized all four of the natural elements. Fire heated the vessel, water filled it, herbs used in spells represented the earth, the steam it created represented the air. Cauldrons were especially associated with feminine magic.

Maybe what she needed was a big black pot and a pointy hat?

And maybe she needed to forget about magic altogether. Just because she had read Nick's mind a few times didn't mean she was a witch.

Maybe she had inherited a bit of psychic power from her biological father.

And maybe it was all just a coincidence.

Chapter Thirty-Eight

Edna smiled at James. It was their second date. Earlier, they had gone bowling, something she hadn't done in longer than she could remember. And her dismal scores proved it. She hadn't even broke a hundred on their first game. She had done better the second two, scoring 129 and 142. James, the stinker, had bowled a 275, a 260, and a 280. It had been a great deal of fun. But then, just being with James was fun. She realized with something of a shock that laughter and good times had been sorely lacking in her life until now. Odd, she had never noticed it before.

Now, they were sitting on a park bench, holding hands and just enjoying each other's company. She had grown very fond of the man. He was such a sweet guy, with a warm, ready smile and a dry sense of humor.

"So," he said, apropos of nothing. "How long have you been a vampire?"

Caught completely off guard, Edna squeaked, "Who, me?"

James laughed softly. "Don't look so shocked," he said, squeezing her hand. "Monroe told me."

"But . . . how did he find out?"

"From Anita, of course."

"I can't believe she told him."

"She didn't have to tell him. We already knew. That stuff you're wearing to hide your scent, I've used it myself. So, even though you didn't smell like a vampire, only vampires use it."

"And hunters," Edna said.

"Really? Damn, I didn't know that."

She nodded.

"Have you and Anita been friends a long time?"

"Oh, yes, years and years. We were turned on the same night by the same vampire."

"I thought maybe you turned each other."

"Heavens, no! Who brought you across?"

"Monroe. His son brought him across."

"Really? I can't imagine anyone *asking* for the Dark Gift."

"Well, Monroe had only a few weeks to live and he asked his son to bring him across. And I asked Monroe a week later."

"I was turned against my will. Anita, too. But, all things considered," she said, smiling at him again. "I'm glad it happened."

"So am I," James said, his gaze intent upon her face, "or I never would have met you."

If she'd been able, Edna knew she would have been blushing. Pearl was always accusing her of being boy crazy and in a way, it was true. She'd always had an eye for a good-looking man. As a young woman, she had been a bit of a flirt. So, she liked men. There was no law against it. Still, she couldn't remember the last time she had been *this* attracted to a man. Sighing, she wished suddenly that she was younger, prettier.

"Brittany? Did I say something wrong?"

"No. I . . . you . . . we just met."

He shrugged. "I don't suppose people's feelings have anything to do with the calendar."

"No," she said, feeling as though the sun was shining in her heart. "I guess they don't."

"Coming to New Mexico is the best decision we ever made," Pearl remarked as she finished unpacking her suitcase.

"You won't get any argument from me." Edna frowned as she watched Pearl hang several dresses—all in bland or neutral colors—in the closet. "I'm getting awfully tired of brown and beige and navy. Aren't you?"

Pearl nodded. "But better safe than sorry, I always say."

"I guess so."

"I know so," Pearl said, and then grinned. "Did I tell you that Monroe said if he ever met the person who killed Lou McDonald, he'd pat them on the back and buy them a drink? You don't know how hard it was for me to keep from telling him the truth."

"Hmm. I'm not sure that's a truth we should *ever* tell *anyone*."

"Exactly. Which means that as hard as it is, we can never let the guys know who we really are. Every hunter and vampire in the country knows Edna Turner and Pearl Jackson killed the McDonald sisters."

Edna sighed. "Things seem to be moving so fast with me and Jim . . . I'm not sure what to make of it."

"I know what you mean, dear. I think I'm falling in love with Monroe and it's only been a few days."

"When are we going to open the motel?" Edna asked, abruptly changing the subject.

"I'm not sure. We'll have to hire someone to run the place during the day, you know."

"Maybe one of the guys can recommend someone?"

"Maybe. We need to install some heavy-duty security doors on our apartment and new locks on all the windows right away. We should have done it before we moved in."

"Do you really think we're in danger here? I never even heard of Dune, New Mexico, before."

Pearl nodded glumly. "I hate to say it, dear, but I think we'll be in danger of one kind or another for as long as we live."

Chapter Thirty-Nine

Abbey leaned on the shovel and blew a strand of hair out of her eyes. She didn't mind cleaning up after the horses. She didn't mind the smell of the manure or find the task unpleasant. Usually, she enjoyed it because it gave her time alone to think about things. But today, she didn't want to think, yet her mind seemed determined to replay her conversation with Nick.

What would she do if he turned her against her will?

Would she hate him forever?

Or wonder why she hadn't asked him to do it sooner?

Dragging her thoughts from Nick, she thought about her father, the warlock. She had tried several times to summon fire, but never with any success. Reading Nick's mind seemed to be her only supernatural power.

Glancing at the hose coiled by the side of the corral, she focused her thoughts on the faucet, willing the water to turn on and fill the horse trough.

A minute went by.

Two.

Five.

Chiding herself for being an idiot for trying again,

she went back to mucking out the stalls and spreading fresh straw.

When she finished her chores, she saddled Freckles. Several days had passed since her conversation with Nick, and she hadn't had a peaceful moment since. One day she decided being a vampire wouldn't be so bad and the next, she was certain it wasn't for her. Not now. Not ever. On the other hand, being eternally young and never getting sick might be a fair trade for what she would have to give up. Plus, she would be making life easier for Nick. He would no longer be tempted to feed from her . . . or drain her dry.

But when she thought about the blood, about hunting for prey like a wild animal . . . why was accepting that so difficult? It was what her whole family did. She knew it, although they had always shielded her from that part of their existence. Was it as horrible and gross as it was in the movies and on TV? She just couldn't imagine her mother dragging some hapless person into the shadows and ripping their throat out. She had often wondered why movie vampires were such sloppy eaters, blood dripping from their fangs, staining their clothes.

It wasn't horrible when Nick drank from her, Abbey thought. He was very gentle, very . . . very tidy. Of course, maybe it was different when he hunted. She had never seen him search for prey. Or feed. Not that she wanted to.

To her chagrin, the idea suddenly held a strange, morbid appeal.

Shaking off her troublesome thoughts, she stepped into the saddle and urged the mare into a lope. A nice long ride was just what she needed to clear her head.

* * *

Abbey was about two miles from home when a pair of riders emerged from the woods to her left. As they drew closer, she could see they were both women, and not accomplished riders, judging by the way one woman held the reins and the other clung to the saddle horn.

One of them, dressed in jeans and a red flannel shirt, waved to her. "Hello, there! Can you help us? I'm afraid we're lost."

Wary of strangers, Abbey reined Freckles to a halt a good distance away. "Where did you come from?"

The second woman, clad in jeans and a long-sleeved T-shirt, jerked a thumb over her shoulder. "Back that way. I don't know how we ended up here," she said, laughing. "Wherever 'here' is."

"You're on private property," Abbey said. "I suggest you turn around and go back the way you came."

"Sure. Thanks," the woman said, but she wasn't looking at Abbey, she was watching something in the woods beyond.

Freckles snorted and shook her head.

Abbey turned to look behind her, let out a cry as a dart embedded itself in her left shoulder. Belatedly, she realized it was a trap, but by then it was too late.

Too late to run away. Too far from home to cry for help.

Her vision narrowed and grew dark as she toppled from the saddle.

When Nick woke late that afternoon, he knew immediately that Abbey wasn't in the house. Guessing that she had stayed late to visit her parents as she often did after taking care of the stock, he willed himself into the city in search of prey.

He found new pleasure in hunting these days. Odd, he thought, how being without his preternatural powers for a short time had given him a deeper appreciation of them when they returned.

Eager to see Abbey again, he fed quickly, then willed himself to Rane's house, thinking to drive back home with Abbey.

A quick sweep with his preternatural senses told him no one was home.

He willed himself to the barn, thinking Abbey must be working late.

But she wasn't there, either. And neither was her horse.

Nick frowned. It wasn't like her to ride so late. Leaving the barn, he sought the bond between them, grunted thoughtfully when he couldn't find it. What the hell? Was she blocking him?

It seemed unlikely. Expanding his preternatural senses, he sorted through the myriad scents that surrounded him—dirt, grass, trees, hay, straw, the horses in the barn, the cattle in the corral—until he found Abbey's unique scent. It guided him unerringly out of the yard. With preternatural speed, he moved past the tree line and into the pasture beyond.

Nick uttered a vile oath when he spied Freckles grazing on a patch of tall grass, reins trailing. There was no sign of Abbey and that worried the hell out of him. No way on earth would she have gone haring off on her own without looking after her horse first.

Where the devil was she?

Walking toward the mare, he caught the scents of two other women. A glance at the ground showed the tracks of three shod horses heading south.

Nick approached Freckles slowly so as not to startle her. Taking up the reins, he swung onto the mare's back and followed the trail of the other three horses. The fear he'd kept tamped down fought free when he neared the tree line and caught the scent of a man.

Genuinely worried now, he kicked the mare into a lope.

Abbey's scent led him unerringly to the service road that paralleled the southern boundary of Rane's property. He found a horse trailer parked there. Three horses were tied in the back. The vehicle that had towed the trailer was gone.

Abbey's scent, and those of the other three people, ended at the side of the road.

Nick sat there a moment, his arms crossed on the pommel as he tried to contact her through their shared link again.

Abbey? Abbey, love, where are you?

He had no sense of her and that scared the hell out of him.

Either she was unconscious.

Or she was dead.

Rane and Savanah were home when Nick returned.

"What do you mean, she's missing?" Rane glared at Nick as if it was his fault.

"Just what I said. I found her horse in the south pasture. There was no sign of Abbey. I located the tracks of three horses. Abbey's scent was mingled with that of two other women and a man. I followed their trail to the service road and then it just disappeared."

"She wouldn't go off like that without letting us know," Savanah said, worrying a lock of her hair. "And she certainly wouldn't leave Freckles loose in the pasture without removing the tack."

"Someone's taken her," Nick said. "And it doesn't take three guesses to figure out who it was."

A muscle throbbed in Rane's jaw. "Hunters." He spit the word as if it tasted bad.

"Right the first time," Nick muttered. "How many people know about those damn books?"

"How the hell should I know?"

"We don't know that this has anything to do with the books," Savanah said, glancing anxiously from one man to the other.

"That's true," Rane agreed. "But it's a pretty good bet."

"I don't give a damn what they want," Nick said, his frustration growing with every passing second. "All I know is she's gone."

Savanah clasped her hands tightly in her lap, her face paler than usual. "You don't think it's the same hunters who came here before, do you?" she asked.

Nick shook his head. "It's unlikely the compulsion Rane used has worn off. Besides, I didn't recognize the scents of the three who took her."

"Let's go," Rane said. "We can follow the car that took her."

Nick shook his head. "I already tried that. I followed it as far as I could. The kidnappers ditched the truck that pulled the horse trailer near a freeway on-ramp. There's no way to tell what car or truck they transferred to."

"What about the horse trailer?" Savanah asked. "Any clues left there?"

"No. I made a call to the police department. It was stolen from a lot in town, along with the horses."

Rane swore again.

"What do we do now?" Savanah glanced from one man to the other.

"We wait until Abbey regains consciousness," Nick said, his voice ice cold. "And then I find her. And rip the heart out of whoever the hell kidnapped her."

Chapter Forty

Voices.

Darkness.

Her head ached.

She felt sick to her stomach.

With a groan, Abbey rolled onto her side and vomited her breakfast.

"What the hell!" A man's angry voice. Rough hands jerked her upright. "Clary, get over here and clean this up."

"Do it yourself."

Abbey blinked to clear her vision. She was lying on a cot. A length of heavy cord was knotted around her ankles. The woman, Clary, stood on the far side of the room. She cradled a mean-looking rifle in her arms. Abbey recognized her as one of the riders she had seen in the pasture. Where was the other woman?

Muttering under his breath about women's work, the man grabbed a towel and clumsily mopped up the mess on the floor.

They were hunters. The knowledge scudded across Abbey's mind. And then she frowned. How had she known that?

"What if he doesn't come?" the rifle-toting woman asked.

"Don't worry, he'll come." The man wadded up the towel and tossed it in a corner.

"And if he doesn't?" the woman persisted.

"Let's not look for trouble."

Still feeling a little groggy, Abbey wondered who they were waiting for, and what would happen when whoever they were expecting showed up. What would happen if no one came? What if it was Nick? Nick! Of course it was Nick. Or her father.

And she was the bait.

Abbey glanced at her surroundings, looking for something she could use as a weapon. They were in what appeared to be a bunker of some kind. There was a sink, a hot plate, two chairs, and the cot she occupied.

The man glanced out the window. "What the hell's keeping Berta? She should have been back here by now."

Clary shrugged. "Maybe the takeout place was busy."

"Maybe she chickened out and decided to cut and run."

"My sister wouldn't do that," the woman retorted, though her tone lacked conviction. "She'll be here."

Abbey felt a tremor deep within her, as if someone— or something—had touched her very soul. *Nick?*

I'm coming. Are you all right?

Yes.

Sit tight, love. I'll be there soon.

Abbey smiled, her former fears evaporating. Hunters or not, these two would be no match for Nick Desanto, vampire extraordinaire.

The man looked at her sharply, his little pig eyes narrowing. "What have you got to look so friggin' happy about?"

"Who, me?" Preternatural power whispered through the room. At first, Abbey thought it was coming from Nick, but then she realized it was coming from inside herself. It reminded her of Nick's power, but it was different somehow.

The man felt it too. Frowning, he glanced around. "What the hell! Clary, do you feel that?"

"Feel what?"

"I'm not sure."

Abbey stared at him. She should have been afraid, she thought, afraid of the power unfolding within her. Instead, she found herself embracing it, molding it, shaping it. In her mind's eye, she imagined picking the man up and throwing him against the wall. To her amazement, the thought no sooner crossed her mind than, with a startled cry, the man flew backward and slammed into the wall.

The woman raised her rifle, her worried gaze sweeping the room. "Who's there?"

"Maybe it's a ghost," Abbey suggested. She focused her will on the woman, sending her stumbling across the floor to stand beside the man. "Or a witch," she murmured, astonished by the strength thrumming inside her.

A moment later, the door crashed against the wall as Nick and her father burst into the room.

Abbey's heart skipped a beat when she saw her rescuers. She looked at Nick, thinking how surprised he would be when she told him what she had done.

As soon as she stopped concentrating on the man and the woman, her hold on them broke.

The woman quickly raised the rifle to her shoulder. At the same time, the man reached for the pistol tucked into the waistband of his jeans.

Faster than the eye could follow, Nick jerked the rifle

from the woman's hands and tossed it aside. A quick twist broke her neck.

Rane didn't move quite as fast as Nick. The hunter squeezed off a round, striking Rane in the shoulder, before Rane plucked the gun from his hand and shot him in the chest. The man stumbled backward as a bright red stain blossomed across his shirt front.

Nick knelt in front of Abbey, his hands deftly untying the rope that bound her ankles. "Are you hurt?"

She shook her head, unable to take her gaze from the bodies on the floor. It had happened so quickly. Alive one minute. Stone cold dead the next. Her nostrils filled with the acrid smell of gun smoke, the coppery scent of blood.

"Nick, get her out of here," Rane said. "I'll take care of these two."

Rising, Nick swept Abbey into his arms and carried her out of the building.

She stared up at him, her face pale. "I think I'm going to . . ."

"Faint," Nick muttered as she went limp in his arms. Well, who could blame her?

Abbey ran through a nightmare landscape. It wasn't night and yet there was no sun. A river of blood followed her. No matter how she tried, she couldn't outrun the crimson tide. Faceless people sprang at her, their eyes hollow and empty of life. Blood poured from hideous, gaping wounds in their throats. Shadowy creatures hovered out of reach, their bony fingers reaching for her, their mocking laughter like the whisper of dead leaves rustling across tombstones.

She tried to cry out, to call for help, but she couldn't

speak. She opened her mouth again, knowing that if she didn't wake now, she would die a horrible, lingering death.

"Nick!" His name was torn from her throat.

"Abbey! Abbey, wake up, I'm here."

Light flooded the room when he switched on the bedside lamp. Moments later, his arms gathered her close.

She clung to him, sobbing incoherently.

"Shh, hush, love, it's all right now. I'm here."

"Nick!" Her arms tightened around him. "Oh, Nick, I had the worst nightmare!"

He stroked her back. "Do you want to talk about it?"

"There was blood. So much blood. And it followed me." She drew in a deep, shuddering breath. "And there were people . . . with dead eyes . . . bleeding . . . And shadows . . ." She buried her face in the hollow of his shoulder, some of her terror fading as his familiar scent tickled her nostrils. His skin was cool against her cheek, his hands gentle as he stroked her back, his voice soothing as he assured her there was nothing to fear.

He rained butterfly kisses on the top of her head. When she looked up at him, he covered her mouth with his, his tongue sweeping across her lips as his hand slid up and down her back.

She moaned softly, her nightmare fading, forgotten, in the magic of his touch.

"Abbey?"

She nodded, her hands moving over him, drawing him down on top of her.

In moments, her nightgown was gone and she was naked in his arms, reveling in his touch. "Take me," she whispered. "Taste me."

She closed her eyes, pleasure flowing through every

nerve and fiber of her being as his tongue stroked the side of her neck. Moments later, he thrust into her. She moaned softly when his fangs pricked her flesh, the sensation sending her to heights of pleasure she doubted few humans were ever lucky enough to know.

"What do you think my nightmare meant?" Abbey asked sometime later.

They were sitting side by side, their backs against the headboard, Nick's arm curled around her shoulders.

"I doubt if it means anything. You had a good scare this afternoon," he remarked. "It was probably just your mind's way of dealing with it."

She nodded. "Maybe you're right." She straightened abruptly. "Nick! I forgot. You should have seen what I did before you and my dad showed up."

"What do you mean?"

"I was sitting on the cot, afraid, because they were waiting for my dad, or maybe for you, and I knew they were going to hurt you and suddenly I felt this . . . this incredible power flowing through me and I concentrated on the man and the next thing I knew, he was pinned against the wall, unable to move. And then it happened to the woman, too. I had this power and I don't know where it came from." The words tumbled out. "Earlier in the day, I tried to turn on the faucet at the barn, you know, with my mind, and nothing happened. But in that shack . . ." She stared up at him. "It was amazing."

"They didn't look immobile when I came through the door."

"I know. As soon as I saw you and my dad, it broke my concentration." Her gaze searched his. "You believe me, don't you?"

He nodded. "Sometimes preternatural power lies dormant until you need it. Today you needed it."

She sagged against him, wondering what it all meant. Had it just been a fluke of some kind, like reading Nick's mind? Or had she really inherited some kind of witchy power from her biological father?

She closed her eyes and then sat up, frowning. "What happened to the other woman?"

"What do you mean?"

"She'd gone out for food, but she never came back."

"Maybe she had second thoughts about what they were doing and left town."

"Maybe." Determined to put it all behind her, Abbey rested her head on Nick's shoulder.

His fingers massaged her neck and scalp. "Do you think you can sleep now?"

"Why?" She sent him a sideways glance. "Are you tired?"

He snorted softly. "Me? Are you kidding? It's not even midnight."

Lifting his hand, she ran her tongue across his palm. "I want to taste you."

"Anytime, love."

Watching Nick bite into his wrist excited her in a way she didn't quite understand. She didn't hesitate to lick at the blood that welled from the shallow wound.

His blood hummed through her veins, turning her own blood to fire. She straddled his hips, her arms wrapping around his neck as she fell back on the mattress, drawing him with her.

His eyes glowed hotly as his body covered hers. One quick thrust carried her over the edge, past mortal pleasure into a world of ecstasy beyond anything she had ever known.

Chapter Forty-One

Pearl wasn't sure how it happened, but almost overnight their little café turned into a vampire hangout. Not that she was complaining. Most vampires had money to burn, whether they had saved it over centuries or stolen it from their prey two days ago.

She and Edna had stocked the bar with nothing but the best, but as mortal customers were few and vampires many, they began stocking a new brand of imitation blood that was popular with younger vampires but rejected by most of the older ones.

"You can't beat the real thing," Monroe said one night after he and Pearl had gone hunting together. "That imitation blood has no kick to it."

Pearl couldn't argue with that.

Now, she smiled at Monroe as he strutted into the bar. "What are you looking so pleased about?" she asked.

"I made a decision last night," he said, easing onto the barstool beside hers.

"Is that right?"

He nodded. "Yep. I need to ask you something.

Something important. I think I know what your answer will be. If I'm wrong . . . well, hell, I can't be wrong." Reaching into his pants pocket, he withdrew a small, square, black velvet box and lifted the lid, revealing a ring with a diamond the size of a golf ball. "Will you marry me, Brittany?"

Pearl stared at Monroe. At the ring. And at Monroe again. "Do you mean it?"

He held up the box. "Darlin', does this look like I'm joking?"

"Of course I'll marry you!" She plucked the ring from the box and put it on her finger. "Yes! Yes! Yes!"

Laughing, Monroe lifted her into his arms and swung her round and round until she was dizzy. And then, with her head still spinning, he kissed her. "Name the day, darlin'."

Pearl blew out a sigh. What would Edna say when she told her the good news?

Edna and James came in later that night. Arm in arm, they joined Pearl and Monroe, who were sitting at one of the booths in the back of the room.

"Hi, you two," Edna said, grinning from ear to ear.

"Hi," Pearl said. "You look like the cat that finally caught the canary."

"So do you," Edna said. "Why are *you* so happy?"

Pearl smiled at Monroe. "We're getting married!"

"So are we!" Edna looked at James. "Did you two plan this?"

James nodded. "It seems like you two do everything else together. So we thought you ought to get engaged on the same night."

"You darling man!" Edna exclaimed, throwing her

arms around him. And then she glanced at Pearl. "Are you thinking what I'm thinking?"

"A double wedding," Pearl said, clapping her hands.

"I told you so," Monroe crowed, looking at James. "Pay up, old buddy."

Grinning good-naturedly, James pulled a fifty out of his pocket and slapped it on the table. "I never should have doubted you."

Pearl sighed as she sat on the edge of the bed and kicked off her shoes. "Edna, I've been thinking. . . ."

"Well, don't. It's always bad news when you start thinking and I don't want anything to ruin this night."

"This is important," Pearl insisted. "We've got to tell Monroe and James the truth."

Edna's eyes widened. "Are you insane?"

"I don't know about you, but I don't want to start my marriage on a lie."

"But . . . if word gets out about who we really are . . ." Edna shook her head. "Are you sure it's a good idea? We're safe here. Besides, how do you know Monroe will keep our secret?"

"Because I trust him," Pearl said.

"With your life?"

"Of course. Don't you trust James?"

"Yes, but . . ." Edna stared at the ring on her finger. "I just hope we're making the right decision."

Pearl decided to tell Monroe the truth the following night. With that in mind, she went shopping in Albuquerque, deciding that if she was going to confess all, she might as well do it with style. She bought a long green skirt and shoes to match, and a flowered silk shirt. Back home, she washed the brown dye out of her hair and when that was done, she felt like her old self again.

When Monroe came into the bar that night, he walked right past her. After a few steps, he backed up, his brow furrowed, his eyes narrowed with disbelief. "Anita? Is that you?"

"It's Pearl, actually," she said, annoyed by the nervous tremor in her voice. "Pearl Jackson."

"Well, I'll be damned. I guess I owe you a pat on the back and a drink!"

Pearl laughed, all her fears allayed when he took her into his arms.

"Don't worry, darlin'," he said, waggling his brows like the villain in a stage play. "Your guilty secret is safe with me." And then he frowned. "If you're Pearl, that means . . ."

She nodded. "Brittany is Edna."

"Son of a gun. Does James know?"

"She's telling him right now. Are you angry because I lied to you? I didn't want to, but . . ."

"Hell, no, I'm not angry. And for the record, I like you a whole lot better as Pearl than as Anita. So," he said, his tone brisk, "name the day and let's get married!"

Pearl sipped her wine. "How'd it go? What did James say when you told him?"

"He was shocked at first." Edna sat on the sofa and removed her shoes. "But then he was okay with it. Where did you get those clothes? You look great!"

"I went shopping earlier. I decided Monroe needed

to see the real me before we got married. And you know what? He said he likes Pearl better than Anita."

"I hope James feels the same way." Edna looked down at her drab gray skirt and white shirt. "I'm sick of these frumpy clothes and clunky shoes," she said irritably, and then she grinned. "Although I have to say, blondes really do have more fun!"

Chapter Forty-Two

"Logan, you're not going to believe this."

About to place a red ten on a black jack, Logan muttered, "Believe what?"

"Edna and Pearl are getting married in Las Vegas next Saturday night, and we're invited."

He snorted as he placed a black eight on a red nine. "Who the hell would marry either one of those old bats?"

Moving up behind him, Mara reached over his shoulder and placed a red seven on the black eight. "You know what they say?" she murmured in his ear. "There's a man for every woman."

"Or a weirdo for every dingbat," he said, pulling her down into his lap. "You're not seriously thinking about going, are you?"

"Of course."

Logan shrugged. "Last time I was in Vegas, I was dealing for the house at one of the casinos. I remember there was this pretty little blond dancer . . . Nanette . . . Ow!"

"You get that little blond right out of your head, Mr. Blackwood."

"Well, I'll try, but she was something else. Legs that wouldn't quit. Big blue eyes . . . Damn, woman!" he exclaimed when she pinched his arm. "That hurt."

She glared at him. "It was supposed to," she said, and then her expression softened. "I'll bet I can make you forget all about that little blond tart."

"You think so?"

Mara batted her eyelashes at him as she slipped one hand under his shirt. "I'll make you forget she ever existed," she promised, her voice low and sultry. "And if you ever mention her name again, I'll rip out your heart and feed it to you."

"Married! Pearl and Edna are getting married!"

Sheree looked up from her book. "To each other?"

Derek shook his head. "Of course not, silly. They found true love in some little town in New Mexico."

"My dad always said anything is possible," Sheree said with a grin. "I guess this proves he was right."

"Go buy yourself a new dress, sweetheart. This is bound to be the wedding of the century. We don't want to miss it!"

Rafe laughed as he read the invitation a second time. "You know, Kath, when I turned those two, I never expected them to survive this long, much less find true love in Dune, New Mexico!"

Abbey grinned in spite of herself when she opened the wedding invitation. Most invitations were printed on white or ivory card stock. Leave it to Pearl and Edna to come up with something unique—the invitation was in the shape of a large, sparkly red heart. The text was in bright pink. She couldn't wait to see what they considered appropriate bridal wear.

Nick shook his head when she showed him the gaudy invitation and matching envelope. "Vegas," he muttered. "Why am I not surprised? What do you want to bet the minister will be an Elvis impersonator!"

Chapter Forty-Three

Abbey had never been to Las Vegas. She knew she was acting like a small-town tourist but who could blame her? She had never seen anything like it, not even in New York. The casinos were lit up like Christmas trees. Never in her life had she seen so much neon. Or so many people—some in fancy clothes and expensive shoes, others in torn jeans and T-shirts. Men and women thronged the sidewalks, laughing and talking as they moved from one hotel to another, or stood at the curb, waiting to cross the street. Taxis, cars, air buses, and motor homes waited in queues on the aprons leading up to the casinos.

Logan had used his pull as a well-known movie producer to get suites for everyone in the family at the MGM Grand, which certainly lived up to its name.

The wedding was set for midnight and the family had agreed to meet at the chapel at eleven-thirty.

"So," Nick said, after they had checked into the hotel and dropped off their luggage, "we've got a couple of hours to kill. What would you like to do?"

"Gamble, of course!"

"Feeling lucky, are you?" he asked with a wry grin.

Abbey batted her eyelashes at him. "Always, since I met you."

Nick reached for her, but she slipped out of his grasp with a murmured "Later."

Grumbling about the honeymoon being over, he followed her into the elevator and down to the floor of the casino.

The first thing Abbey noticed when they entered the gaming area was the noise. Bells and whistles, hoots and hollers from the players, the rattle of dice from the craps table, the whir of the Wheel of Fortune. If it was loud for her, how much worse was it for Nick, with his preternatural hearing?

"What's your pleasure?" he asked. "Blackjack? Craps? Roulette? The slots?"

"The slot machines, I think. I don't know how to play any of the other games."

"Slots, it is."

He led her to a bank of machines, stopped in front of a dollar slot, and pulled up a stool for her to sit on.

Abbey tapped her foot in anticipation as she watched the wheels spin, held her breath as they slowed. One seven. Two sevens. She let out a squeal when the third seven stopped on the line. "I won!"

She played for another half an hour, winning more than she lost, and then she was ready to try something else.

Nick headed for the nearest blackjack table, where he bought six hundred dollars worth of chips, stacked half in front of her, and quickly explained the rules. It was a quick game, won or lost on the turn of a card. She didn't know if there was any skill involved. It seemed to be a matter of luck, as far as she could tell. And yet Nick won consistently. When she asked what his secret was, he whispered something about counting cards, but it didn't mean anything to her.

From the blackjack table they went to try their hand at roulette, which really was a game of luck, she thought, since no one could predict whether the little white ball would land on red or white or on the number chosen.

She checked the time on her phone, then tugged at Nick's arm. "We need to go."

"Too bad," he muttered. "I'm on a hot streak."

The Elvis chapel proved to be a dazzling white building surrounded by a white wall and flanked by a pair of trees glittering with tiny white lights. The inside was lovely, with a dark blue carpet and a white stage with four pillars.

Abbey and Nick were the last to arrive. After exchanging hugs and hellos with everyone else, Abbey took the chair next to her mother's. "Has anyone seen the brides?"

"Not yet," Savanah said. "I can't wait to see what they're wearing."

Abbey grinned.

A moment later, a recording of Elvis singing "As Long as I Have You" came over the speakers. Monroe and James entered through a side door and stood in front of the stage. Monroe wore a gaudy pink, orange, and yellow Hawaiian shirt à la *Blue Hawaii*. Going for the *Viva Las Vegas* look, James sported a yellow jacket over black slacks. Both wore colorful leis.

Abbey glanced over her shoulder to see a dead-on Elvis look-alike escorting Pearl and Edna down the center aisle. She bit back a grin when she saw the brides. Carrying out the *Blue Hawaii* theme, Pearl wore a long

Hawaiian dress with a short train. A red hibiscus adorned her white hair, a red and white lei circled her neck.

Edna wore a bright yellow dress reminiscent of the one Ann-Margret had worn in *Viva Las Vegas*. Her lei was pink and white.

The Elvis impersonator wore a skin-tight white jump-suit similar to the outfit the real Elvis had worn during his *Aloha from Hawaii* concert. He was, Abbey thought, the most remarkable look-alike she had ever seen.

When the trio reached the stage, Monroe and James stepped forward to claim their brides.

Elvis took his place onstage.

Abbey couldn't stop staring at him. If she hadn't known that the King had died decades years before she was born, she would have sworn he was standing in front of her. His pompadour was perfect. He had the same sexy bedroom eyes, the same curl to his lips.

"Welcome to Las Vegas," he said in the best imper-sonator voice Abbey had ever heard. "We are here to celebrate the most important day any lovin' couple can have. That day when a man and a woman pledge their undying devotion to their favorite teddy bear.

"James, please take Edna Mae's hand in yours and repeat after me, I, James Harkness, take you, Edna Mae Turner, to be my lawfully wedded wife, to love you tender and always treat you nice, to have and to hold from this day forward."

Abbey smiled as she listened to the two couples repeat their vows.

Elvis twitched his hips. At Monroe's nod, Elvis said, "Monroe, I want you to gaze deeply into the eyes of your beloved—yes, just like that. Now, repeat after me, I give you this ring as a symbol and token of my undying love. I promise I will never, ever, treat you like a hound dog, but will always treat you nice. And that I will love only you for as long as I live."

Abbey glanced at Nick as the couples exchanged rings. She didn't have to read his mind to know he found the whole thing terribly amusing.

After both couples had exchanged rings and vows, Elvis sang "Can't Help Falling in Love" while the newly-weds danced.

When the song ended, Elvis winked at Monroe and James. "Gentlemen, you may kiss your brides."

Amidst a burst of applause, the couples kissed.

Abbey looked over at Nick, who leaned toward her and said, in a fair impression of the King, "Darlin', you'll always be my hunka-hunka burnin' love."

Abbey was laughing as they left the chapel. Vampires being what they were, there was no reception, no cake, only hugs for the brides and congratulations for the grooms. And a not-so-subtle warning from Rafe, reminding Monroe and James that Edna and Pearl were part of the Cordova family and under their protection.

A few last congratulations and they all went their separate ways—the newlyweds hurried off to the hotel, Logan and Mara decided to see the show at The Venetian, Savanah and Kathy dragged their husbands off for a night of dancing; Derek and Sheree opted to go sight-seeing.

Abbey wondered if they would all get together later, after she was asleep, to go hunting.

"Alone at last," Nick said as they strolled back to the MGM. "What do you want to do now?"

Abbey shrugged. "I don't know. What do you want to do?"

"How's this for a start?" Drawing her into the shadows, he wrapped her in his arms, lowered his head, and kissed her.

She leaned into him, her hands fisting in his shirt front, pulling him closer. He slid one hand down her back, drawing her body even tighter against his.

His voice a husky growl, he said, "I think I know what I want to do now."

Abbey was asleep, a satisfied smile on her face, when Nick left the hotel. Even though it was close to three A.M., people still crowded the sidewalks. Of course, it was an entirely different class of people. This late—or early— the underside of the city came out to play.

Nick strolled down the sidewalk, aware of a man and woman coupling in the alley across the street. Several hookers—ranging from young and uncertain to older and wiser—propositioned him along the way. He passed an old man snoring on a bus bench, sidestepped a man and a woman laughing drunkenly as they shuffled none too steadily toward their destination.

So many people, Nick mused irritably, and none of them appealed to him.

He was on his way back to the hotel, and the warmth of his bride's bed, when a man darted out from behind a parked car. Wielding a large knife, he snarled, "Gimme your wallet!"

Nick snorted. "Go to hell."

The man stared at him, rage building in his eyes, and then he sprang forward, his blade arrowing toward Nick's heart.

Nick moved instinctively, easily avoiding the blade as he plucked the weapon out of the man's hand. "You're not much," Nick muttered as he tossed the knife aside. "But it's late and I'm hungry."

* * *

Abbey stared up at the ceiling. Nick had been gone for about an hour. Out searching for prey, no doubt. Or bending over the neck of some sweet young thing.

He had thought her asleep when he left, but sleep eluded her. For a time, she contemplated how much she loved him. How much she loved *making* love to him. Each time proved better than the last.

In the chapel tonight, surrounded by her family, she had felt like an outsider—a sparrow flying with eagles. Were they all out there hunting the night together while she lay here in the dark alone and lonely? Would she be happier if she were with them, preying on some helpless mortal?

She quickly shut the door on that train of thought and focused on the wedding instead. Edna and Pearl were in their seventies, yet they could look forward to hundreds of years with the men they loved. If she was lucky, she might share sixty years with Nick. What would it be like, when she was in her seventies or eighties, and he still looked like a man in his late twenties? Would he stay with her until she passed away? Would she even want him to?

Blinking back her tears, she turned onto her side and stared into the darkness as she waited for him to return.

Chapter Forty-Four

Several days later, Abbey sat on the top rail of the corral fence, her hands resting on her knees as she watched Freckles kick up her heels. It was good to be back home. Nick had wanted to spend a few more days in Vegas, but she had been anxious to get home and sleep in her own bed.

She grinned when Freckles rolled in the dirt, then sprang to her feet and bucked from one end of the corral to the other.

Since returning home, Abbey had spent several sleepless nights, her thoughts in turmoil about her life, her marriage, her future.

She frowned when she saw her mother striding toward her. It was unusual for her mom to be out and about this early in the day. Was something wrong at home?

"Hi, Mom."

Savanah climbed up on the fence beside her. "Hi. Beautiful day, isn't it?"

Abbey nodded. "Is something wrong?"

Savanah took Abbey's hand in hers. "I was going to ask you the same thing."

"What makes you think something's wrong?"

"A mother's instinct, maybe. Is everything all right between you and Nick?"

Abbey bit down on the corner of her lip, debating whether to confide in her mother. It would be great to unburden herself. And surely her mother would understand.

"Abbey?"

She hesitated a moment more, then blurted, "Mom, did you ever feel like an outsider?"

Savanah's hand tightened on hers. "Of course, honey. Everyone does at one time or another. Why do you ask?"

"At the wedding, I wondered if you all got together later, after I went to bed, to go hunting together, and . . . and I felt left out, like I'd been abandoned."

"Honey . . ."

"I know that's not how it was, but I just . . . I don't think I want to live like this anymore, always on the outside looking in. Never really belonging."

"What are you saying?"

"I think I'm going to ask Nick to bring me across."

"Oh, Abbey. Are you sure?"

"No," she whispered. "Nick tried being human for me and it didn't work." She lifted one shoulder and let it fall. "I don't know what else to do."

Savanah shook her head, and then sighed. "I know how difficult this decision can be," she said quietly. "My only advice is to be absolutely sure it's what you want. Not what you think Nick wants. Not what anyone else thinks is best. It has to be your decision, and yours alone."

"I know, Mom. Thanks for not trying to talk me out of it."

"It was tempting," Savanah admitted with a faint

smile. "But I suspect you'll accept the Dark Gift because you can't abide the thought of growing old while Nick stays young. And because it's the only way you can have a truly meaningful, long-lasting relationship with the man you love."

Abbey nodded. "If I decide to do it, it won't be right away. I mean, I'm only twenty-six. I thought maybe I'd wait a year or two." She sighed. "Or maybe three or four."

"Believe me, daughter, I know what you're going through. I thought about it long and hard, contemplating the pros and cons, weighing what I'd be giving up against what I'd be gaining. But in the end, it all boils down to one thing: Do you love Nick enough to become what he is? If not, it's best to end it now and move on."

On the drive home, Abbey thought about what her mother had said. There was no question about loving Nick. She loved him with her whole heart and soul. . . .

Her soul.

She had never considered the religious aspect of becoming a vampire. It brought her up short. If she accepted the Dark Gift, would she be damned for all eternity? Did her mother feel damned? What about her father? And yet, her father had been born a vampire. How could he be punished for that?

Abbey broke out in a cold sweat. Her parents had killed people. She didn't know how many. She didn't want to know. Was it considered murder if it was self-defense? And what about Nick? He had admitted to killing people when he was a fledgling. But he had been turned against his will. Wouldn't those deaths be on

Mara's conscience—if she had one—since she had turned Nick and then abandoned him?

Abbey pounded her fist on the steering wheel. Why did she have to think about this now, when she had almost made up her mind?

Nick was waiting for her in the mudroom when she got home. He took one look at her bleak expression and asked, "What's wrong?"

Avoiding his gaze, Abbey sat on a stool to remove her boots. "Nothing. I'm just tired."

"Uh-huh."

She felt his mind brush hers.

"Is it true?" he asked. "You're thinking about becoming a vampire?"

"Maybe. I was mulling it over today when my mom stopped by the barn."

"I see."

"It wasn't like that. She didn't try to talk me out of it. She just warned me to be sure it was what I wanted before I made a final decision."

He nodded. "Good advice." He followed her into the living room, remained standing, his arms folded over his chest, while she sat on the sofa, one leg tucked beneath her.

Abbey scrubbed her hands up and down her arms. "A fire would be nice," she said, still not meeting his gaze. "I think it might rain."

He glanced at the hearth; a moment later, flames crackled to life. "Spit it out, Abbey. What's really bothering you?"

She cleared her throat, wishing he would just read

her mind because putting her fears into words made them all too real.

"Abbey?"

"Do you ever worry about your soul?"

He looked at her as if she were speaking a foreign language. "My soul?"

She nodded. "Do you think vampires are damned?"

"What brought that up?"

"I don't know." Abbey wrapped her arms around her middle. "I . . ." She shook her head. "I just suddenly started to wonder about all the people I love. I know my parents have killed people. And so has everyone else in the family. You've taken lives. . . ."

"Abbey." He whispered her name as he sat beside her and gathered her into his arms. "I don't know your mom and dad very well, but I'm willing to bet they've never killed anyone who didn't have it coming."

"But that's not true for you, is it?"

"You're sweet to worry about my soul, love. But by now it's probably light years beyond redemption."

"What if I kill someone, Nick?"

Cupping her face in his hands, he gazed deeply into her eyes. "I will never let that happen, Abbey Marie. I swear it on your life."

Tears glistened in her eyes as she buried her face against his shoulder.

Feeling suddenly helpless, Nick stroked her hair, her back. "You don't have to become what I am, sweetheart. I'm yours for as long as you want me. I love you, Abbey. Nothing on earth will ever change that. I promised to love you for as long as I lived, and I meant every word." He tilted her chin up so he could see her face. "Do you believe me?"

She nodded, unable to speak past the lump in her throat.

He made love to her that night, each kiss, each caress, reinforcing his promise to love her forever. In Nick's arms, all her doubts and worries melted away.

But, like noxious weeds after a summer rain, they sprouted anew with the coming of dawn.

Chapter Forty-Five

Still half asleep, Abbey smiled as Nick rained kisses across her cheeks, her brow, the tip of her nose. A soft sigh of contentment rose in her throat as his hands moved lightly over her breasts and belly.

"You awake yet?" he asked, his voice husky.

"Maybe. Maybe I'm dreaming that we're making love."

"Give me an hour and I can make that dream come true."

She shivered as his tongue licked her ear, but then he drew back. Rising on his elbow, he gazed down at her. "What's wrong?"

She blinked up at him. "Nothing, why?"

"You're troubled about something. I can feel it. Taste it."

She would have denied it but what was the point? He would just sort through her thoughts until he uncovered the misgivings that had haunted her dreams and waited to meet her on waking.

She was about to try to explain, but he didn't give her a chance.

"You're still worried about my soul, aren't you?" He

brushed a wisp of hair from her cheek. "Still afraid that if you become a vampire you'll go to hell?" Nick shook his head. Abbey had never seemed like the religious type. Oh, he knew she believed in a higher power, in good and evil, but they had never really discussed religion.

Except for Father Lanzoni, Nick didn't know any vampires who spent much time in church. He had resigned himself to his fate centuries ago. He had done what was necessary to survive, and if there was, indeed, a final judgment, then he would face the consequences of his actions. "I thought we put all this behind us last night?"

"I did, too, but . . ." She shrugged. "I can't stop thinking about it."

"You don't have to become a vampire, love. I told you that. But if you decide to become one, you'll never have to kill. And you won't have to feed on humans if you don't want to. You can feed on me."

She stared up at him, her eyes wide. "You told me vampires don't usually feed on other vampires."

"They don't." He stroked her cheek. "But in your case, I'm willing to make an exception."

"Nick, can I ask you something?"

"Anything, anytime."

"You won't get mad?"

"No."

"Did you ever ask forgiveness for the lives you took?"

"No." In truth, it had never occurred to him. "Would it make you feel better if I did?"

She nodded.

"All right, love. I'll get in touch with Lanzoni and I'll go to confession if it'll ease your mind."

"Oh, Nick!" She threw her arms around his neck. "Thank you!"

"You're welcome. Now, about making that dream come true . . ."

Later that afternoon, while Abbey and her dad went to pick up a load of hay, Nick called Mara for Father Lanzoni's phone number.

"Why on earth do you need a priest?" she asked. "I'm pretty sure you aren't getting married again, and you don't sound like you need last rites."

"Just give me the man's number."

"Not until you tell me why you need it."

Nick bit back an oath. "Did you ever feel the need to confess your sins?"

"My what?"

"You heard me. Have you ever felt guilty about your past, about the lives you've taken?"

"Is that what this is all about?" Mara exclaimed incredulously. "You want to go to confession?"

"Yeah."

A very unladylike expletive slipped past her lips.

"Nice."

"Why do I get the feeling that Abbey has something to do with this?"

"She's worried about my soul."

"I'm worried about your sanity. You're a vampire, Nicky, not a saint."

"Just give me the damn number."

She rattled it off, then disconnected the call, but not before he heard the sound of her laughter.

"This is an unexpected pleasure," Father Lanzoni said, smiling. "Please, come in."

Nick glanced around as he entered the priest's

house, which looked more like a church than a home. There were crosses, large and small, as well as numerous statues and pictures of the Virgin Mary and other saints. A particularly large crucifix enjoyed a prominent place on the wall above the fireplace.

"What brings you here?" Lanzoni asked.

"I promised my bride I would go to confession."

Surprise flickered in the priest's eyes. "Are you Catholic?"

Nick shrugged. "I used to be."

"Very well. Are you ready?"

Nick glanced around. "Are we going to do it here?"

"Do you have a problem with that?"

"If I'm going to do this, I'd just as soon do it in a church, if it's all right with you."

"Of course," the priest said. "That would be my preference, also, but I wasn't sure how you would feel about it. You know how some vampires are," he said. "Once they're turned, they don't want anything to do with religion."

"Yeah," Nick said dryly. "I used to be one of them."

Lanzoni gestured toward the door. "Shall we go? The church is just down the street."

Built of gray stone and red brick, the church on the corner was old, though not as old as the chapel where Nick had married Abbey. Stained-glass windows on either side of the massive front doors depicted scenes from the life of the Good Shepherd. The bell in the tower chimed the hour as Nick and the priest climbed the stone steps and entered the vestibule.

Although he hadn't been to confession in centuries, Nick automatically genuflected, then crossed himself when he entered the chapel. He tensed as he knelt there, waiting for heaven's lightning to strike and burn him to ash.

When nothing happened, Nick followed the priest toward the confessional. Stepping inside, he took a deep breath and then closed the curtain.

Fretting over what was keeping Nick so long, Abbey called her dad and arranged to meet him at the barn, thinking a nice long ride might take her mind off her worries.

"This was a good idea," Rane said as they led the horses outside and tethered them to the corral fence. "We don't do this often enough."

"We'll have to fix that," she said, smiling.

"Is something bothering you?"

Abbey shook her head. Why did everyone keep asking her that?

"You look a little distracted," her father remarked.

Abbey glanced at her watch, noting it was only a few minutes later than the last time she had looked. Had she made a mistake, insisting Nick go to confession? She wasn't Catholic. She hadn't been to church in years. Who was she to tell Nick how to live his life? Whatever guilt he felt, whatever sins he had committed, were between her husband and his God.

"What's up, daughter?" Rane asked when she glanced at her watch again. "You got a hot date?"

"No, I . . ." She ran the dandy brush over Freckles's neck. "I just wondered what was keeping Nick. He said he'd meet me here."

"How are you two getting along, now that he's a vampire again?"

"Fine, Dad. Stop worrying about me."

"I'm your father. It's my job to worry. No regrets, then?"

"Not one." After dropping the brush into a box filled

with curry combs, hoof picks, and a bottle of fly spray, Abbey lifted the mare's front foot and checked the hoof. "Dad, I might have forced Nick to do something I shouldn't have."

Pausing in the act of currying his horse, Rane glanced at his daughter. "Go on."

"Well, I . . . that is, the other night, I was thinking about becoming a vampire . . ."

"What brought that on? You've never wanted it before."

"I know." She pried a bit of dirt out of the mare's hoof. "But I'm the only mortal in the family and I'm starting to feel like I don't belong."

"Of course you do."

"Dad, just listen." Abbey studied the pick in her hand as if she had never seen one before. "I was thinking about asking Nick to turn me and one thing led to another, and I started thinking about all the people Nick has killed and that made me wonder if becoming a vampire would . . . would . . ."

Rane frowned. "If it would what, honey?"

"Put my soul in danger."

He stared at her, speechless.

"Have you ever worried about that?"

"Often enough," he admitted ruefully. "I've done some things I'm not proud of. I've taken human lives." He rested his forearms on the back of the horse. "What does any of this have to do with Nick?"

"I asked him to go to confession."

Rane's jaw dropped and then, to Abbey's astonishment, he burst out laughing.

"Dad! Dad, it's not funny!"

"Man, I'd like to be the priest who hears *that* confession."

"Stop laughing! Did I do the right thing?"

"I don't know, honey. But as old as Nick is, I imagine it'll be a good, long while before he comes home."

Rane thought about his conversation with Abbey as he walked back to the house later that day. He and his brother had become vampires the night after their thirteenth birthday. The guilt of his first kill remained with him to this day. He remembered the face of every man and woman whose life he had taken, but no matter how he had tried to justify what he'd done, in his heart he thought of himself as a monster. But his daughter didn't need to know that.

He had once asked Mara if it ever bothered her to take a life. To this day, he clearly remembered her reply.

I am a vampire. It was not something I sought, nor was it bequeathed to me of my own choosing. I could have spent my existence bewailing my fate. Instead, I chose to embrace what I am. I am Nosferatu. It is my nature to hunt, to kill, just as it is yours. If peace is what you are searching for, you will never find it until you fully accept who and what you are. There is no going back, Rane. There is no magic cure. You are what you were born to be.

It had been good advice.

He wondered what advice the priest had given Nick.

Abbey was a nervous wreck as she waited for Nick to return. She wondered again if she had done the right thing. Maybe he had come to terms with his past. Maybe going to see Father Lanzoni would only stir up old memories of people and places he would rather forget.

She tried to read. She tried to watch TV. She unpacked the last box from the move. And still he didn't come home.

It was near midnight when he materialized in the living room.

"Nick?" She twisted her hands in her lap. "I'm so sorry. I never should have asked you to . . ."

"It's all right, love." He sank down on the sofa beside her. "I had a long talk with the good Father."

"So, you're not mad at me?"

"No." He slipped his arm around her shoulder. "It did me a lot of good."

"So, what did he say? Did he give you absolution?"

"Hey, that's between me and my priest."

She quirked a brow at him. "*Your* priest?"

"Lanzoni gave me hope," Nick said after a moment. "He said the Lord is merciful, that He judges each of us individually, according to the times we lived in, the intent of our hearts . . . you know, the usual. He had a lot more to say, but that's between him and me." Nick squeezed her hand. "He's a good man."

"So are you, Nick Desanto," Abbey murmured fervently. "So are you."

Abbey was at the barn bright and early the next morning. Feeling lighthearted, she hummed softly as she fed the stock. Nick had gone to confession, and even though he hadn't told her everything Father Lanzoni had said, he admitted it had done him good. It had done her good, too, she thought. Maybe vampires weren't cursed, or damned for eternity.

She had decided to put thinking about becoming a vampire on the back burner for a year or two. As she'd told her mother, she was young and healthy. There was no hurry.

She smiled as she filled the water barrels. Life was good and only promised to get better. She loved Nick more with every passing day. She loved having a home of her own. There were things she missed, now that Nick was a vampire again. Little things, like sitting down to dinner with him, but, all things considered, she had never been happier.

She puttered around the barn for a while and then, thinking it was too beautiful a day to spend working, she decided to exercise Freckles. Forgoing a saddle, she bridled the mare and led her into the exercise corral.

She soon grew bored riding in the arena. After saddling Freckles, she rode out of the yard. She had stayed close to home since the kidnapping and she had every intention of doing so today. But Freckles was feeling frisky and eager to run.

"All right," Abbey said, patting the mare's neck. "We'll ride out to the shack, but no farther."

Abbey sighed as she turned Freckles toward home. Given her druthers, she would have ridden for hours.

She was thinking about what to fix for lunch when something slammed into her chest and knocked her out of the saddle.

Stunned, she lay there a moment, wondering what had happened. It was only when she tried to sit up that she felt the pain. When she touched her chest, her hand came away bloody. Horrified, she glanced down. Her shirt was covered with blood.

She'd been shot.

Her vision blurred and she closed her eyes. When she opened them again, a woman stood over her. A woman who looked vaguely familiar. "Berta."

"Know who I am, do you? Good. You killed my sister, you vampire-loving whore. In another minute, you'll be dead, and then I'm going after the rest of your blood-sucking family."

"Nick . . . no . . ."

Nick!

Abbey's vision narrowed. The world grew dark, darker. In her mind, she screamed for Nick, but it was too late.

A black pit yawned before her. Helpless to resist, she slid over the edge into oblivion.

Nick!

Abbey's voice penetrated the darkness that surrounded him. Rising from his lair, he followed the link between them with all the speed at his command. Nearing the shack, he dissolved into mist when he sensed the presence of a hunter. When he was behind the woman, he resumed his own form. Grabbing the rifle from her hand, he tossed it aside, then turned her to face him.

He felt the rage build inside him. He had vowed to rip the heart out of whoever kidnapped Abbey. Time and circumstance and Abbey's presence had prevented him from fulfilling that vow with the other two, but Fate had kindly granted him one more chance.

The hunter stared at him defiantly. "What are you waiting for, bloodsucker?"

"I just wanted you to know who killed you," he said.

And kept his promise.

After tossing the body aside, he wiped his hands on his jeans, then lifted Abbey in his arms and willed them home.

In their room, he laid her gently on the bed and peeled away her shirt. He stared at the ugly bullet wound above her heart, at the blood smeared across her breasts.

So much blood.

Had he arrived too late to save her?

Eternally too late?

Chapter Forty-Six

Nick dropped to his knees beside the bed, Abbey's hand clutched tightly in his. She couldn't be dead, not now. Not after all they had been through. But even with his preternatural hearing, he couldn't detect a heartbeat. She wasn't breathing.

He bit into his wrist, praying that he wasn't too late, that there was still a spark of life deep within her. Parting lips that were already turning blue, he held his wrist over her mouth, watched anxiously as each dark red drop dripped onto her tongue.

"Drink, love." He stroked her throat in an effort to make her swallow. "Dammit, Abbey, don't you dare die on me!"

He felt a rush of power as Mara and Logan materialized on the other side of the bed.

Mara glanced at Abbey, lying still and silent, her clothing drenched in blood. At the blood on Nick's hands. "What happened?"

He answered without looking up. "She was shot by the other woman who kidnapped her. Drink, Abbey. Come on, love, drink."

"Is this what she wants?" Logan asked quietly.

"We discussed it," Nick said. "She wanted to wait a few years, but that's no longer an option." He bit into his wrist again, deeper this time, so that a steady stream trickled into her mouth. She swallowed once. Twice. "That's it, love." Relief swept through him when she reached for his arm.

Some of the color returned to her cheeks as she continued to drink.

Mara laid a hand on his shoulder. "Nick, you can't give her enough blood to sustain her through the change."

"I don't care if she takes all I've got."

"Let me help."

"No!" He shook his head. "She's mine."

"She'll still be sired to you, Nick, but my blood is more powerful than yours. She won't need as much."

Reluctantly, he withdrew his arm and let Mara take his place. Ordinarily, when a vampire turned a mortal, the vampire drank the mortal's blood and then gave it back. In this case, there had been no blood left for Nick to drink, but that didn't matter. He had tasted Abbey before. She had tasted him. There was already a bond between them. It would be stronger now. Unbreakable as long as one of them lived.

Minutes later, her heartbeat was steady, her breathing and color normal.

"She'll be all right." Mara licked the wound in her wrist, sealing it. "Have you contacted Rane and Savanah?"

"Not yet. I thought she was . . ." Unable to say the word, Nick brushed a few blood-stained strands of hair from Abbey's cheek.

"And the woman who did this?"

"She's dead. Shit! I left the body in the pasture."

"Logan, why don't you go dispose of the body while Nick and I get Abbey out of these bloody clothes?"

With a nod, he left the room.

"Nick, go wash up."

He was reluctant to be away from Abbey for even a few minutes, but he did as Mara said.

He returned carrying a wastebasket. He dumped Abbey's bloody shirt inside. "Do you think she'll be all right?"

"Why wouldn't she be?" Mara removed Abbey's boots and slid her jeans over her hips.

He shrugged as he removed Abbey's bra and dropped it into the basket. "She was as close to being dead as you can get. What if I didn't get to her in time? What if . . . ?"

"Stop worrying. With your blood and mine in her veins, I'm sure she'll be fine."

"I hope to hell you're right."

Between them, they got Abbey into her nightgown. Nick tucked her in, then stood by the bed, gazing down at her. He could have lost her tonight. It was a sobering thought.

Mara laid her hand on his arm. "Do you need anything?"

"No."

"Don't worry about her. You should get in touch with her parents tonight."

He nodded. "Thanks for coming," he said, but she was already gone.

Nick caressed Abbey's cheek. It was cool to the touch. Her breathing was shallow now, her heartbeat slowing, as she sank into the dreamless sleep of his kind.

She would sleep through the night and tomorrow,

and when she woke tomorrow evening, she would be a fledgling vampire, albeit a very powerful one. All that remained was to see how she would handle the transformation. In spite of her decision to accept the Dark Gift in a year or two, talking about the possibility and actually becoming a vampire were two very different things. But she was alive.

And for now, that was the only thing that mattered.

Dreading the call he was about to make, Nick moved away from the bed and punched in Rane's number. He hadn't finished explaining what had happened when Rane and Savanah materialized inside the bedroom.

Savanah immediately knelt at her daughter's side, a pair of crimson tears sliding down her cheeks as she took her daughter's hand in hers.

"She's going to be all right," Nick said quietly. "I got to her in time."

"What happened, exactly?" Rane asked, his gaze on Abbey's face.

"She took Freckles out for a ride."

Rane frowned. "I'm not sure that was a good idea."

"What did you want me to do? Lock her in the house? Believe me, I thought about it, but I knew she was afraid that if she let her fears rule her life, it would cripple her. I didn't want that to happen."

"And the one who did this?"

"Is rotting in hell," Nick said curtly.

"Who was it?"

"The other woman involved in the kidnapping. Logan disposed of the body."

"I know I haven't treated you with the respect you deserve," Rane said. "It's no secret that I was against this marriage from the start, but—" He took a deep breath.

"You saved my daughter's life tonight and for that, I'm forever in your debt." He squared his shoulders, then held out his hand. "Thank you."

Nick regarded the other vampire for a moment, then grasped his hand. "It's all in the past, Cordova. All that matters now is Abbey."

She struggled to breathe, to fight off the repulsive creature that was slowly killing her. His fangs tore into her throat, ripping through flesh, piercing her jugular. He was drinking her blood. She could hear him swallowing, feel him stealing the life from her body, taking more and more. Taking it all. She grew weak, weaker. She tried to scream for help, to beg for Nick to come and save her, but she couldn't speak, couldn't move.

Darkness closed in around her, thicker, deeper than anything she had ever known. She tried in vain to run from it, but the world around her grew darker, until an endless black void opened in front of her. Helpless to resist, she felt herself being dragged toward it, sliding over the edge of the precipice, falling, falling into a yawning chasm as wide and deep as eternity as all that she was, all that she had hoped for, slowly slipped away into nothingness.

And then, like a miracle, her mouth filled with liquid fire. It scorched her tongue as it slid down her throat, burning through every cell and fiber of her body, relentless as death itself, until it found the last flickering spark of life smoldering in the very core of her being. Found it and embraced it, ignited it, until that last faint ember blazed with new strength, new life, stealing her soul from eternity's grasp.

Clawing, gasping for breath, she fought her way out of the stygian darkness, searching for . . .

"Nick!"

"I'm here, love. I'm here."

Strong arms wrapped around her, crushing her close. A familiar hand stroked her hair. She felt his tears on her face as he whispered her name.

Content, she rested her head on his shoulder . . . and frowned.

Suddenly overcome with a wave of sensations, Abbey drew back, her gaze searching his face. He looked the same, yet different somehow, as if someone had taken blinders from her eyes and she was seeing him, really seeing him, for the first time.

Her gaze swept the room. It, too, looked the same, yet different. Colors were brighter, more intense. The lights were off, yet she could see everything in sharp detail—the faint cracks in the walls, the tiny black spider tiptoeing across the ceiling. Her fingers detected each individual thread in Nick's shirt. Without trying, she heard people stirring downstairs—her parents were here, as well as everyone else in the family. They were talking softly amongst themselves but she heard each word as clearly as if they were in her bedroom. They were all worried about her. Glad she was alive. Grateful that Nick had found her before it was too late.

Too late? She frowned. *Too late for what?*

Her confusion growing, she looked at Nick again.

And read the truth in his eyes.

"Forgive me, love," he murmured, squeezing her hand. "You were a heartbeat away from death." He shook his head. "I couldn't let you go."

She stared at him, her thoughts chaotic. This wasn't supposed to happen, not yet. She needed time to prepare, to make sure it was the right decision. And now the choice had been taken out of her hands. Her first thought was to rail at him, to scream that he'd had no right to make such a life-shattering decision for her.

She wrenched herself out of his embrace. She wanted to hit him, to make him hurt. . . .

"Go ahead. Hit me if it'll make you feel better."

Hands clenching, Abbey stared at him, shocked by the force of her anger. She rarely got mad, and never like this.

"Everything is heightened," Nick said quietly. "All your senses. All your emotions. You'll learn to control them, in time."

She took several deep breaths, her anger cooling. How could she be angry with him when he had saved her life? Snatched her from the very jaws of death?

She still had time to think it over, she reminded herself. She was a new vampire. If, in the next few days, she decided being a vampire wasn't for her, there was always Pearl's cure. Hadn't Mara said it always worked on fledglings?

"Abbey? Say something."

"I'm sorry I got mad. I should be thanking you for saving me."

His gaze searched hers, his expression wary. "You don't hate me, then?"

"Of course not. But I feel so strange." She wrapped her arms around her middle. "So empty inside."

He nodded. "You need to feed, but don't worry. Like I told you, you don't have to hunt. You can drink from me."

She nodded, but it wasn't Nick's blood she craved. Far off in the distance, she could hear many hearts beating. The steady thrumming called to her like sweet music, promising relief from the horrible pain swelling inside of her.

She knew she should feel revulsion, horror at the mere thought of preying on humanity. She tried to summon a sense of guilt, but to no avail. She glanced at Nick. If she said the word, he would let her drink from him.

But it wasn't vampire blood she craved.

It amused her that he was treading so lightly, watching her so carefully, as if he was afraid she might explode.

"Abbey, we should go downstairs. Your parents and the rest of the family are anxious to see you."

"Later."

He nodded. Her eyes were bright and tinged with red as she stood and effortlessly pulled him to his feet.

"I'm thirsty, Nick. Take me hunting."

Chapter Forty-Seven

After Abbey changed into a pair of jeans, a black sweater, and boots, Nick transported the two of them to Sacramento. On the way, he explained that it wasn't a good idea to hunt where you lived, at least not too frequently.

Nick glanced at her often as they strolled hand in hand down Main Street. It felt strange, hunting with Abbey at his side, stranger still to think she was now a vampire.

He watched her carefully. She had been very close to death, but she didn't seem to be suffering any ill effects from her ordeal. He was surprised that she had accepted it so readily, that she didn't hate him. Then again, she had grown up with vampires. And there was always Pearl's cure to fall back on.

He grunted softly. He had told Abbey he didn't care if she accepted the Dark Gift or not. If she decided it wasn't for her, he wouldn't love her any less, but, deep in his heart, he hoped she would accept the change.

Watching Abbey hunt was an amazing experience. She didn't need a great deal of guidance, but seemed to know instinctively how to call her prey to her. He had expected her to be squeamish about feeding, since she had expressed a good deal of concern about it previously. Once again, his fears were groundless.

"I think you were born to be a vampire," Nick remarked as they left her third victim behind.

"Maybe I was. I never knew hunting could be such fun. Is it always like this?"

"Pretty much."

She laughed. "If I'd known how wonderful it was to be a vampire, I might have asked Mara to turn me years ago." She smiled up at him. "But I'm glad I waited for you."

"So am I."

She flung her arms out to the side and twirled around. "Everything looks so amazing! I feel wonderful! Strong. Invincible."

"Don't get carried away, Lady Dracula," he said dryly. "You're not immortal, you know."

She stuck her tongue out at him. "I know."

"We should get back home. Your parents are waiting."

"Along with everyone else," she muttered.

"They just want to welcome you into the family," Nick said. "When you were dying, Mara gave you a little of her blood. It made the difference. There are vampires who would do anything, sacrifice anything, to have her blood running in their veins. There is none more powerful anywhere on earth."

He stroked her cheek, thinking she had never looked more beautiful, more desirable. "I understand you're feeling a little uneasy, facing everyone as a vampire for the first time. Don't let it worry you. We're all related now, in more ways than one. Mara's blood connects us all."

Sighing with resignation, she said, "Let's go get it over with."

* * *

Entering the house, Abbey felt like some foreign oddity on display as every eye swung in her direction. As Nick had said, they were all there—her mom and dad, Rane and Kathy, Brenna and Roshan, Vince and Cara, Derek and Sheree, Logan and Mara. Even Edna and Pearl had shown up, along with their new husbands, James and Monroe.

There was a moment of silence. At first, it made Abbey uncomfortable. She could feel their individual power pushing against hers—taking her measure, so to speak. Without realizing it, Abbey was unconsciously doing the same and as she did so, she knew what Nick had meant. They were all connected by Mara's ancient blood. Should the need arise, Abbey knew she would be able to find any one of them whenever necessary, just as they would always be able to find her.

And then the moment passed.

"Abbey!" Savanah hurried forward to embrace her, then drew back, her gaze probing her daughter's. "You're well?"

"I'm fine, Mom," Abbey said cheerfully. "Never better."

Savanah nodded, then stepped aside so Rane could hug his daughter. After that, they each came forward in turn, to hug her and welcome her into the family. Mara last of all.

"You are truly one of us now," Mara said. "Blood of my blood. If you ever have need of me, you need only call and I will hear you."

Abbey nodded. "Thank you for sharing your power with me."

"You have always been family," Mara said with a dismissive wave of her hand. "But now the bond runs deeper, stronger."

"Family," Abbey murmured. For so long, she had felt like she didn't quite belong. Now she understood why. Not only had she gained a measure of immortality and a husband she loved more than life itself, she had finally, truly, come home.

**If you've enjoyed *Night's Surrender*,
don't miss *Beauty's Beast*,
available wherever print or digital books are sold!**

"In this lovely, sexy retelling of *Beauty and the Beast*, Ashley hits the mark. The mysterious change that the hero goes through and the depth of his curse will keep readers intrigued until the very last page. The relationship between the two main characters is set to a slow simmer and becomes more beautifully passionate as the story unfolds. When it comes to a sensual romance, Ashley never disappoints."

—*RT Book Reviews*, **4 stars**, on *Beauty's Beast*

The rattle of the guard's keys roused her from a troubled sleep. She bolted upright, fearing that it was morning and they had come to take her to the block. Stomach churning with fear, she stared at the guard, blinking against the light of the lamp.

"That's her," the guard said. He stepped into the cell and lifted the lamp higher. "Stand up, girl. His lordship wants to see yer face."

She had learned long ago to do as she was told, and to do it quickly. Hardly daring to breathe, she scrambled to her feet.

It was then that she saw him, a dark shape that looked like death itself shrouded in a long black woolen cloak. The garment fell in deep folds from his broad shoulders to brush the tops of his black leather boots. The hood of the cloak was pulled low, hiding his face from her view. Black kidskin gloves covered his hands. He stood there, tall, regal, and frightening.

"Her name's Kristine," the guard remarked. "Don't recall her family name."

The hooded man nodded and made a circling motion with his forefinger.

"Turn around, girl," the guard demanded brusquely.

She did as the guard asked, her cheeks flushing with shame as she felt the hooded man's gaze move over her. She was barefoot and filthy. What was left of her hair was dirty and crawling with lice. Her dress, once the color of fresh cream, was badly stained, the hem torn. And worst of all, she smelled bad.

She heard a faint noise, like the rustle of dry paper, and realized the stranger had asked the guard a question.

"Just turned seventeen," the guard replied with a leer.

She heard the rasp of the hooded man's voice again and then he turned away, melting into the shadows beyond her cell.

The guard followed him, pausing at the door to look back over his shoulder. "This be yer lucky day, girl. Seems his lordship has taken a fancy to ye."

"I don't understand."

"He just bought yer freedom."

Kristine staggered back, overcome by a wave of dizzying relief. She wasn't going to die.

"He'll be comin' by to fetch ye tomorrow night."

Coming for her. Tomorrow night. Relief turned to trepidation. "What . . . what does he want with me?"

The guard threw back his head and barked a laugh. "He says he's going ta marry ye."

"Marry me!" Kristine stared at the guard in shock.

"Aye."

"But . . . he doesn't even know me."

The guard shrugged. "What does it matter?"

Why would a stranger want to marry her? And why did she care, if it would get her out of this terrible place with her head still on her shoulders? "Can you tell me his name?"

"Why, don't you know? That's his lordship, Erik Trevayne."

Stunned, Kristine stared at the guard. She would rather lose her head that very night than become the wife of the infamous Lord Trevayne. A beheading, at least, would be swiftly and mercifully over. "And he wants to marry me? Are you sure?"

"Aye, girl. It seems a fittin' match. A murderin' wench bein' wed to the Demon Lord of Hawksbridge Castle."

GREAT BOOKS, GREAT SAVINGS!

When You Visit Our Website:
www.kensingtonbooks.com
You Can Save Money Off The Retail Price
Of Any Book You Purchase!

- All Your Favorite Kensington Authors
- New Releases & Timeless Classics
- Overnight Shipping Available
- eBooks Available For Many Titles
- All Major Credit Cards Accepted

Visit Us Today To Start Saving!
www.kensingtonbooks.com

All Orders Are Subject To Availability.
Shipping and Handling Charges Apply.
Offers and Prices Subject To Change Without Notice.